BOTÁNICOS

Botánicos

A novel

ALAN MEEROW

Griffinia Press

Tempe, Arizona

1

The phone's insistent ring cut deep into Kovac's REM sleep, and he woke grasping at the last fading tendrils of a vague erotic dream. He withdrew one arm from under the sheet that covered him, and, in his daze, reached for the offending instrument without looking at the screen. He likely would have passed on the call if he had done so.

"Hello?" he murmured.

"Anton, it's Kevin Hobart," perhaps identifying himself lest Kovac had purged his number from his contacts (which he had).

Kovac shot upward in his bed. "Kevin," he replied. "It's been…"

"Twenty years," Kevin Hobart interrupted. Hobart was the most well-known botanist on the planet and director of the most extensive research botanical garden in the United States. He had also once been Kovac's employer. Twenty years ago.

Kovac swung out of bed and traipsed into the small kitchen in his boxers and t-shirt. The shirt, old, thin, and stretched out, had a graphic of an incandescent plant with beautiful flowers. It was a Brazilian species that Anton had himself described a quarter century ago. He started the coffee machine while framing his next words in his head.

"Anton?" Hobart queried.

"Uh, yeah, Kevin … sorry, I just got up." He paused, closing his eyes and leaning against the counter. "What's on your mind?"

"A mutual friend," Hobart continued. "Garwell Sorrentino."

Kovac grunted and muttered, "You feeling sentimental, Kevin?" He regretted it immediately.

Hobart sighed theatrically, then cleared his throat before speaking again. "I have it on good counsel that he's still alive. I thought you would want to know."

Kovac suddenly grew light-headed and pulled a small wooden chair away from an equally small table he could easily reach in his starkly apportioned kitchen. He fell, more than sat, onto it heavily. "That's ridiculous," he said.

"There was no trace," Hobart replied

"Yeah, I know. And given the preponderance of animal scavengers in the area, no one was surprised."

Garwell Sorrentino was solo piloting an ultralight aircraft above a primary site in southeastern Peru twenty-five years ago, when its engine stalled and caught fire, causing the ultralight to plummet a thousand feet towards the treetops. The craft was smashed to smithereens by the expansive canopy of a forest giant. When a recovery team arrived weeks later (it took a minor miracle to get one into the trackless tropical wilderness at the height of the rainy season), no trace of the botanist's remains was discovered. Sorrentino was widely crowned as the world's most knowledgeable authority on tropical forest dynamics and biodiversity and had been conducting canopy surveys of a region rumored to be the richest tract in the southwestern corner of the upper Amazon basin. Despite entreaties by his collaborators to involve others in these surveys, Garwell had thrown caution to the wind and went aloft by himself that time. His collection numbers were a legend unto themselves; over a hundred thousand unique herbarium specimens bore his name as the primary collector. Gar, ten years Kovac's senior, had also been his doctoral academic mentor at the midwestern botanical garden helmed by Kevin Hobart, through a collaborative relationship between the Garden and the Ohio State University. In more ways than one, Sorrentino had shaped the caliber of scientist that Anton Kovac had once been, and had also, across the decades of their association, become his closest friend.

"So, Anton," Hobart said. "What's your schedule like in the next few months?"

♦ ♦ ♦ ♦ ♦

"He wants you to do what?" Nell exclaimed, eyes growing wide as she lowered her wineglass to the table. Kovac leaned back in his chair and eyed Nell Sorrentino with a bemused look. They were seated at a table for two at Kovac's favorite restaurant in Little Italy.

Nell was Garwell's widow, though truth be told, they had separated shortly before his ill-fated field trip to Peru. Kovac often wondered why she retained her married name all the years since. He paused while their server deposited another basket of warm bread on the table between them. Sorrentino had been a legendary philanderer; some would have said a predatory one at that, based on the average age of his universe of bedmates, starry-eyed female graduate students for the most part, at least those with whom Anton was familiar. The great irony was that Sorrentino treated them badly, casting them off with heartless abandon once he grew bored or they became too besotted. It was the one character flaw in his friend that Anton judged harshly, but he wasn't beneath being the young ladies'

7

rebound comfort when the opportunity presented itself. Nell had built a productive and awarded career with the New York Botanical Garden as a specialist in the coffee family, a successful, sprawling inter-continental assemblage that included not only coffee but quinine. She had recently accepted a generous offer for early retirement. She had shifted her work on the family to its Asian branches after their separation, and then to Brazil. Both of her children with Garwell, son and daughter, were each pursuing careers in zoology and medicine, respectively. Anton had been something of a Dutch uncle for them in the absence of their father. Nell was nearing 63 but was fit and lithe. Her long gray hair was typically tied up in a bun; that night, she wore it down, and Kovac almost didn't recognize her.

Kovac turned to survey the other patrons at various stages of their meals. His eyes caught those of a middle-aged man of indigenous South American appearance, a phenotype he knew well from years of field experience in the region. The man held his gaze, and a small smile twitched at the corners of his mouth.

"Says he'll pay for the entire trip with a generous per diem," he said, turning back to the still-warm bread.

"To look for my dead husband," Nell snorted.

"In a nutshell."

Nell inhaled deeply and raised herself up in her chair. "I'm coming with you," she said forthrightly.

"No, you're not," Anton replied. "That's a non-starter—end of story. I haven't even said 'yes' yet."

"Oh, you will," Nell retorted. "And I'm coming with you. I'll buy my own ticket."

Kovac sighed. He'd known Nell long enough to be familiar with her powerful obstinance. "What will you tell the kids?"

Nell smiled sweetly. "That their uncle and I are taking a field trip to Peru."

2

Cusco had changed in the twenty or so years since Kovac had last been to Peru. For one, virtually everyone walked the streets of the old city with their noses pointed down to a cell phone screen. Internet cafes alternated with coffee shops and bars, and myriad 5-star hotels were clustered in the city center. Kovac and Nell were bivouacked in adjoining rooms in one of the best.

The elevation had laid Nell low, so while she slept, Anton roamed the streets of the Incan capital, surprised by his familiarity with the city after so many years. After climbing a steep cobbled street, he was forced to pause to catch his breath. Tourists were everywhere, seemingly outnumbering the locals. Machu Picchu awaited them via the Inca Trail or by train to Aguas Calientes, which he remembered as an absolute pit of a town, apparently now grown into an only slightly seedy tourism hub. Kovac envied their cosseted exploration of a long-departed empire's once-secret hideaway. Where he and Nell were headed, there would be few creature comforts.

Kovac sat down at an outdoor coffee house veranda and ordered a *café con leche*. He was both relieved and apprehensive about having Nell along for the ride. Anton had only the slightest sense of where they would head once they arrived two days hence in Puerto Maldonado, gateway to the Madre de Dios region. He had written a letter to Oscar Crescente, his and Sorrentino's frequent field companion back in the day, during the two weeks of preparation for the trip, but had yet to receive a reply. Crescente was a half-Belgian

Peruvian naturalist, primarily self-taught, whose familiarity with the sparsely inhabited forests of southeastern Peru was second only to Garwell Sorrentino. Kovac didn't know if Oscar was still alive; he wasn't even sure if he could pick him out of a lineup, although he was only a few years older than himself. Oscar had loved Gar like a big brother. They had traversed countless square miles of primary forest together. Kovac had hired him as a guide for some of his own field trips. "For you is cheap," Oscar always greeted him in self-parody.

While he nursed his coffee, Kovac reviewed the trip preparations. He and Nell had flown directly to Cusco from JFK. His ticket had been business class, but halfway through the flight, he graciously exchanged the comfort of his accommodations for Nell's coach seat. Wandering toward the back of the plane, the aisle was choked with passengers embroiled in conversation with family members and friends, a melange of Spanish and Quechua. He caught the gaze of a man seated alone with a few rows in front of Nell. He paused, and his brow furrowed, while a slight chill crawled up his spine. The man nodded, and Anton was positive that the same fellow had locked eyes with him in the restaurant two weeks ago. He shook his head to dispel the odd feeling the stranger's stare inspired, both now and in the recent past. All had spooked him.

Twenty years ago, Anton was caught in *flagrante delicto* with Kevin Hobart's first wife deep in the bowels of the herbarium of the Cincinnati Botanical Garden by no less than Hobart himself. The scandal that erupted soon led to Kovac's termination as a research botanist for the institution, and ultimately to Hobart's divorce. Kovac moved to New York and managed to obtain a nine-month per year teaching post with a local community college in Queens, a position he viewed as mostly penance for his folly. His research career ground to a halt, as no other botanical garden dared risk the ire of a cuckolded Kevin Hobart. Over the following two decades, Anton passed by fifty, cultivated a beer belly, and found professional solace in the occasional student who discovered a love of botany and successfully climbed the academic ladder. He lived in a studio apartment close to the college and spent a lion-sized share of his time feeling miserable. He dated sparingly, always short-lived affairs, the epitome of which was a spate of one-night-stands in his early forties with married women who'd momentarily tired of their husbands. The *aprés* sex talk generally resulted in Kovac agreeing that yes, they were far better off sticking with their husbands. Nell Sorrentino was his only friend.

When he returned to the hotel, Nell was up and about and had procured herself a large mug of *coca* tea, which helped alleviate the symptoms of altitude sickness. She was writing in a notebook when he knocked on the door that separated their rooms. "Good morning," she said brightly.

Kovac glanced at his watch. "Afternoon," he replied with a wry smile. "Feeling better?"

Nell lifted her mug of tea in a silent toast to the efficacy of the ancient remedy for *soroche*. "I thought we could maybe head up to Sacsayhuamán." The ancient Incan fortress was one and a quarter miles from the city's central plaza, and the highest point in Cusco. "We can take a bus up and walk back down."

Anton shrugged. "*¿Porque no?*" he answered. "We have all day. Finish your tea."

♦ ♦ ♦ ♦ ♦

It was pleasant to leave the crowds that overflowed the city's narrow streets. Their busload of mostly tourists soon dispersed across the grassy meadows that intervened among the ruins, now brown during the dry season. Anton and Nell strolled in silence, except for the sound of their labored breathing. Llamas grazed at the base of the structures, only the largest stones of which remained since the conquest. Here and there, a few *qantua* shrubs, the sacred flower of the Incas and both Peru and Bolivia's national flower, held out a few early blossoms, over which several hummingbirds competed aggressively, the metallic buzz of their wings rising and falling in pitch as they flew close to their ears and then retreated.

"What are the odds?" Nell suddenly said. Kovac knew exactly of what.

"Not very good," Anton replied.

"Then why are we doing this?"

Kovac sighed. *Why indeed,* he thought. "Unfinished business, I guess," he answered.

Nell nodded in assent and wandered off by herself. Kovac continued on his own way towards the structures known as the "Bastions," zigzag walls of limestone that stood on terraced platforms. He was overcome by weariness suddenly, but he knew it had nothing to do with altitude this time. It was accompanied by a deep sense of foreboding, as if the ghosts of the ancient Inca surrounded him. They were surely mocking him. The sun disappeared behind a cloud bank, and he perceived the cold on his skin, which the thin air and sunlight had momentarily disguised. He turned around a blind corner and immediately collided with someone, landing square on his backside. "*Discúlpeme señor,*"[1] said a figure dressed in local garments, who extended a hand to help him to his feet. For a brief moment, as the short-statured stranger assisted him, their eyes locked, and Anton visibly started. He was absolutely certain it was the same man he'd seen in the restaurant in New York and on the flight to Cusco. "*¿Está todo bien, señor?*"[2] the man inquired.

Kovac just stared at him, his mouth agape. "*¿Yo a usted lo conozco?*"[3] he stammered.

The familiar stranger was already bounding away, but before he disappeared behind another wall, he glanced over his shoulder at Kovac and flashed a wide smile. "*Todavía no,*" he answered — Not yet.

◆ ◆ ◆ ◆ ◆

On the way back down from the fortress, Anton told Nell about the odd encounters. "Why would we be followed?" she asked.

Kovac threw up his hands. "The only possible explanation I can come up with is Kevin."

---

[1] Excuse me, sir.

[2] Are you O.K., sir?

[3] Do I know you?

"Why on earth would Kevin have someone tailing us?" Nell wondered.

"Because he doesn't trust us," Kovac replied. "At least not me."

"You mean he doesn't trust you to tell him the truth? Anton, that's absurd."

The streets lost grade as they neared the central plaza of the city. "I'm starving," Kovac said, changing the subject. "I'm up for barbequed *cuy*."

3

When the engine of his aircraft suddenly stalled with a cough and a plume of smoke, Garwell Sorrentino realized he had perhaps fifteen seconds to react. He reasoned quickly that he had to separate himself from the ultralight just as the wheels neared the forest canopy. Gar unbuckled himself and began scanning the treetops for a suitable candidate to intercept his fall without breaking too many of his bones. A large well-branched *guarumo* tree stood out in the distance by its large silvery, palmate leaves, a fast-growing tree gap colonizer whose supple branches might slow and eventually halt his descent. Sorrentino had to estimate his forward motion, and precisely choose the optimal time to jump. He prepared as the tiny plane dipped towards the ground, lowering the visor of his helmet over his eyes. He counted down the seconds, preparing as seamless a pitch over the side of the ultralight as could be managed. His chosen target loomed ever larger, green arms beckoning like a forest siren. When he reached 15, he threw himself out of the craft, clutching his small pack and knees to his chest. "Oh baby," he whispered, whether to the tree, some god or a distant shadow from the future he didn't know.

The highest branches of the *guarumo* barely stopped his momentum, but as the greener branches piled up, rather than fell to the lower canopy, they cushioned the blows. Without the helmet, he would have been knocked senseless, if not killed. He was finally halted about the mid-trunk of the tree, some thirty feet from the ground. Every bit of bare skin was lacerated; his legs and arms were severely contused. However, as best he could tell, prone in his nest

16

of piled *guarumo* branches, nothing was broken. Gar winced as he gingerly shifted his position, causing some branches to bounce up and down. There was a sharp crack, and one side of his platform listed downward. His pack was miraculously still with him. Inside was 30 feet of nylon rope. He hoped he hadn't underestimated the distance to the ground. Availing himself first of two aspirins from the pack, which he was forced to chew as his water supply had gone down with the ship, Garwell carefully extracted the rope from his pack, along with a pulley connected to a grappling hook. He reconnoitered his savior tree, looking for a place to secure the line. *Guarumo* belonged to the genus *Cecropia*, the species of which harbored fiercely defensive ants inside their twigs in a mutualistic relationship. For the ants, the trees provided room and board in the form of protein bodies, and they, in turn, kept the trees clean of pestiferous insects and even invading plants. Sure enough, he became aware of the burn of multiple ant bites, which added impetus to his industry. He fastened the hook and pulley assembly to the rope.

Not too far from his perch, and at about the same height, he sighted a branch of an adjoining tree, a species of Spanish cedar in the mahogany family, seemingly thick enough to support his weight. Carefully, he lifted himself to a seated position. He took a sufficient lead line and swung the hook back and forth, weighing just how much strength to put behind his toss. He was fortunate that it was a clear shot, free of intervening branches, and his eye didn't fail him. "Fuck all," he whooped, as the four hooked arms of the grappling bit into the wood of the *Cedrela* branch. A few explorative yanks on the line convinced him he could proceed successfully. Moving slowly, in an effort not to rock his cradle, he tied his pack to the free end of the rope, and lowered it slowly towards the ground where it landed with a satisfying thump. To his gratified ears, it was the loveliest sound that he'd ever heard. Gripping the rope with his ant-bitten hands, Sorrentino rolled out of the *guarumo* into the open space between the two trees, dangling only a few feet below the anchored grappling, his aching legs wrapped around the rope. Slowly, he commenced his descent, inching his way downward in a reverse rope trick. Gar was tall and wiry, but muscular, with a phenomenal ability to block out pain, and his descent was relatively easy.

After trying in vain to dislodge the grappling from the cedar branch with several painful yanks, Sorrentino reached into his pack and took out a lightweight 9 mm semi-automatic pistol. "More than one way to skin a cat," he muttered. That had been his old man's favorite aphorism. The Cincinnati Botanical Garden's field office in Lima at the National Museum was well-apportioned with accouterments for surviving field trips into the tropical wilderness, and he had two more clips in his pack. He took sight of the cedar limb that held his hook and pulley assembly. Bullet by bullet, he blasted the wood away from the points of the hook. Garwell was a very good shot. Still, it took most of the 13-round clip to liberate the grappling, and with a last pull, the assembly and rope tumbled to the forest floor. He cleaned the sharp hooks off carefully, capped them, and returned the rope to his pack.

The events of the day at last overcame him, and he sank to the ground, growing light-headed. His body ached again, but the thought of chewing two more aspirins made him grimace. He glanced at his watch. It was 3 pm. He had about 3 hours before darkness to find some food and water, especially the latter. *I should make a shelter*, he thought. His eyes grew heavy. "No!" he said aloud. But his chin fell to his chest, and he was soon asleep.

He woke with a start. "Shit!" he exclaimed as he rose to his feet. Sorrentino now had only an hour of gloomy daylight left at his disposal. Gar surveyed the area. He was amid primary *terra firma* forest, and so successfully did the rooftop canopy intercept and consume the sunlight that there was a park-like understory that needed no machete blade to clear a path. Sorrentino spied the trunks of two sub-canopy trees that would serve as posts to string his hammock. And the rope tied higher on the same trees would allow him to erect a tarp roof to stay dry, under which he could hang his mosquito netting. The dry season was nearing its close, and the intermittent storms that occur periodically during the dry months were increasing in frequency. As if to add credence, he heard the distant rumble of thunder. He set off to make his camp, extracting one of two energy bars that he had in his pack, savoring small bites as he labored.

As his bedroom took shape in the last light of day, the forest sounds transformed into the night suite of nocturnal birds, the hum of insects, and myriad sounds for which Sorrentino could only guess an identity. A spectacled owl began its low whooping call in a nearby tree. Gar fished in his pack for the last energy bar; tomorrow, he would search for breakfast in the forest. He was fairly confident of finding at least some errant fruit at the tail end of the dry season when many of the tree species would be flowering. But water was his foremost concern. And insect repellent, as the mosquito hordes gathered wherever bare skin presented itself. He applied it lavishly, withstanding the painful stinging that exploded across his ant bites, and then set about making a small fire using the lighter in his pack. Dry fiber from the old leaf bases of an *inayuga* palm served as tinder, followed by some fallen dead tree branches that snapped sharply across his knee (only the right one, as his left was swollen with a bruise).

Garwell pulled a headlamp from his pack and pulled the woven elastic band around his head. He clicked it on, and a bright LED beam bathed his encampment in harsh light. Sorrentino intended to always keep his fire in sight but hoped to either spot some edible fruit or a stem he could tap for water. To his satisfaction, only a few yards from the large *inayuga* palm, he found a younger and shorter individual that bore a cluster of ripe fruits. Gar peeled the tough skin of the fruit with his knife and popped it skinned into his mouth. The pulp was sweet and refreshing, allowing him to swallow three aspirin whole. He ate his full, placing the seeds in his satchel to crack open later and eat the oil rich endosperm inside. "Not bad for a start," he mused.

The thunder had not abated, had in fact grown closer. A gusty wind rustled about the canopy trees. Gar made his way back to the fire. The air below the forest giants was yet still. The owl had ceased to call. He checked the tie-downs for his tarp rain fly, threw another few pieces of wood on the fire, and sat down, but not before checking the immediate surroundings for tarantulas, scorpions or snakes. Garwell was as home in the Amazon basin forests as he had been in the temperate Ozark woodlands of his Arkansas boyhood, an only child of a Christmas tree farmer and his flower grower wife, both now departed. He had walked those woods for days at a time as a boy during spring especially, when the understory erupted with ephemeral exhortations of magnificent wildflowers: trilliums, spring beauty, violets of various sorts, lady slipper orchids; the rarest he sought out with particular acumen and success. His friend Kovac once remarked about Sorrentino's dogged focus, suggesting that he lay somewhere on the Asperger's spectrum. Certainly, he internalized nothing, and that more than anything may have accounted for his seemingly guilt-free extramarital adventures. He could also be an imperious asshole, caustically scolding when a student mis-identified a plant.

As the rain fell above, he poked at the fire with a stick and attempted to devise a plan. He was confident that his GPS would fail to find any satellites unless he could stumble upon some open sky. Nevertheless, he would give it the college try in the morning. With a lurch of aggravation, he remembered removing his satellite phone from his pack and laying it on the ultralight's small console, along with his canteen. "Strike two," he sighed. Rivers were the byways of the Madre de Dios forests, and he needed to find flowing water that would eventually lead him to some human contact in the least inhabited portion of the Peruvian *selva*. He looked up, feeling the first drops from the drip-tip leaves of the upper canopy. Gar found a spot on his rain fly with frequent drip activity and fashioned a conduit to collect and funnel water to one spot. He used his helmet as a bucket reservoir. The precipitation increased perceptibly, and Sorrentino called it a night. He scooted below the tarp and netting, and gingerly lowered himself onto his hammock. He was suspended to about one and a half feet from the ground. His tightly zipped pack he hung from a hook that he screwed into the trunk of one of his post trees. Gar heard the comforting gurgle of a steady stream of water echoing in his helmet. Sorrentino wrapped himself up in a Mylar thermal blanket and inched around for a comfortable position. The temperature would drop ten degrees before daybreak. He watched his fire die, and the fading flames lulled him to sleep. He awoke only once during the night. Some animal he could not recognize was emitting the most mournful sound he'd ever heard. It sounded like the wail of some creature knowing that death was approaching. It repeated itself maybe six times before moving off or passing on.

Garwell woke as soon as daylight penetrated the primary forest canopy. It was cool and humid; he kept the thermal blanket around himself for a while until it became an encumbrance to activity. The fire was out, and he didn't relight it, since he wished to move on as soon as possible. But he was thirsty, and his helmet was full. He pulled a collapsible plastic cup from his pack and dipped it into the water. The water tasted like divine nectar to his parched lips. He slugged down four cups, reducing his reservoir to half its volume.

From inside his pack, he withdrew a collapsible plastic bottle, which he extended and filled with the remainder. Thirsty no longer, Sorrentino tried to bring his GPS to life, but he quickly turned it off when it warned that no satellites could be found. He concluded it was time to find breakfast.

He walked with his short machete out, putting small blazes onto the side of tree trunks he would most readily see on his return. Garwell used his compass religiously, maintaining a northeastern track. A huge, buttressed forest giant, a fig, he surmised, was his traveler's tree. He never let it out of his sight. He knew how bewildering the forest could be. Gar had not proceeded half a mile before he found a fruiting *ñejilla* palm, a clustering and ferociously spiny species of *Bactris* that also produced delicious fruit pulp. A single cluster of the purple fruits, looking to be at peak ripeness, dangled from one stem. Sorrentino would have to maneuver his hand through a labyrinth of sharp, black spines to extract the fruit, or do some judicious pruning. He cut off some stems that were in his way, removing thorns from the bigger stems, until he created a clear path to cut off the fruit cluster. Coupled with the remaining *inayuga* palm fruits, he would be well sated before commencing his trek. He made his way back to his soon-to-be abandoned camp and made good on his bounty of palm fecundity.

On the way back to his camp, he identified a *sangre de grado* tree, the sap of which was a powerful healer of wounds. He made several blows to the trunk with his machete, and it immediately exuded the red sap. He used the sticky liquid from the injured tissue to make a poultice, which he applied to the cuts on his arms and legs. Gar knew from experience that the cuts would start to heal as the gummy sap dried.

Sorrentino broke camp with customary efficiency, rearranging his backpack to keep essentials near at hand. He hung the water bottle and helmet from external loops using sturdy clips, and placed the pistol in his waistband below the pack. He tested his reach and clenched the firearm easily. When his tasks were completed, there was little trace that the encampment had ever been there. He reasoned that maintaining a southeasterly track would most likely lead him to creeks and streams that would eventually flow into a navigable river.

Garwell moved through the forest on his compass track, which he wore around his neck from a leather thong. He paused now and again, to strike a glancing machete blow at a tree trunk, observing the color of the sap, the smell of the freshly cut wood. From these clues, Gar could frequently identify trees to family, and half the time to genus. He read the forest only as someone with a rare intimacy with it could, which gave him a deep and, by most estimation, peculiar satisfaction. Most of all, he experienced no fear. His own death was as much an abstraction to him as the emotional lives of his wife and children. Yet when in his company, the fearlessness was contagious, and Anton Kovac could remember those moments over a quarter of a century past as the truest instances of freedom he'd ever experienced, deep in the sodden womb of tropical rainforest.

As he pushed forward into the forest, Sorrentino kept his eyes peeled for a tree gap. An open stretch of sky was his best hope for getting a GPS connection to some Southern Hemisphere satellite. Instead, the canopy remained unbroken, as the temperature rose as morning ebbed. He passed below a rare deciduous tree of the forest, a pink trumpet tree, or *ipê*, which, judging by the sheer abundance of its fallen large flowers, was in peak bloom. He had sailed over a few on his ill-fated canopy survey. A blast of sunlight up ahead stopped him in his tracks. His luck remained consistent. A forest giant had come down recently, and he had a shot at determining where in southeastern Peru he stood.

Garwell made his way to the tree gap, which was no more than perhaps twenty feet in diameter. He dropped his pack, found the GPS, and powered it up. The instrument's search seemed interminable, but the device finally contacted a single satellite. Gar hoped the latest maps had been downloaded to memory. A map view suddenly burst into focus. He zoomed in as more features appeared. Sorrentino immediately identified the Las Piedras River and estimated that where he stood now lay over a hundred miles to the northwest. He had departed the previous morning from the small river town of Lucerna and had maintained a northwest bearing. Gar zoomed in, hoping that smaller and closer tributaries of the river, itself a significant branch of the Madre de Dios, would resolve on the screen and be situated much closer to where he found himself. A small squiggle appeared on the GPS screen. If he maintained his southeast track, he'd intercept the nameless river in about twenty miles. He had little hope of encountering any boat traffic on the closest tributary of the Las Piedras. It was the dry season, and significant lengths of the smaller rivers were likely passable only by canoe with lots of intermittent portage. Another trek of 60-70 miles would bring him to the Las Piedras, where he assuredly could find boat passage to Lucerna and ultimately Puerto Maldonado. He turned off the GPS. He was at about 900-foot elevation. If he stayed on course, he'd intercept the small river at 700 feet. He figured he had at least five days of forest slogging ahead, longer if he botanized, which he most assuredly would. Sorrentino had penetrated the Madre de Dios Territorial reserve. The only humans living in the reserve were tribes that forsook a contact with the modern world. The odds of encountering any were infinitesimally small, though even if he did, they'd likely remain invisible to him.

Gar drifted through the forest understory, across the gently rolling terrain, taking compass readings every twenty minutes or so to maintain his path. He spied little in the way of animal life, aside from insects in the dark understory of the forest. Most of the birds and arboreal mammals would be high in the canopy. Descending a gentle slope, he surprised a troop of brown capuchin monkeys, who seemed to deride his presence with sharp guttural vocalizations. They peered down at him with their perches in the lower branches of an *abiu* tree, which bore a smattering of fruiting branches. He circled the trunk of the tree, eyes glued to the blanket of leaf litter. Gar found six relatively unscathed fruits. He cut into the yellow drupes with alacrity, involuntarily closing his eyes as he bit into the sweet and astonishingly delicious white pulp that surrounded the black seed. The genus *Pouteria* to which *abiu* belonged was a goldmine of forest fruits in the sapote family.

The hours slipped by rapidly as he walked. High above him, toucans and macaws serenaded him. The toucans occasionally dropped into the sub-canopy and regarded him with a mixture of defiance and indifference. It surprised him to see how late it was when he glanced at his watch, nearing four in the afternoon. He anticipated that he'd accomplished half of his first trip. Tomorrow, by this time, he should be on the bluffs overlooking the tributary of the Río Las Piedras.

He searched his vicinity for a campsite. As always, his first objective was two trees close enough together to support his hammock. One half mile further into the forest, he found two small trees that sufficed. Everything else proceeded by rote. A swift movement caught the corner of his eye. He deftly turned toward the spot and immediately caught sight of a fat *paca* foraging in the leaf litter about twenty feet away. Stealthily, Gar reached for the pistol in his waistband. He was not a vegetarian, and this forest cousin to *cuy* (guinea pigs), would fill his belly that night.

Sorrentino skinned and cleaned the *paca* about twenty yards away from his camp to dissuade predators. If a jaguar paid him a visit, perhaps the organ meats would be satisfactory booty. He erected a spit over his fire and felt the protein's siren call as the flesh roasted. His stomach gurgled in anticipation. Gar chased his *paca* with the remains of his water that night.

He didn't sense any indication of rain in the short term. Sorrentino had to rely upon condensation on his rain fly in the morning and then scout out a liana whose stem, if cut, would yield water. He bedded down for the night and was immediately asleep. He never saw the jaguar slink from around a tree near where he'd deposited the entrails. With a glance over its shoulder at the fire still blazing in Sorrentino's hearth, it made quick work of the heart and liver, before silently moving back into the darkness.

The following morning, he harvested only a quarter cup of condensate off his rain fly. He sipped it slowly, savoring each taste. He found a liana not too far from his camp, and with his machete, first tested the sap. It was clear and had no unappealing odor. Sorrentino cut several feet, first from a spot over his head, and next below, about a foot from the ground. Holding the vine segment vertically, he first filled his water bottle, then collected the excess in his helmet. Gar collected over a quart of water. He drank all that he had accumulated in his helmet. Garwell found another half dozen *abiu* fruits on the forest floor and made quick work of them. He opened a small leather bag attached to his belt and withdrew a wad of coca leaves and some crushed shell powder from a corked vial. Gar wrapped the lime with the leaves and placed the mass into his mouth and gently chewed it before pushing it against his cheek. That side of his mouth grew numb, and he was soon energized, focused, and no longer hungry. He quickly broke camp, packed his things, and continued through the forest.

Sorrentino had a preternatural sense of how the forest changed, with differences in soil composition, elevation and slope. His prescience was confirmed when he saw pink flowers fallen from a tree with buttresses and stilt roots he recognized as a *brea-caspi*. This species was typically found in wet, even swampy places, and its presence in *terra firma* forest meant that he was descending and nearing water. Sorrentino listened carefully. Gar could hear the music of a creek, perhaps a spring, no more than a hundred yards distant. He drew nearer and was greeted by as welcome a scene as he could hope for, clear water burbling over a few rocks as it made its way to exactly where he was headed. Gar filled his helmet and dumped it over his head. The cool water revitalized him, and he filled his water bottle to the brim. There was little sediment in it.

Garwell figured to follow the creek downstream. He withdrew a handful of palm seeds and cracked them open with the blunt edge of his machete. The meat tasted like coconut; it was oily and slightly sweet. He hoped he might surprise another *paca* for dinner when he made camp.

The creek meandered in roughly a southeastern direction, speeding up when the terrain dropped a few feet, slowing down on the more level passages. The forest was changing again, opening slightly. Higher light inspired exuberant growth in the understory, which slowed his pace for the last few miles.

The trees abruptly came to a halt on the cliffs above the river. He had to hack his way through a final curtain of head-high grass and herbaceous vines before he could see the waters perhaps a hundred and fifty feet below. His companion creek merely tumbled over the edge and formed a small cataract on its descent. Gar welcomed the sun on his face and grinned happily. A few more days, and he'd be on his way to Puerto Maldonado.

Sorrentino figured that at some point he would encounter a low area along the bluff that allowed him to approach the river's edge. The current was steadfast, but the river often broke off into three or more branches that swept past islands of water-smoothed rock. Plants colonized very few of them, for during the rainy season, the river became a raging torrent, rising in places at least thirty to fifty feet above its current bed.

To his surprise, the riverbed suddenly widened enormously where a broad meandering loop had been isolated into a small oxbow lake. On his side of the river, the forest floor gently sloped to a sandy beach. A grove of *aguaje* palms stood at the terminus of the beach, and he was gratified to see that several females held fruit. The first thing he did was shed his clothes and bathe in a deep pool along the river's main course. The water was surprisingly cool. He washed his clothes as best he could, set them on river rocks to dry and made his way back to the palms. The *aguaje* fruits wore their relation to Asia's high climbing and speciose rattan palms in the form of brown scales on the skin of the fruit. Below this was a thick layer of nutritional and comestible enough yellow pulp. The silvery palmate leaves were a common sight throughout the wetter parts of the Amazon basin, sometimes forming immense colonies in swampy places, and the fruit was much loved in South America, especially for making ice cream.

The absurdity of standing naked in the middle of the Madre de Dios watershed consuming *aguaje* after *aquaje* suddenly occurred to him and he laughed. As he feasted, he roamed the perimeter of the oxbow lake, searching for a site accommodating to his camp gear. He came across two male *aguaje* palms that were properly sized and spaced to hang his hammock, in addition to a rope line for the mosquito netting and rain fly. Few animals other than visiting insects would be attracted to the male palms, he reasoned.

Sorrentino had only been lost once during his many field trips into the Amazon. It had happened almost ten years ago, accompanied only by Oscar Crescente, over six hundred miles closer to the equator, deep within the wilderness northwest of Iquitos. It was also the single instance where Oscar had lost his nerve, convinced that they would stumble about for days without food or water, despite their combined knowledge of the forest's ability to quell both hunger and thirst. Gar had somehow dropped his compass while traversing a log bridge across a small but swiftly flowing stream a few miles from their base camp, and much as they tried, failed to retrieve it. Garwell hid from Oscar the fact that he was feverish, a re-blooming of malaria that he had contracted for the first time three years previously, and his illness had made him careless. As the day waned, Sorrentino sank deeper into fever-induced lethargy, while Crescente mumbled a collusion of prayer and curses. To their surprise and no small amount of relief, on the third day they suddenly burst into a clearing, no doubt an abandoned slash and burn agricultural site. Clustered at one end of the opening, was an array of fluorescent tents, with a handful of *gringos* standing around, mouths agape at this apparition of two dirty and sweat-soaked young men bursting out of the forest. "Ho," Gar hailed them, raising his arm in a salute. He then collapsed into a heap amid their small circle, while Oscar paced, reciting "*¡El está loco!*" — He's crazy! —, over and over like a mantra. They were ornithologists, chasing rumors of an unnamed parrot species. The leader of the expedition, which had been dropped by helicopter into the old clearing, knew Sorrentino by name, when Oscar told them who they were. The scientists administered water and several quinine tablets to Gar and carried him into one of the tents. He slept for six hours. The next day, one of the ornithologists' indigenous guides led him and Oscar back to their camp. In the intervening years, Crescente never let him forget the incident.

Gar collected his sun-dried clothes and dressed as the air grew cooler and the shadows long. He doused himself with DEET. He rummaged through his pack for his fishing line and hook and strolled over the forest edge. Just inside the canopy, he found a clump of bamboo and sliced off a narrow stem to use as a perfunctory pole. Moving riverside, he caught a grasshopper to use as bait, and was rewarded with a bite after a few minutes, a twelve-inch *pavon*, or peacock bass. Garwell landed it easily and swiped its head off with his machete. He cleaned the fish by the river, and returning to camp, made a fire to roast his catch. Roasted *pavon* and a handful of *aguaje* fruits made for a comfortably filling dinner.

While he sat ruminating, a family of capybaras emerged from the forest to drink and swim in the lake. For a moment, he considered harvesting one to provide protein for the rest of his trek downriver. But he found the scene so bucolic, he let it go, figuring that the river would provide abundant fish for the next few days. The idea of having to smoke the meat and haul it with him was also unappetizing. Sorrentino was not sentimental. He took no pleasure in dispatching animals for their flesh, but did what was necessary to survive.

His thoughts turned to Nell. Their separation was likely heading towards divorce. Marriage, children—it all seemed like a dream that he haplessly sleep-walked through, with little attention to detail. It had been his friend Anton Kovac who had taught his son to throw and catch a ball, not Garwell. Lord knows, he'd been a terrible husband and a lack-luster father. He sighed deeply. Gar spent half the year in the field, and it was only deep in the tropical forests that he loved did he feel at peace with himself.

Birds gathered to settle into their roosts for the night. A troop of noisy scarlet macaws settled among the female *aguaje* palms, but only stopped to dine before moving on. A harpy eagle wafted soundlessly to its nest in the canopy of a forest giant. The fading diurnal chorus was transformed as nocturnal voices joined the fray. He recognized the moaning call of a great patoo, which would likely sound throughout the night.

As the shadows deepened, he perambulated along the forest edge, gathering fruits of a *sacha inchi* vine that clambered over the other vegetation. Roasted, the seeds lost their toxic principles and were loaded with protein and nutritive oils. He picked a single ripe *tumbo* fruit and sucked the tart juice from around the seeds. Returning to camp, he finished his bed preparations and added wood to his fire. He wrapped the *sacha inchi* seeds in the banana-like leaves of a heliconia that flourished at the forest edge and buried them in the river sand near but below the fire. The coals would roast them slowly through the night.

He woke at first light. A wispy fog of water vapor crowned the forest treetops, the breath of the *selva* returning to the troposphere. He dug the seeds out from where he had buried them in the sand. They were still warm, and a couple of handfuls made a tasty breakfast. He broke camp and filled his bottle from a small waterfall where another creek joined the river.

Gar figured he'd follow the river until its bed became impassable. It was almost eight miles before the channel narrowed through a canyon that forced him to climb back into the forest. Passing the base of a huge Brazil nut tree, he surprised a red brocket deer, which stared at him for a moment before bounding away through the forest. He kept the river to his left as he trekked, and could hear the water's brisk tempo in its passage through the canyon.

Sorrentino suddenly experienced a sharp sting in his neck. Gar reflexively brought his hand up to the spot and touched something feathery. He pulled it out of his skin and glimpsed a dart fashioned from a palm spine attached to a small iridescent feather. He turned but saw nothing as his knees gave way and he crumpled to the ground.

4

Kovac slipped into the auditorium stealthily, just as the moderator of the session was introducing the speaker. The room was packed, forcing Anton to stand along the wall at its rear. "With great pleasure, I introduce our keynote speaker, Dr. Garwell Sorrentino of the Cincinnati Botanical Garden. The title of his talk: 'Evolution of Neotropical Plant Diversity.'"

It was Kovac's first year of graduate school at Ohio State University. He was 25 years old, and attending his first botanical society meetings, which were being held that year at his institution, likely the only reason that he could afford to attend. He had yet to settle on a mentor for his graduate work, but the speaker who ambled to the podium was high on his list. OSU had a cooperative graduate program in botany with the botanical garden where Garwell Sorrentino worked as a curator, and he was one of several Garden scientists with adjunct appointments as graduate faculty. He was notoriously discerning in selecting new students with whom to work.

Sorrentino was lanky, with a light Mediterranean cast to his complexion, black hair that just swept his collar, and a short, scruffy beard. When he spoke, someone even toned his voice, with a trace of a Texarkana accent. He had a piercing gaze over an aquiline nose that swept across the audience, pausing now and then, Kovac noted, on attractive women in the front rows of the auditorium. Gar was, at thirty-five, something of a legend already. Sorrentino's early work was on the taxonomy of the kapok trees and their relatives. Only a handful of tropical botanists rivaled his knowledge of the western

Amazon flora. Garwell demonstrated an uncanny ability to process botanical information. Seeing a plant for the first time, Gar never forgot its scientific name or the plant family to which it belonged. At thirty, he had developed a technique of forest sampling plot design that had become the de facto standard for censusing plant diversity in nature, and had since published comparative studies of equatorial African and Amazonian rain forests. Sorrentino spent no less than half of every year deep in the jungles of the Americas, and the amounts of unique collections that bore his numbered series totaled tens of thousands.

Sorrentino's talk was riveting, as he unwound his own and other scientists' theories about what accounted for the staggering number of species that populated the diverse ecosystems of the tropics. He livened up the slides of statistics with intervening photographs of life, from plants to insects to even humans. A question period followed, and Kovac moved closer to the podium, raising his hand as strode forward. "Yes, the fellow moving up the center aisle," Sorrentino said. A student volunteer ran up to Anton with a wireless microphone. "Thank you, Dr. Sorrentino, for a peerless presentation," Anton began. Gar acknowledged the compliment with a curt nod. "There are certain plant families that are hyper-diverse in tropical forests, but there are also monotypic[4] families found there as well," Anton continued. "Are you able to make any generalizations about the characteristics of the so-called winners versus the losers?"

---

[4] Monotypic: containing only a single species.

Garwell nodded. "Good question," he conceded. "We're just beginning to get some ideas." He went on for a while, listing some likely factors that contributed to such disparity. "And there is a degree of serendipity. The losers may be on their way out; you know, evolve or die."

Anton grabbed a seat near the front as he handed the microphone back to the volunteer. He hoped that his question had impressed. After a few further queries, the moderator thanked the speaker and announced a coffee break. "Perhaps Dr. Sorrentino will be available around the coffee urns for more discussion," he said hopefully.

Kovac grabbed a cup and loitered at the periphery of the ring of students, predominantly female, that surrounded Sorrentino, who clearly enjoyed the fawning attention. *I thought he's married*, Anton said to himself. Nell Sorrentino was a well-known plant taxonomist herself.

At last, the crowd thinned and Kovac drew closer. "Dr. Sorrentino, could I have a word?"

Gar's brow wrinkled, as if he was trying to place Kovac in his mind. He suddenly brightened. "Oh, hey, you were the guy with the smart question. Sure, what can I do for you?"

Anton extended his hand. "Anton Kovac," he introduced himself. "I'm a first-year grad student. I was hoping I could work with you for my Ph.D."

Sorrentino took his hand in a firm handshake. "Always interested in students who ask good questions. Tell you what," he continued, extracting his wallet from his pants' pocket. "Here's my card; give me a call. I'll be at the Garden for the next couple of weeks."

Kovac could hardly cloak his elation. He took the card and slipped it into his shirt pocket with a smile. "You can bet on it," he said. "Thanks; I'll be in touch." Garwell nodded in assent and clapped him on the shoulder.

Anton felt like clicking his heels as he rushed to the next session of the conference that he wished to attend. He'd seen no one actually do that and doubted he could manage it himself. "It's the thought that counts," he muttered.

He let a week go by before calling the number on the card. "Dr. Sorrentino's office," a female voice answered.

"Is Dr. Sorrentino available?" he asked.

"One moment. Who is calling, please?"

"Anton Kovac," he replied. "A student."

"Anton!" a familiar voice boomed into the phone. It surprised Kovac that Sorrentino appeared to remember him.

"Dr. Sorrentino," Kovac acknowledged. "I… I'm calling to discuss the possibility of working with you for my Ph.D."

"Yeah, yeah, sure. I remember you. First of all, please call me Gar. So, any chance you could come down to the Garden?"

"Absolutely," Kovac said enthusiastically. "I'm free all week."

"Great; how about Wednesday? I'll set you up with a bed in the visitor's housing."

"Fantastic; I'll see you then."

Kovac had a class he would have to miss. He liked the professor, and the subject, evolutionary genetics, was interesting. He'd already done the readings and had a few friends also taking the course on whom he could depend to share their notes.

The next morning, he set off in his old Dodge Dart for Cincinnati; a trip taking less than two hours. He parked in the large visitors' lot and made his way to the front entrance. Spring was at its peak, and tulips and late *Narcissus* filled the beds, the air redolent with fragrance, and still cool with the last touch of fading winter at this hour of the morning.

He told an attendant that he had an appointment with Garwell Sorrentino. She called the research building, which sat in the middle of the garden, and handed a visitor pass to Anton. "You know the way?" she asked. He nodded.

The azaleas were in peak bloom as he strolled towards the herbarium where Garwell had told him they'd meet. Two bronze busts, one of Charles Darwin and another of Carolus Linnaeus (Carl Linné), the acknowledged father of modern taxonomy, flanked the entrance to the building. A pigeon was currently perched on Darwin's bald pate; Anton's approach made it take wing.

Sorrentino was waiting for him at the herbarium reception area. "Anton," he hailed him. "Welcome. Let's go into my office." Curators' offices were arranged along the main walkways that led down the aisles of specimens housed in special cases. The air held a faint tang of mothballs. Gar's office was at the far end, and he motioned Anton to a well-worn chair in the room's corner as they entered. One wall was lined with bookshelves, interspersed with curios accumulated from many adventures in the tropics. Sorrentino slid into a leather chair behind his expansive desk, which was covered with piles of manuscripts and stacks of scholarly reprints. "I looked over the resume that you sent. You did a master's with Bruce Stauber at Duke. Impressive." He paused and smiled. "What made you decide to jump ship?" Anton wondered if Gar had phoned his previous mentor.

"You pretty much," Kovac answered. "There is no one I'd rather work with more."

Sorrentino considered this in silence, absently stroking his beard. "Well," he finally said, "that's all quite flattering, but why should I care?"

"I've published a dozen papers," Kovac responded forthrightly. "I worked at the National Tropical Botanical Garden in Hawaii before I started my master's degree. And I'm a pretty decent tree climber."

Sorrentino chuckled. "OK," he replied. Gar absently drummed his fingers on his desktop. "That's all good. But why do you want to work with me?"

Anton leaned forward in his chair. "Because you're the best. Your work is impeccable. Just point me in the right direction. I've got a few ideas of my own."

Garwell grinned. "I'll listen to them," he said, "sometimes." He stood, and Anton suspected he was subtly being dismissed. To his surprise, Sorrentino asked him what he was doing that summer.

"I'm open," Kovac replied.

"I could use a field assistant. We'll be in Peru, starting in Iquitos. Your expenses will be covered plus a small stipend. What do you say?"

The unexpected opportunity to spend time in the field with Garwell Sorrentino rather blew Anton away. "Wow! I'd be hon…"

"Don't say it," Gar interrupted; he grinned again. "The important thing is you said you're good at climbing trees."

Gar invited Anton to dinner at the Sorrentino's that night. He knew Nell Sorrentino by reputation and publications. He picked up a nice bottle of wine on the way over. Gar greeted him at the door of their small home in a tree-lined neighborhood near the Garden. Native azaleas were in extravagant bloom around the house.

"Nell, this is Anton Kovac, my new student." Kovac found Nell Sorrentino strikingly beautiful, a mix of European, Caribbean and Brazilian genotypes that conjoined had created perfection.

Nell Sorrentino entered the room from the back bedroom where she and her mother had just placed the baby to sleep in her crib. She corralled her energetic four-year-old son off to bed with apologies. Nell also maintained an apartment near the New York Botanical Garden, her place of employment, and she spent two to three weeks each month there. Gar visited for at least a week when he wasn't in the field. Fortunately, Nell's mother currently lived with them; it would otherwise never have been possible to make it work. She was a reserved woman of advanced middle age, who, Anton sensed, was slightly disapproving of Gar. She kept her own counsel on that during the evening. The dinner was a delightful melange of Brazilian and Caribbean fare. "Mom handled most of this," Nell revealed. Anton bade his compliments to the chef, who smiled and nodded in acknowledgement.

Gar brought out *cafezinho*, the heavily sweetened Brazilian espresso; Nell followed him from the kitchen with the classic Brazilian dessert, "Romeo and Juliet," slices of slightly salty, creamy soft cheese topped with a slice of molded guava paste.

"So, Anton," Nell asked, "what group are you thinking of working on?"

"Well, I'm open to suggestions, but I've always fancied *Clusia*," he replied. *Clusia*, perhaps the largest genus in its family, Clusiaceae, was a group of several hundred species, found only in the Americas. More than a few began life as stranglers, beginning life as a seed left behind by a bird, and eventually engulfing its aerial host. Many had exquisite flowers.

"Good choice," Gar said. "There are some sections of the genus that are a complete mess taxonomically." This was standard fair in the realm of systematic botany research—the term most of the practitioners preferred for taxonomy. Pick a group of plants to study and generate a treatment of the species, culminating in a monograph allowing other botanists to identify them; assign the dried specimens interred in museums, universities and botanical gardens to the various species; and attempt to puzzle out their evolutionary relationships. Using DNA sequences to assist in the latter, which eventually dominated the literature, was still in its relative infancy.

Nell's mother excused herself, and they rejoined to the living room, to comfortable chairs and a couch. Gar explained why he had turned from taxonomic botany to biodiversity studies using his famous plot sampling strategy, while Nell read the first draft of a student's dissertation. At a lull in the conversation, Kovac glanced at his watch. "I'd better get back to the apartment," He announced. Sorrentino walked him to the door.

"I'll be in touch as summer draws near," he told Anton. They shook hands, as if signing an agreement. "*Clusia*. Good choice," he stated again. "*Clusia amazonica* is usually in our plots. You'll probably get to climb one."

♦ ♦ ♦ ♦ ♦

"How the hell am I supposed to climb that?" Anton exclaimed.

Kovac and Sorrentino stood at the base of a thirty-foot tall *Clusia amazonica* in forest along a tributary of the Pastaza River in Peru. "You don't have to," Gar assured him. "We'll find more, smaller ones to make specimens in this plot. But we want to make a note of this one; it's clearly engulfed its host and may be the oldest individual in this population." His last comment was addressed to a Peruvian who stood nearby, a man a few years older than Kovac, named Oscar Crescente.

"*Claro, jefe*," Crescente proclaimed.

"I hate when he calls me *jefe*," Gar muttered.

"I heard that," Oscar teased. His English was good, though he seldom spoke it.

"Let's be sure to get all the ground trash," Sorrentino commanded. He used that pejorative term for anything non-woody growing in the primary forest understory.

The evening was spent getting their samples into the plant presses. They were set to dry over a gas burner in a frame that Oscar put together while several pacas roasted over the fire that Kovac built at their campsite. Gar made copious notes in his field book for each specimen, a total of 100 different numbers. The ease with which Sorrentino identified everything to genus impressed Anton, and at least half to species.

Gar and Oscar had met at the National Museum in Lima five years ago, Oscar recounted when work was completed, as a flask of pisco made its way around their circle. Crescente identified the sounds of the night; he clearly was well versed in Peruvian natural history, learned at his father's knee, a Belgian expat who fell in love with the Amazon and married a local woman from Tarapoto. Oscar obtained a bachelor's degree in natural science from the National University in that city. He earned a living as a guide for biologists and tourists operating out of Iquitos, but always made time for field work with his friend and mentor Garwell Sorrentino.

Kovac had experienced nothing like those six weeks in northeast Peru. They literally lived off the natural bounty: game and fruit from the forest, fish from the river. Their water came from the clear streams that fed the river. Sorrentino was a brilliant teacher; he tested Anton's botanical acumen constantly. "Crush that leaf; smell it. That should give you the family;" he cajoled often, thrifty of praise when Kovac succeeded, and almost malevolently mocking when he didn't. Anton noticed Oscar gave as good as he got from Gar; *I guess with time comes privileges*, Kovac thought to himself.

Indeed, so they did. After successfully defending his dissertation, which focused on a hotspot of diversification in the genus *Clusia* that Gar had discovered in the *"ceja de la montaña"*[5] cloud forests of the eastern Peruvian Andes, Kevin Hobart hired him as an assistant curator at the Cincinnati Botanical Garden. One of the dozen new species that Kovac described became *Clusia sorrentinoana*. Over the next five years, the mentor/student relationship between Garwell and Anton became a friendship as deep as any Kovac had experienced in his 20's. He became an adjunct member of the family, quietly head-over-heels in love with Nell, and frequent babysitter for the children after Nell's mother returned to Brazil.

Anton spent cumulatively months in the field with Gar and Oscar, traversing hectares of northeastern Peru and with Oscar alone after their friend disappeared. He watched uneasily as the Sorrentino's marriage faltered amid Gar's myriad infidelities. He never discussed this with either of the two, both friends that he valued as treasure. But Nell's sadness grew ever more apparent as time went by, until one day, when both she and Anton were at the New York Botanical Garden, she informed him of their separation. Nell and the children moved permanently to New York. Five years

---

[5] Eyebrow of the mountain.

later, Gar was lost, and in another five, a disgraced Kovac joined her back east.

5

Puerto Maldonado was a classic Peruvian river town, rough-hewn, but beginning to develop a slight cosmopolitan facade as its population inched over eighty thousand, and for the fact that the Interoceanic Highway passed directly through it. This huge, overwrought project steeped in corruption was designed to link Brazil to Peru's Pacific coast ports, but evidence suggested that relatively little shipping was taking advantage of the road's existence. Instead, the paved highway was turning into a thoroughfare of deforestation in both Peru and Brazil, penetrating miles into primary forest on either side of the road. Kovac hoped he'd be able to locate Oscar. He'd half-expected to see Kevin Hobart's presumed spy on the small plane from Cusco, and he was almost disappointed when he did not.

Anton and Nell took rickshaw taxis to a decent hotel far enough from the city center to suppress the cacophony of downtown. The humid swelter of six hundred feet of elevation was a difficult adjustment from the mountainous thin-air coolness of Cusco. They dropped off their bags in their rooms, and took taxis back to the city center, choosing, of all things, an Italian restaurant that made passable chicken parmigiana. Nell chose a local fish grilled with capers, white wine, and butter.

The town had few tourist attractions; most travelers were pass-throughs on the way to one of the jungle lodges that lay down river. The Guillermo Billinghurst Bridge over the Madre de Dios, which connected the town to the outside world, was a big draw in its first months after completion, so they walked the one and a half miles to see it. *"Progresso,"* Anton declared with deliberate irony. The Interoceanic Highway cut through primary *terra firma* forest, and its construction had incited deforestation along both sides of the road, especially after it crossed into Brazil.

"Tomorrow, we'll try to find Oscar," Kovac announced, to which Nell nodded. "We can't expect to make any headway without him," he added.

The heat had hardly abated as night fell, and they took the rickshaws back to their hotel. Nell excused herself to read, while Kovac flipped through the 8 channels available on the small tv. He settled on a soccer game between the national teams of Peru and Argentina but watched with only vague attention. Kovac felt the dark cloud of depression creeping across his mind. *Hello darkness,* he thought to himself. He got up and checked the mini bar, extracting three equally lilliputian bottles of whiskey, knocking back one after the other. Satisfyingly drunk, he threw himself onto the narrow bed and slipped into welcome unconsciousness.

Both Anton and Nell woke early; they had to wait twenty minutes before breakfast would be served downstairs. They walked over to a small park that was shaded by a large Brazil nut that had been spared the ax. A profusion of bird life milled about the expansive canopy, rising from their roosts and commencing their own day. He and Nell tried to outdo each other naming the species; she won hands down.

After breakfast, they strolled into the central district. Anton looked for shops that Oscar was likely to patronize, and a store called "La Selva," which dealt in used camping gear, was as good a start as any. An over-solicitous young man greeted them. Kovac noted that a large section of the store bore wares for gold mining.

"*¿Señor, conoce a Oscar Crescente?*"[6] Kovac asked.

"*Claro,*" the young man said, subdued as the prospect of a solid sale evaporated. He motioned with his hand for them to follow him outside the store. "*A tres cuadras directamente de aquí. Busque 'Vistas Manu.'*"[7]

"Well, that was hard," Kovac said ironically to Nell as they walked the three blocks. A large painting of the cliffs in Manu where thousands of parrots and macaws gathered to consume the red clay, thought to aid in detoxifying some elements of their diets, adorned a sign above the entrance. The artist was skilled; the details on the birds were luminous.

They entered the shop, which was arranged with desks in the front two-thirds, and two small offices in the back. One young man sat with prospective clients at one station, an equally young couple who spoke English with European accents that Kovac couldn't place. Another agent waited on an older Black American couple. A young

---

[6] Sir, do you know Oscar Crescente?

[7] Three blocks straight from here. Look for Vistas Manu.

woman emerged from one of the offices in the back. *"¿Puedo ayudarle?"*[8] she chirped.

"Buscamos a Oscar Crescente, por favor," Anton answered. *"¿Está aquí hoy?"*[9]

The young woman frowned. *"Lo siento. Me temo que el Sr. Crescente está en el campo con un grupo. Debe regresar mañana."*[10]

Tomorrow. Anton requested a piece of paper and a pen. He wrote out his and Nell's name, and that of their hotel. *"Gracias,"* he said when she told him that she would make sure Mr. Crescente received it. They left Vistas Manu and continued further along the commercial main street of the town, stopping to buy freshly processed *camu camu* juice, sweetened just enough with sugar. It was getting almost painfully hot and humid. Kovac contrived to place a wet bandana over his head underneath his wide-brimmed hat.

"Oscar's done well for himself," Nell commented.

"It would seem," Kovac agreed.

"Let's head back," Nell said. "Our hotel does have a pool."

While Nell made good on her promise to soak in the pool, Kovac pulled out his web book for the first time since they'd arrived in Peru. It was clunky in performance, but lightweight enough not to be a bother on the road. He owed Kevin a message. He waited

---

[8] Can I help you?

[9] Please, we are looking for Oscar Crescente. Is he here today?

[10] I'm sorry. I'm afraid Mr. Crescente is in the field with a group. He'll be back tomorrow.

interminably for it to connect to the hotel wireless. When it finally did, he whipped off a terse email to Hobart:

"Greetings. In Puerto Maldonado. Seeing Oscar tomorrow. – AK."

The next day began with little but waiting around the hotel for Oscar to contact them. Having no idea of his schedule, they were reluctant to lurk around the office of Vistas Manu, waiting for Oscar to show up. Early in the afternoon, a white SUV came roaring up to the front of the hotel. A magnetic "Vistas Manu" sign was affixed to both front doors, miniatures of the large sign above their office. Out popped a slightly paunchy middle-aged gentleman, who flashed a huge grin when he spied Anton heading over to greet him. He struck a theatrical pose, threw his arms out and roared, "For you is cheap!" He enveloped Kovac in a bear hug, but his eyes opened wide when he caught sight of Nell. "Nellita!" he exclaimed, and she came forward, somewhat bashfully. The embrace was transferred to her. "Aieee, come. We have a lot to talk about." He ushered them into his truck. "Daniela insists you have dinner with us. *¿Eso está bien?*"

Oscar threw the truck into gear, and they headed out to peripheral parts of the city. Eventually the tarmac gave way to gravel and finally just graded dirt. Here and there, small tracts of secondary forest elbowed their way among the crowded settlements of the poor. The SUV suddenly swung into a drive that terminated in a few minutes near a giant kapok tree, a lonely sentinel of a fractional domain. The immense tree was leafless but swelling flower buds heralded the approach of the wet season. They came to a halt by a large house circled by an ironwork fence and gate. The front yard was a riot of fruit and flowering trees. A large dog came bounding out of the house and barked wildly at them, tail wagging. "Don't worry about him. He's dangerous only if you have *un corazon negro*."[11] Oscar grabbed their bags and brought them to the front, which was an archway into a shaded lanai that circled the house. The actual entrance was set back from the lanai. The door opened, and Daniela Crescente welcomed them into the house. When last Anton had seen her, she was a young woman with long black hair, now cut short and graying. "*¿Recuérdame?*" Kovac said with a smile. Remember me?

"*Claro*, Anton!" she remonstrated. Nell stepped forward and hugged Oscar's wife, kissing both cheeks in the Latin way. "Welcome to you both," she continued in English. "Come, Nell; help me in the kitchen." Daniela was a teacher in town, Kovac remembered, or at least had been. He asked her if she still taught, and she shook her head. Vistas Manu was apparently doing quite well. Daniela explained that they'd bought the land and built the house ten years ago, after moving from Iquitos. Their oldest son, Antonio, lived with his young family in a house on a parcel adjacent to theirs about a half mile through the disturbed forest. Kovac remembered him as a wiry six-year-old.

Oscar appeared with a tray of pisco sours over ice. He dropped off two for the women and motioned Anton to the lanai with a tilt of his head. They sat in a shady corner around a metal table in

---

[11] A black heart.

comfortable wicker chairs. Oscar told him how the genesis of his ecotourism business began, fifteen years old at this point. He still assisted biologists in the field, mostly during the rainy season when business was much lighter at Vistas Manu.

Crescente leaned back in his chair and eyed Kovac with a mischievous twinkle in his eye. "So, amigo, what brings you back to Peru?"

Anton asked him if he'd received the letter that he had written. Oscar shook his head. "Really?" Kovac says with surprise. "So, you have no idea?" Another shake of the head. "Kevin Hobart thinks that Gar may be alive."

Oscar stiffened in his seat and placed his cocktail on the table. "What? That's crazy. We found the wreckage; it was torn to shreds. He can't have survived."

Kovac shrugged. "What else did you find?"

"We found no trace of him. You know that." He took a long pull of his drink. "Did he explain why he thinks so?"

Anton nodded. "His Garden has an active team working in the Madre de Dios watershed. They collaborated with several acculturated indigenous communities in the Reserve. Several of them are rife with rumors of a gringo living with an isolated group in the forests northwest of the Río Las Piedras." Kovac had almost said "our Garden," as if his links hadn't been sundered two decades ago.

"Seems like a fool's errand," Crescente remarked.

"*Tal vez*," Kovac agreed. "And we're the fools."

They grew silent as dusk enveloped the lanai, and mosquitos buzzed around their heads. "Come, I want to show you something." Oscar stood and waited for Anton to finish the rest of his drink before following him inside the house. They strolled into a room deep in a corner of the house, set off by beautiful French doors carved from mahogany. This was, of course, Oscar's office and library. Books had long outgrown shelves and were piled all over the main workspace. An old Mac occupied part of the desk; the monitor displayed Vistas Manu's iconic sign.

Oscar opened an herbarium case filled with unmounted dried plant specimens. The mothball fumes were over-powering. "These were his last collections. Half of them are undescribed species." He reached up into the top slot and pulled out a slim notebook, battered and smudged. "His last field book. I think you should have it."

The gesture genuinely moved Kovac. He put his arm around his old friend. "This is yours as well as mine." Oscar gestured with his chin towards the herbarium case.

"*Tengo las especímenes*," he said. "They'll get to Cincinnati sooner or later."

Dinner was a feast of *salton*, an Amazonian catfish prized for its flavor, bathed in a pineapple and mango sauce. Oscar and Daniela's daughter, Amelia, arrived just before dinner. She was a striking young woman, about twenty-five years of age, and it was she who had painted the arresting clay lick scene that adorned Vistas Manu's emblem. Soon after, Antonio arrived with his wife Rosa and two young sons. Oscar swooped up the elder and soon had him emitting peals of toddler laughter.

After supper, the group adjourned to the great room next to the dining area. Replete, and a little besotted from a second pisco sour, Kovac grew silent, and reminisced inwardly about some of his memorable trips with Oscar into the forests of Peruvian Amazonia. He remembered once following a trail in the forests of the Tocache river northwest of Tingo Maria, some six hundred miles distant. Anton was poised to step off the trail, entranced by an unfamiliar plant with intense cerise flowers. Crescente suddenly commanded *"¡Parada!"* and abruptly thrust his arm across Kovac's chest, nearly knocking the breath out of him. He pointed to a nearly invisible line of taut monofilament fishing line. Kovac followed Oscar's indicating finger to the terminus of the trip line; a shotgun set up to fire at roughly ankle height. "Unlicensed coca growers," he declaimed. "They cripple you, then come finish you off later." He grimaced. "Stay on the trail."

Antonio offered to take Anton and Nell back to their hotel. As they departed, Oscar pulled Kovac aside. "Tomorrow, we begin." Oscar declared. Anton threw him a quizzical look. "But of course, I am going with you on this fool's errand." He grasped Kovac's forearm and gave it a squeeze. "But remember this. Maybe Gar chose to stay lost."

6

Sorrentino had been deposited into a hammock strung within a small hut. Six tribal elders, all in breechcloths, surrounded him. Their cloths were dyed red, with ornamentation along the lower edge. Younger males gathered just outside the hut, while children darted between their legs, battling for a better view. The stranger didn't stir in his hammock.

Garwell's possessions were neatly arrayed across a large woven mat set on the ground. One of the crouching elders was picking through a subset of the items. "<He knows the forest>," he said in his language, inspecting the small satchel of roasted *sacha inchi* seeds and palm nuts, along with the remaining coca leaf.

"<What do we do with him?>" A middle-aged tribesman spoke up. He directed his question to another older man who stood leaning against his spear. His bearing suggested he was the chief.

The leader sighed. "<Now we let him sleep.>" He motioned to the others to clear the hut. "<We will decide this another time.>"

Garwell stirred. His head was throbbing with a cloying ache, and he had trouble at first focusing his eyes. He swung his legs out of the hammock, while waves of nausea ran over him in counterpoint to his splitting head. He glimpsed his water bottle on the mat with his other things, and he retrieved it, gratefully swallowing several large gulps. Gar took stock of his surroundings. He could hear voices outside, and the occasional child's laughter.

57

Gar rose somewhat unsteadily to his feet. He had no idea in what the blowgun dart had been dipped, but it was certainly effective. He stepped outside, shielding his eyes from the blaze of sunlight. A well-beaten clearing extended for about 100 yards. It was ringed by palm thatch-roofed structures of variable size, twenty, he counted, on stilts of *huacapú* trunks. A long house stood in the center of the oval-shaped clearing, constructed of palm and tree trunk walls, and the ubiquitous thatched roof. At the far end of the clearing were yuca plots, and a managed area of useful forest trees and shrubs with edible fruits and nuts, as well as a papaya grove, stands of sweet potatoes, cassava, beans, and cotton. His hut was set apart from the main community at the edge of the clearing. The forest began immediately behind the wall of the shelter.

At the sight of him, the people milling about in front of the nearby huts grew silent. Young children cautiously slipped behind their parents' legs. An old man was rushing towards him. He slowed when he drew near and extended a handful of leaves while pantomiming putting them in his mouth and chewing them. Gar did as he was told, and the old man nodded in approval, and just as quickly retreated. The foliage was astringent at first, but soon innocuous. What was truly miraculous is that it dispelled the residual drug hangover symptoms after fifteen minutes.

Everyone in the tribe roundly ignored him the rest of the day. He guessed that there were perhaps thirty-five adults and about seventeen children of various ages in the community. As he strolled around the clearing, he noticed that there were none of the usual signs of acculturation: no second-hand t-shirts, no flip-flops, no cheap Asian-manufactured gym shorts, no shotguns, not even machetes or metal cooking pots, which a number of supposedly isolated tribes had obtained in generations past via trade. Adults and children alike wore breechcloths made of woven fabric and dyed various shades of red and blue. The women were as bare-chested as the men. Both ornamented themselves with feathers and armbands made of hide. Some adults were tattooed, though not elaborately. Clearly, these people had been spared the pox of missionaries, whom Sorrentino detested. Perhaps they had never been contacted. Garwood hadn't expected to encounter remote indigenous tribes, but he still got vaccinated against the flu before his trip. He thought it unlikely that a single outsider would prove infectious, but his foresight pleased him.

That evening, the same old man arrived unexpectedly with a wooden bowl of steaming capybara meat and chunks of boiled *yuca*. He placed it at the opening of the shelter and then crouched a few yards outside the hut. He pointed to the bowl and pantomimed eating.

Sorrentino dined under the sharp gaze of the elder, who remained perched outside. When he finished his meal, he laid the empty bowl near the old man, and gestured in what he hoped appeared to show gratitude.

The old man stood and made a quick sweeping motion with his arm, indicating the forest that surrounded them. He then pointed to Gar and next to himself. He mimicked a walking motion with two fingers as legs, then pointed again to the forest. Sorrentino signaled his understanding with a nod of assent. Tomorrow, they'd walk in the forest together. The old man then once more abruptly spun about and made his way to the central longhouse, where the chief and other men were gathering around a fire. He wondered if he was to be the subject of their discussion. In any event, he wasn't invited. Gar retrieved his GPS from his belongings, stepped into the clearing, and powered it up. He had marked his previous coordinates, and the single satellite he contacted placed him perhaps ten miles south of the river that he'd been following before they waylaid him. He guessed that someone had carried or dragged him on a sled of palm leaves for that distance.

Gar heard several voices grow strident from inside the longhouse. If he was the agenda item, there was some discordance regarding his fate. He considered packing his belongings and continuing his trek towards Puerto Maldonado, departing the next morning, but something inexplicable gave him pause. He continued to eavesdrop on the conversation. The language was a dialect of Piro, a language group common throughout the area, and he recognized certain words from the small vocabulary he had learned by osmosis over the years. Gar gleaned little from those few phrases.

As darkness fell, the village grew quiet as people went off to their own family huts. Sorrentino was not sleepy, so he strapped his headlamp across his forehead and slipped in the forest darkness. He was completely unmoored, unsure of what he should do: leave or stay with his hosts for at least a few days. Garwell's contact with indigenous people had always been limited to acculturated tribes, few of whom still followed the old ways of their people. Only once before had he encountered a true shaman of the forest, and this took place far to the north, another elder male who at first found the lithe stranger amusing. He had learned what he could about the immense pharmacography of the upper Amazon northwest of Iquitos, until the shaman grew wary of his constant queries, and became sullen, even somewhat hostile. He later learned that the old man had been killed on one of his solitary forays into the forest by a member of a neighboring tribe who was convinced that he was responsible for the death of one of his family through some dark application of spirit magic.

Sorrentino carefully trod a short distance into the forest, entranced by the nighttime cacophony of animal voices. Scorpions festooned some of the tree trunks, and he toyed with a tarantula that soon scurried under the thick accumulation of leaf litter that lay across the bases of the forest giants. He suddenly heard the faint sounds of an animal's passage, and spun around, his lamp reflecting in the eyes of a melanistic jaguar that froze in its approach. He wondered if the cat had been tracking him. Gar threw his arms up over his head, attempting to make himself appear as large as possible and growled loudly while bouncing the beam of his lamp off his machete blade. He wished he had brought his handgun with him, if only to fire a warning shot and make the animal turn tail. The jaguar eyed him seemingly without malevolence before slinking off into the darkness of the forest. He hurried back to the clearing, his heart beating resoundingly in his chest. It took him time to settle into his hammock, and sleep was punctuated by disturbing increments of dream that fled his memory as soon as his eyes opened.

When Garwell woke in the dim early dawn light, the apparition of the old man standing startled him near his hammock. He held out a steaming wooden pot of manioc porridge with various pieces of fruit floating within it like a multi-colored archipelago. Gar took the bowl appreciatively and wolfed it down. It was better than agreeable, and had been sweetened with honey, no doubt foraged from nearby.

Sorrentino threw what he considered essential into his pack and tossed it over his shoulders. The old man had already entered the penumbra of the trees, and waited for him below a hugely buttressed fig. He had a woven bag over one shoulder, and a blow gun fashioned from a tree stem, with a small quiver of darts, the points probably dipped in curaré.

When Garwell arrived alongside him, he held up his hand to indicate a pause. Then to Sorrentino's utmost surprise he drew his arms up in an exaggerated mime of Gar's reaction to his encounter with the jaguar the previous night, then burst out laughing, his dark eyes twinkling. When he regained his composure, he smacked his chest and uttered a terse statement in his language, which Gar could not decipher. "<That was me>," he had said.

The pair made their way through the forest, following a path that Garwell could not see but which the old man navigated with secure familiarity. Sorrentino stopped frequently before trees that caught his attention, and the old man would name it in his lexicon. Gar took notes at each stop, which amused the elder to no end. An unfamiliar species of *Strychnos* caught his eye, a genus that figured in many recipes for the poison curaré, and the shaman (for that he most surely was), identified it. He pointed to his blowgun, and then to Gar. "<I used that one on you. But not full strength>," he said, from which Garwell got the gist. Gar then pointed to himself and said, "Gar." The shaman grunted, pointed to himself, and said something that sounded like "Aku-na-yaz." *OK then*, Sorrentino thought. *A'kunayaz it is.*

They reached a short rise, and as soon as they ascended, Garwell heard the flow of water spilling over rocks. A stream about six feet wide lay over the other side of the rise. They were barely over a half mile from the village. A sizable beach bordered an oxbow lake that would disappear under water during the rainy season. This was no doubt the tribe's water source, outside of rain, which they collected off their roofs in roughly hewn hollowed palm stems. Both drank from the swift water of the river. Howler monkeys resounded around them in the treetops. Gar forded the stream where it had split into three channels. Halfway up the embankment a colony of amazon lilies, a genus of the amaryllis family, was blooming. It was a smaller flower than the more northern species, and he detected the faint traces of its perfume.

The shaman was gathering shoots of a shrub in the coffee family. Garwell recognized it as a species of *Faramea*, one of his estranged wife Nell's specialties, and pointed to it, saying "*Yacu sanaga*," as some members of the genus were called widely in the Amazon. The shaman seemed to confirm that Gar was more or less correct in his nomenclature and pantomimed a sneeze and then a cough to indicate how it was used in his administering to the people of the village. They crossed back to the other stream bank and continued through the forest along the rise. Sorrentino halted before the woody stem of a vine that rose high into the canopy. "*Yagé*," he said, followed by "*Capi*," the two indigenous names for the liana with which he was most familiar. The old man shrugged but nodded in assent. The inner bark of the stem was a major ingredient in preparing *ayahuasca*, the potent hallucinogenic brew that was a mainstay of shamanic divination and visionary experience. Garwell had never tried it, despite ample opportunities over the years in the Amazon. The shaman seemed pleased. He pointed to Garwell and then to himself. "<Tomorrow we take *ayahuasca*>," he said while pantomiming a drinking motion after pointing to the vining stem. Then he turned and led the hapless gringo back to the village.

7

It took four days to outfit the trek into the Madre de Dios Reserve. Both Anton and Nell became volunteer employees during preparations. Oscar ran a tight ship. He had trusted indigenous associates who knew the forests as well as he, who, though well-paid, still chose to live in their now acculturated but remote communities, picking and choosing from the tools of western civilization, but preferring forest life over whatever Puerto Maldonado had to offer. Two such stalwarts would accompany them. Antonio handled most of the tourist trade, allowing his father to focus on organizing his venture with his *gringo* friends. Kovac was sure that the son would run Vistas Manu in short order.

The first part of the journey would be via a compact riverboat as they penetrated the vast domain that extended unbroken to the northwest. They would first head up the Madre de Dios from Puerto Maldonado for about five miles until its confluence with the La Piedras River. They would remain on the Las Piedras for nearly 100 miles. The final roughly fifty miles west into the Reserve would be along the bed of a tributary, possibly bereft of canoe passage so late into the dry season. The Cincinnati Botanical Garden's research encampment was located about forty miles towards the headwaters of this river, and Crescente had already contacted them and arranged their arrival. From there, they would head by foot and with a single mule — courtesy of Kevin's research team.

The captain of the boat struck Anton as a bit of a scoundrel, but he deferred to Oscar's years of experience. Christened the *"Ana*

Cariniña" (Kovac wondered if with irony) was about 45 feet long with twin engines and two decks. At the marina, the boat was already filling up with other passengers, mostly indigenous or mixed blood, returning to villages upriver. Below the lower deck was stowage, which was rapidly filling with items bought in the city. The crew consisted of two young men, one who remained with the stowage to discourage theft. Oscar's two hands, Alvaro and Isidoro, quickly set to work, claiming as much space as they could for their supplies. Crescente was in animated discussion with the captain. The conversation ended with laughter, so Kovac and Nell assumed that all was well. Oscar told them the captain anticipated navigable waters to the point where he had arranged for two motorized canoes. They would rely on those to bring them to the Botanical Garden's research station.

This late in the dry season, the Las Piedras rarely exceeded a tenth of a mile in width, and its main channel was likely only 15 feet deep. Oscar told Anton that rain was expected in the higher reaches of the great Amazonian piedmont, which would raise river levels several feet sometime in the night.

As they left the marina, and turned into the Madre de Dios channel, Anton and Nell planted themselves in a shady spot where they could easily survey the riverbank. In short course, they came to the mouth of the Las Piedras, turning sharply to the northwest. The forest edge now met the riverbanks, occasionally fronted by small beaches. There were periodic clearings on the starboard bank of the river, and pockets of rural habitation; the port bank, where the reserve began, was yet unbroken forest. Boat traffic fell away quickly as they wound through several loops of the La Piedras. Nell spied several black caiman nests, and Anton pointed to several adults on a sandy stretch of beach. One slid into the water and followed their wake at some distance. Another beach hosted a family of capybaras, who all lifted their heads as they motored past. Nell identified virtually every bird that they passed; birding had become an obsession of hers since retiring as a research botanist. Kovac enjoyed her skills, but he concentrated more on trying to identify the arboreal giants flowering in the *terra firma* forests above and behind the floodplain of the river. Alvaro handed a late lunch of rice and beans with a few filets of smoked fish to them. From her knit bag, Nell withdrew two mangos, the smaller yellow types that were Anton's favorites.

After lunch, and as the temperature rose to the afternoon peak, Kovac fell into a drowsy reverie. He watched Nell's face grow increasingly beatific as they penetrated further and further into the forest's embrace. Nell's botanical work in the last two and a half decades had shifted away from the Amazon, but her time in Amazonian Peru had been concentrated in the Loreto Region. Her other experience in the Madre de Dios territory had been with Sorrentino and Oscar many years in the past. "Anton," she suddenly said, snapping him out of his thoughts. "Thank you," she continued.

"Thank me for what?" he replied, a trifle annoyed at being propelled out of his half dreams.

"For being such a good friend all these years. For helping me raise my children. For doing this."

"Do you seriously think he's still alive?"

"I don't know anymore. I'm not even sure it matters." She took his hand in both of hers and gently lay her head on his shoulder. "Either way, he left us. Me, you, our kids." She sighed. "The fucker!" she abruptly snarled, and Anton himself recognized a corresponding bitterness of betrayal rise in his own chest. He'd wept when he had first heard the news of Garwell's death, and then went on a bender for two days, waking afterwards on the floor of his Cincinnati apartment in a pool of his own vomit.

A pair of scarlet macaws crossed the river in front of them and landed in a grove of *aguaje* palms along the river's edge. Like all macaws, the pair were monogamous mates for life, living for up to 50 years. Was this a random flick of evolution's genetic wand that had imparted some unmeasurable uptick in the lineage's fitness such that no known species of these resplendent avian savants had ever abandoned their sexual fealty? Did they ever know temptation? Kovac shook his head to dispel such useless thoughts, squeezed Nell's hand and stood. "I'm going to take a walk." He climbed the stairway to the upper deck, where the buzz of the engines was slightly muted. He nodded to several other passengers, most of whom muttered "*Buenas tardes*" as their eyes met.

The *Ana Cariniña* made reasonably good time moving upriver, and over half of the other passengers soon disembarked near their villages. Nell and Kovac watched them melt into the riverine woods, beyond which there was likely a settled clearing. More than a few were met by family members who helped them with whatever burden they had accumulated in the city. As dusk settled onto the river, Oscar and the captain surveyed the riverbanks for a decent place to anchor. They found a mutually acceptable spot just off the main channel, where a sandbar rose above the water. The crew killed the engines and set two anchors, bow and stern, in the deeper water. There was ample play in the lines to accommodate the expected rise in water level that night.

With the engines off, the air filled with the late soundings of myriad birds now roosting in the forest canopy. Both Anton and Nell had small, single person tents and planned to pitch them on the upper deck. The crew, Oscar, Alvaro and Isidoro, and the few remaining passengers, strung hammocks from hooks strategically positioned in various places on the boat. The captain would sleep in a small compartment in the wheelhouse. He was busy casting a fishing line near the sandbar and pulled out an astonishing number of striped bass. His two crewmen built a fire on the sandbar, and the fish were soon cooking in coconut oil. Oscar and Isidoro went on shore and brought back a satchel full of *abiu* fruits.

Over dinner, Oscar told them they had only about thirty miles left to reach the mouth of the tributary, informally called Río Progresso, where the canoes awaited them. If they didn't meet any bottlenecks involving portage, they would reach the Botanical Garden station in two days. Kovac perceived that Oscar was much more standoffish since they began their journey. He thought back to his five years of intensive fieldwork with Crescente when Gar was still alive and concluded that his old friend had always been all business when they were in the field, lightening up only after a shot or two of pisco around the fire late at night, surrounded by unbroken forest for hundreds of miles.

Indeed, the river had risen sometime in the night; the sand bar was nearly submerged. Oscar was buoyant. "We'll make excellent time today." They stopped once to unload the remaining few passengers. They arrived at the appointed spot upriver, where the two outboard canoes awaited them on a narrow beach, guarded by a young man in gym shorts, flip-flops and a Miami Dolphins t-shirt, armed with a shotgun. "*Gracias, amigo*," Oscar said to him, counting out a wad of Peruvian *soles* from the leather satchel draped over his shoulder, which he pressed into the youth's hand. The kid nodded and disappeared into the forest, the shotgun slung over his shoulder. Oscar settled with the boat captain and exchanged some good-natured banter as the *Ana Cariniña* turned and headed back downriver. Alvaro and Isidro were carefully transferring their satchels and supplies, piled up on the beach, to the stern of the canoes, which were fifteen feet long and six feet wide. Isidro erected a nylon canopy over the stowage in both canoes, and then the duo pushed them further into the water to gauge how well their cargo was seated, making a few adjustments along the way. Nell and Anton botanized along the forest rim. "*Vámonos,*" Oscar called from behind them after a short time.

The tributary mouth was only a half mile upstream. Alvaro and Isidro each carefully steered the canoes through the smaller channel which meandered continuously throughout its length. Oscar stood in the bow of the lead craft, surveying the water ahead while Alvaro steered, with Anton seated in the middle. Nell rode with Isidro in the second canoe, following behind. The day quickly drew hot and humid, alleviated only by stretches of the sinuous river that allowed them to reach full speed. Anton poured water over his canvas hat; the moving air cooled his head as it whisked the moisture away. Nell did the same. Once they passed a small beach where several indigenous women and their children played in the water. They were dressed traditionally; the women bare-breasted and wearing loincloths. Two men stood on the forest embankment behind them. One shot an arrow, clearly meant as a warning; it fell far afield of the canoes. After that, they saw no one. Rounding a sharp meander, they surprised a tapir foraging near the shore. Navigating another turn, they caught an enormous kapok in full flower, the white blossoms erupting in profusion across the spreading canopy.

That night, they camped on a beach that Oscar deemed protected enough from high water (at least not without warning). Alvaro and Isidro demonstrated their angling skills yet again. Kovac and Nell found a level plateau at the forest's edge to pitch their tents, and Crescente joined them in a third. A thunderstorm woke the world sometime in the dead of night, rushing in from nowhere, it seemed, dousing them, and then moving on.

Water level had risen again overnight, and their canoes sliced easily through the center of the serpentine river. They arrived at the Cincinnati Botanical Garden's research station shortly before sunset.

"Anton!" a burly and bearded fellow called out. "I had no idea." Kovac recognized his last graduate student from 20 years ago. He was now the director of the Garden's Madre de Dios project. "Anton fumbled for his name in his mind.

"Hello Luis," he finally replied.

Luis smiled. "*Si, mucho tiempo,*" acknowledging Kovac's momentary lapse of memory. "And Nell Sorrentino! We're honored. Come, let me show you to your quarters." He led them into the main lodge, built sturdily from forest products. Solar panels were set into the roof, and there were storage batteries in a small walled off area. The large hostel-like bedroom was a mix of bunk beds and hammocks draped with mosquito netting. Currently, there were only four people present aside from their party of five, and Luis. There was a large table set for specimen preparation in the front great room, and a large open kitchen. Dinner appeared to be cooking.

Kovac shared a small table with Luis. Over rice and beans, fried yuca, and chorizo, they shared pleasantries and memories. After a few glasses of the wine Oscar had brought to the table from his duffel, Luis grew more reflective. "You know, he is a legend around here. We all owe him a debt. He had so much more to teach us."

"He's dead," Anton uttered sharply.

Luis shrugged. "*Tal vez.*"

♦ ♦ ♦ ♦ ♦

They got an early start in the morning. Alvaro and Isidro packed the mule, burdening the poor animal with what both Anton and Nell considered excessive. The mule ultimately seemed nonplussed by the weight of their packs and kept pace as they penetrated the *terra firma* forest. Oscar led their small band, pausing only now and again, compass in hand, to true their bearing through the arboreal cathedral. Anton was incredulous that Oscar had a clue as to where they were bound. All manner of bird song filtered down from the canopy. Brilliant blue morpho butterflies seemed to suddenly materialize in front of their faces, accompanying them for a short while before pausing, their dull brown underwings now exposed, blending back into invisibility against the carpet of brown leaves on the forest floor.

By midday, they'd covered 10 miles, and took a break beside a swiftly flowing creek. Oscar and Isidro disappeared deeper into the forest and returned with *nejilla* palm and *abiu* fruits, which made fine companions to the cooked chorizo and cassava flour bread.

"You doing OK?" Anton queried Nell, who nodded. Kovac's sense of trepidation had begun to increase since they left Puerto Maldonado. He wasn't sure why, reasoning amid the uncertainty that it was because two decades had transpired since he had done anything like this.

"I'd forgotten this feeling," she replied. "You know, the sense of being out of time. I only experienced it in the Amazon." Nell was slim and fit, even at 63. She was probably more comfortable with the heat and humidity than he was, five years her junior.

The expedition finished for the day at 15 miles through the forest, bearing southwest. Anton found his jungle legs, and he, too, was enraptured by the overwhelming fecundity of nature that surrounded them as they walked. Near another creek from which they filled their water bottles, Nell pointed out another small population of Amazon lilies in full bloom. Metallic blue bees were busy among the white flowers.

The spot Oscar chose for camp was not near any water; perhaps he anticipated rain. It was relatively flat and accommodated their tents nicely. Alvaro took his shotgun and went off to find game. He was gone for about an hour when the muffled sound of gunfire echoed from somewhere in the forest. Alvaro returned with two pacas and a large bird that Nell identified as a forest tinamou. Oscar and Alvaro, who already had a fire going, cleaned and dressed the meat, which was soon cooking on the flames.

After dinner, Oscar, Anton and Nell sat around the fire, passing a flask of pisco among themselves. "So," Kovac spoke up, "when do we know we've arrived?"

Oscar shrugged. "Somewhere in all this," he said, motioning across the forest expanse, "there should be a settlement. The plan is to give it four days. If we find nothing, we turn around and go home."

Anton said nothing in reply. He glanced at Nell, who didn't appear to react. She rose to her feet, announcing, "I'm going to bed." Kovac followed soon after, stumbling a little from the alcohol.

In the morning, after a light breakfast, Oscar handed out pouches of coca leaves and ground shell. "We want to make over 30 kilometers today," he declared. "This should allow us to skip lunch. I'm sure we'll find fruit along the way." Nell was entranced by the diversity of her iconic coffee family in the understory, the most alluring of which was the "hot lips" plant, *Palicourea tomentosa*, whose small flowers were enclosed by two large brilliant red bracts that bestowed its common name.

Despite the stimulation of the coca leaves, they stopped for a rest after about six hours alongside another stream that allowed them to replenish their water supply and take quick baths in the cool waters. Refreshed, they continued on their way. Alvaro had pushed on ahead and waited for them to catch up, whereupon he delivered fresh *abiu* fruits to each of them.

They resumed their trek across the gently undulating forest floor. Two hours later, Oscar signaled for them to halt. They could hear voices, a mix of Spanish and indigenous syntax. A band of eight men was visible up ahead. "Wait here," Oscar instructed, and continued towards the men, hailing them with a thunderous "*Buenos dias*," as he approached. He conversed with the apparent leader for ten minutes or so, then returned, calm but unsmiling.

"Gold miners," he stated flatly when he drew alongside Nell and Kovac. "They're fortunately going in the opposite direction. They're panning in all these small streams we keep crossing. Completely illegal. I told them we are botanists working for the National Museum."

Two of the men, a rough-looking pair, strolled closer to observe the two gringos. One, nodding towards Nell and then Anton, made some inaudible remark that drew laughter from the other one. Alvaro and Isidro, their shotguns slung visibly over their shoulders, casually neared the two gold miners, who then retreated to their base. "Let's get the hell out of here," Oscar said.

As they left the gold miners behind, Oscar drew alongside Kovac and Nell. "These prospecting bands are growing bolder every year. There's going to be trouble eventually if they contact an indigenous village. It's a ticking time bomb. And with the Interoceanic complete, the cartels are getting involved. They tear their own roads into primary forest, extracting the valuable timber, while they send gangs like this into the wilderness to look for gold. Any promising river is soon poisoned with mercury."

It was particularly hot this day, and Anton found himself hitting the coca leaf frequently whenever he lagged from the heat. It helped, but he was out of shape, and his jungle legs had abandoned him. In the afternoon they came to a wider stream than they had so far encountered, fording it where it became shallow and had deposited large rocks that served as stepping stones. "We'll stay here tonight," Oscar told them once they all were on the far shore. Dinner was only rice and beans, and a smattering of fruit Isidro culled from the forest's cornucopia. The never-ending forest. Here, in southeastern Peru, miles from anywhere, it was difficult to believe that human impact could ever diminish its breadth across the piedmont that eventually fell to the Amazon River itself. But Kovac had seen the most recent photographs of deforestation along the Interoceanic highway in Brazil. The consequences were being met out miles beyond where the clearing ended. So far, Peru's Madre de Dios Reserve, amid which some indigenous tribes lived in voluntary seclusion, had remained relatively untrammeled. For how much longer was a prophecy Anton had rather not pursue.

Oscar surprised them with hot coffee in the morning. "I brought very little; it's celebrating the halfway point of our ecotour." Anton's mood lifted with the familiar taste. Just one of the vegetable kingdom's many exceptional gifts to humankind.

The mule, whom Alvaro called "Blanca," largely took care of its own provision, seemingly to know precisely which shrubs were suitable for browse. It was often the mule who first spied edible palm and tree fruits near the ground. Alvaro supplemented with a handful of oats from a waterproof bag. Both Anton and Nell were eternally grateful to walk among the trees without packs on their backs.

The day transpired without incident or any further unforeseen encounters. It rained in the later hours of the afternoon, the lightning invisible but audible thunder echoing around them. It took about an hour before they discerned the first drops rolling off the leaf surfaces high above them. Nell and Anton donned rain ponchos as the shower strengthened. A band of emperor tamarin monkeys descended from the upper canopy to the second story trees and regarded them with faint curiosity, emitting a series of long calls until their procession passed by. With their long white facial hair that curved downwards at the tip, they resembled nothing so much as wizened old men in miniature. As the rain tapered off, howler monkeys began sounding from some distance away.

Crescente called for a halt while a few hours of daylight remained. He told them he wished to make some collections from the trees in the immediate area, which was particularly diverse in species composition. They would remain encamped there for the next day while this was accomplished. Kovac was secretly pleased; the heat, the rain, and the insects were sapping his fortitude. He remembered his younger days when he could trek through the primary forest for days without getting tired, without even chewing coca leaves.

While Oscar and his employees unloaded their supplies from Blanca, Anton meandered about a huge fig whose trunk was festooned with clusters of ripe fruits. Stepping between two of its buttressed roots, one of his legs suddenly sunk deeply into a hidden crevasse of soft leaf mold. He lost his balance, toppled, and gashed his knee on the ferociously armed stems of a sarsaparilla vine that clambered across the fig's roots. Oscar told him to stay put and disappeared briefly, returning with a mass of sticky red latex that he had gathered by wounding the trunk of a forest tree. "*Sangre de grado*," he informed Kovac, as he placed a sizable poultice of the sap on his wound. "Stay still and let it dry," he instructed. "It'll fall off on its own." While Alvaro built a fire, which the earlier rain had made no small task, Isidro went off in search of dinner, returning with a half dozen medium-sized peacock bass plucked from a small but swift river that flowed a mile and a quarter distant. Isidro brought a haul of *camu camu* from out of the forest and began preparing the juice drink that would quench their thirst during tomorrow's hard work, climbing and collecting tree specimens. Oscar told them that he didn't expect their help the next day. Nell demurred, and Oscar eventually relented. "OK, how's this? Have a leisurely morning, and then join us. At the very least, you can help load specimens onto Blanca."

That night, a harpy eagle circled above their camp for several hours, its keening dominating above the cricket and frog chorus. Such behavior was odd; I did not know them to be nocturnal. For some reason, Anton found it unnerving. By the fire, passing the customary pisco, he checked his leg. The poultice had hardened, and there was no soreness.

Oscar, his men, and Blanca the mule set out early. Both Anton and Nell emerged from their tents at the same time, to find hot coffee and cacao fruits awaiting them. Kovac cut open the hard fruits to expose the seeds covered with a sweet and refreshing whitish pulp.

Anton stood and pulled a roll of toilet paper from his tent. "Excuse me," he said to Nell and walked further away into the forest. As he neared their camp on his return, he was suddenly sure that he was being followed. He spun about and was greeted by the sight of a slender but muscular indigenous man dressed in a loincloth and wearing a necklace of brilliant-colored feathers, following three yards behind. His long gray hair fell thickly past his shoulders, and he had a closely cropped beard of corresponding color. Kovac judged him to be somewhere around 65. He leaned casually against a long stick, a spear Kovac realized, at the same time as he knew that his initial assumption of ethnicity was wrong. And the man was smiling.

When he spoke, the voice was unmistakable, and Kovac suddenly grew unmoored.

"Hello Anton," Gar said softly. "I live here now."

8

A'kunayaz the shaman woke Gar before dawn. He had a lit torch in his hand, made from a piece of woven cotton that had been soaked in the sap of a local tree. It burned slowly and gave off a pleasant fragrance. Gar was cautioned in mime not to eat. Water he could imbibe, nothing else. They set out into the forest, still cloaked in the half light of dawn. After a short amble, they came to a small hut roofed with palm thatch. The shaman motioned Garwell to be seated at the entrance. From a basket that he had carried strapped to his back, he removed two small wooden vessels, placing one in front of Sorrentino. "<Drink>," he said, bringing the second container to his own lips. Then he threw down a cotton mat and sat cross-legged, watching Sorrentino carefully.

Gar hesitated; he knew enough about *ayahuasca* to expect the brew's noxious flavor. He wasn't disappointed. Nonetheless, he downed the bitter liquid, finishing with a gasp and a look on his face that made the old man laugh.

The forest was fully alive in the first hours of the morning. Within a half hour, his fingers tingled. The old man gestured for Gar to walk away from the lean-to shelter. As he did, the first waves of nausea hit, and a bilious rumbling in his guts presaged a voiding of momentous dimension. He no sooner lowered his pants and squatted, then he gave way to contemporaneous torrents of vomit and foul-smelling diarrhea. The cycle repeated itself one more time.

He stood and was stunned by what he saw. The entire forest was lit with a dim cerise luminescence that connected everything around

81

him. The color changed sometimes when the network crossed kingdoms of life. Even his bodily waste glowed, a soft green as it became colonized by the simplest forms of life.

He rejoined A'kunayaz by the shelter, where he had laid out a second blanket for Sorrentino and bade him sit. As far as he could tell, the shaman had not experienced the furious purge that he had. The old man gave him water to drink which he attacked ravenously. "<Close your eyes now and listen>," the shaman instructed, demonstrating by closing his eyes and pointing to his ears.

Garwell did as he was told, and almost immediately he heard an incredible expression of music emanating from the forest. Birdsong became spinnerets of sound, not melodic so much as harmonious improvisation. The rhythmic piping of tree frogs interlaced with the crickets' violin chorus.

When he opened his eyes, the old man was gone. He wandered through the forest, with which he experienced a connectedness that he had never before encountered. It was as if before, the forest and he had a one-way intellectual bond; this was indescribable.

Gar came to a massive Brazil nut; upon a buttressed root, colonies of delicate mushrooms, glowing blue, emitted the sweetest bell-like tones that brought tears to his eyes. The fungi beckoned to him; an urgent need to reach down and consume some overcame him. Suddenly a black jaguar leaped out from the darkness, landing deftly on two closely spaced buttresses. It raised a paw, bared its teeth and growled, before bounding off again into the forest. The message was clear, and he wandered deeper into the *selva*. It was then that he realized the trees were talking to him.

Their language was mostly via images and song. He paused before a member of the cashew family. Closing his eyes, he understood immediately that the leaves would ease digestive upset. A large liana that snaked along the ground then rose up the trunk of a kapok, imparted its ability to quench fevers. It was almost too much, and he retreated to the shelter.

The shaman was waiting for him, again cross-legged on his mat. "Did the forest speak to you?" the old man asked. Gar abruptly realized that he understood every word the shaman spoke. He accepted this incongruity and sat down on his mat.

"It did," he replied. A'kunayaz nodded; he seemed pleased.

"The chief's son wanted to kill you," the old man said matter-of-factly, "but the *ayahuasca* had told me you would come, a white man of the forest."

Gar said nothing. He was overwhelmed by the ease of their conversation, even as he realized he was not speaking with his mouth, but via some other mysterious faculty that could only be considered telepathy. "How do we speak?" he suddenly asked.

The shaman gestured at the surrounding trees. "Through the forest," was all he said. "The *ayahuasca* makes this possible."

"Why didn't you shit and vomit like I did?"

A'kunayaz smiled. "My *ayahuasca* contained a plant mixture that fights that. I wanted you to have the full experience the first time."

Sorrentino suddenly was overcome by a wave of what he interpreted as fatigue. He lay down on his mat. It was as if the earth itself was pulling him downward, to which he surrendered. He closed his eyes and descended below the forest floor. When he opened his eyes, he saw the incredible network of plant roots and fungal mycelia that pulsed with a shifting aura of colors and again an almost celestial type of music. He moved through the tableau with the speed of thought.

His perspective suddenly shifted. He was over the forest, above the canopy. A sharp keening echoed inside his head, as if he himself was making the sounds. Gar gave himself over to the sensation of flight, riding updrafts with the skill of the harpy eagle that he had become. He spied movement in the canopy of a giant fig and prepared to drop silently upon a band of squirrel monkeys gamboling across the outstretched branches of the tree. He dove soundlessly, enormous talons stretched, and felt them strike the small primate as he swept back up into the air.

His consciousness was again aligned with his own body. He opened his eyes and saw that the old man had disappeared again. He had no sense of time, whether hours or minutes had transpired since he first sensed the tingling in his fingers. The forest was still alive with effervescent music and the glow of its network's aura. He only had to set his eyes upon a particular tree or shrub to learn of its gift to corporeal human existence. And like the hidden babble of an underground stream, a message was imparted wordlessly in a low, sibilant tone that rolled over him in waves of unexpected joy. "*You belong here. This is your home.*"

The shaman abruptly appeared beside him. "Come," he said, "the *ayahuasca* is almost finished with you for today."

Gar followed him soundlessly through the forest back to the village. He was surprised to see that the sun was low in the sky. The old man laid a hand on his shoulder, then pantomimed sleep, for which he needed no further encouragement.

Vivid dreams visited Sorrentino all night. They ranged through a temporal landscape; past, present, and future weaving a tapestry that entreated him to plumb their hidden meanings. They dissipated when he woke.

A basket of fruit sat on the same cotton mat that A'kunayaz had bestowed upon him at the *ayahuasca* ceremony. Next to it was a cotton loincloth, dyed a deep brown. After eagerly dispatching the fruit, he removed his field clothes and shoes and tied the loincloth around his waist. He stepped out into the clearing, where the villagers were beginning their day. A band of young men prepared to hunt game in the forest, a bow and quiver of arrows around each of their shoulders. A group of women were weaving cotton; they eyed him and tittered as he strolled past. Their children were bolder; they ran circles around Sorrentino, giggling and chattering.

He had stepped into a new world.

9

I live here now, Anton echoed in his mind, astonished at just how lame it sounded, the first words of Garwell Sorrentino that he'd heard in twenty-five years. He clenched his fists, feeling a spike of anger rising up inside him. "That's it?" he loudly asked. "You live here now," he continued in a mocking tone. Gar said nothing, but the smile faded from his lips.

Having heard Kovac's angry tone, Nell hurried over from their campsite. Her eyes grew wide, and her mouth fell agape, while her hands rose to sandwich her cheeks. A sound like no other that Anton had ever heard rose from somewhere deep inside her. Gar raised a hand in greeting. "Nell," he addressed her gently.

With a banshee wail, Nell charged at her ex-husband and began beating him with her fists, pounding his chest in rage, then slipped to her knees before him. She was weeping now. "You selfish prick!" she screamed, and covered her face with her hands, two and a half decades of uncertainty, anger and humiliation wracking her body. Anton rushed to comfort her, but Gar raised a hand to signal forbearance. Garwell kneeled and placed his hand on Nell's head.

"Nell," he whispered. "Nell, please..." She brushed his hand away and rose unsteadily to her feet. She shuddered, suppressing a final sob. Sorrentino gathered her to his chest, and oddly murmured a song in a language that neither she nor Kovac understood. It sounded like a plea for forgiveness.

"My God, you stink!" she exclaimed. Gar had always been notoriously haphazard about personal hygiene when he was in the field. Somewhat self-consciously, Gar sniffed his armpits and grimaced. "There's a shrub in your plant family that kills the bacteria. I must gather some."

Anton had meanwhile slipped away, heading to the part of the forest that he knew Oscar and crew would be working that morning. He soon could hear their voices, and he quickened his pace. He was seething with anger. When he stood a few feet from Crescente, he began sputtering. "You knew! All this fucking time, you knew he was alive!"

Oscar's shoulders slumped. He drew a deep sigh. "*Cuando tu hermano te pide algo,*" he said, "*no te queda otra.*" [12]

"He was my brother, too!" Kovac spat.

"And only he can tell you why, Anton. Gar is a complicated man."

Kovac's anger suddenly fled, leaving him light-headed. "When did you find out?"

"A year after the crash. He walked into my office one day." He laughed and snapped his fingers. "Just like that." He shook his head. "A small tribe had tracked him as he neared their village on his way back to the Las Piedras. They knocked him out with some form of curaré and brought him back to their settlement. It was a miracle that they didn't just kill him." He smiled wryly. "Their shaman saved his life. Said he had a vision about a white man who came out of the forest." Oscar turned towards his men and told them that he was

---

[12] "When your brother asks something of you, you have no choice."

going back with Kovac. "He picked up two dozen notebooks and several boxes of indelible pens to take back with him." Oscar continued as they walked back to their encampment. "Gar told me that he'd finally found his place on earth, and that I would probably never see him again."

"Did you?" Anton asked.

"Not until six months ago. Like before, he just appeared, this time at my house. He told me you and Nell would come to Peru."

"How did he know?"

"He said he'd seen it in an *ayahuasca* vision."

Nell and Garwell were in conversation when they returned. Nell had regained her composure. While Sorrentino and Crescente conversed in Spanish, she and Anton went off by themselves. He asked her what they had talked about.

"Mostly about the kids. I told him everything that he had voluntarily missed in their lives."

"And?" Kovac interjected.

Nell sighed. "He took it all rather mutely. It was almost as if I was describing what, for him, was a past that no longer had any meaning. The only thing he said right before you guys came back was, 'My life has found its heart here in these forests. I'm sorry if it has made a fiction of what came before.'"

◆ ◆ ◆ ◆ ◆

Dinner was a collared peccary that Gar and Oscar bagged on a short hunting expedition. While they were gone, Kovac and Nell helped prepare specimens from the wealth of material that Blanca had borne on her back. This was the grunt work of botany, trimming the samples while being careful not to eliminate important features of the plant. A curated specimen was placed between a sheet of newspaper, labeled by collection number with indelible pens, then placed between two blotters. This was sandwiched between corrugated aluminum sheets, adding another every four to ten specimens. Finally, the samples were transferred to wooden herbarium presses tightened with strong canvas straps. A propane heated drying rack was assembled by Alvaro and Isidro, which would run all night, directing heat through the corrugates. They constructed a frame from forest wood to support a rain tarp over the drying frame. It was tedious work but formed the basic collateral of botanical research in the tropics.

At dinner, Gar spoke about his people. They called themselves the "A'kun," which translated as "children of the forest" and had lived in the Madre de Dios watershed for as long as they could remember. Once, Gar told them, they had been much more plentiful, but the diseases that had followed wherever the missionaries made contact had split their people into small remnants. The A'Kun retreated further and further, losing contact with other villages with which they once shared ties of trade and kinship. Gar's group remained isolated by choice, and the population had been growing steadily, nearing fifty adult individuals.

"So, what…," Anton stammered, "what do you do?"

Sorrentino shrugged. "I'm their shaman," he replied calmly.

10

In the ensuing months after his arrival among the A'Kun, Garwell gradually acculturated himself to the rhythms of life in the village. There was much leisure during waking hours, but never indolence. Men and women both tended their children. The women gathered in inter-generational groups and gossiped while weaving cotton or processing manioc bread. The men went off to hunt, usually twice per week, sometimes more if the results were poor. Children and teenagers, sometimes supervised by adults, tended the gardens. Whatever the activity, there was always abundant laughter.

On the surface, A'kun society appeared patriarchal; closer intimacy revealed the importance of the women in maintaining the secular fabric of the tribe. Their husbands always consulted wives before council meetings in the longhouse, which the chief's wife always attended. The women's circle, whether embroiled in weaving or food preparation, and always well-attended, was as important to the functioning of the tribe as the council meetings themselves.

Garwood applied himself to learning the A'Kun's language. In that endeavor, the children were immeasurably helpful. They were content to spend hours with him, telling him the names of everyday objects. His vocabulary increased each week, and he began halting attempts at conversation with other members of the tribe. When he stumbled into some malapropism, he'd evince gales of laughter from his audience.

At least every other day, Gar and the shaman ventured into the forest to collect healing plants. He had impressed the old man with his ability to climb trees, and A'kunayaz took full advantage of it.

The *ayahuasca* communions with the shaman also continued, though henceforth the preparation included an ingredient to temper the explosive digestive symptoms that initiated his first experience. Sometimes it was administered in the evening, and the experience differed from the daytime excursions. The music of the forest changed at night, but it was just as entrancing as in daylight. The accompanying glow of the network of life was even more vivid in the darkness, and it pulsed in syncopation with the song.

One day, the chief's son, Te'bayna'kun, gave Dar a bow and a quiver of arrows. In a way, the gift served as an apology for Te'bayna'kun's initial suggestion that Gar should be killed. He invited him to join in the hunt the next morning.

They set out shortly after dawn, Te'bayna'kun and four other young men of the tribe with Garwell. Sorrentino was still getting used to walking barefoot through the forest and soon fell behind. The chief's son, who appeared to be in his mid to late twenties, stopped periodically to allow Gar to catch up. At one point, he handed Gar a rolled-up leaf containing a viscous substance. He instructed him to rub the goo over his exposed skin, and with a buzzing noise, made it clear for what the material was intended. Sorrentino did as he was told, and soon discovered that the forest's myriad biting insects left him alone. He made a mental note to ask A'kunayaz about the lotion.

The men had paused up ahead; Te'bayna'kun motioned back to Gar to come forward silently. Fortunately, being barefoot allowed for a stealth approach. Several collared peccaries were ahead in a tree-fall gap. The chief's son pointed to the largest of the animals and then nodded at Gar to take the first shot.

Sorrentino had spent his boyhood stalking feral boars with bow and arrow in the Arkansas woods. He raised his bow, soundlessly positioning the shaft and drawing the string taut. He let loose, and the point found its mark, entering just above the haunch that gave the peccary its name. With a single grunt, it fell dead in its wallow. The other peccaries quickly took flight.

A resounding cheer was raised unanimously among the men, and several slapped Gar on the shoulder or back. Several of the young men began constructing a frame to bear the beast back to the village. Te'bayna'kun turned to Sorrentino and said, "<You surprise me>." Sorrentino sensed the meaning. He could think of nothing to say in reply, so he just smiled. The chief's son pulled the arrow from the dead animal and handed it back to Garwell, but not before cleaning the lower shaft and stone tip with a mass of crushed leaves that he'd harvested from a copal tree. He dipped two fingers into the wound, coating them with the peccary's blood and painted two lines in red on both of Gar's cheeks.

They headed back to the settlement. The tribe enthusiastically welcomed the hunting party home. The word of whose kill would feed the village that night must have spread quickly; several men and women patted him on the back as he passed. Several men were already hard at work, butchering the large male, taking care not to disturb the dorsal gland that could give off a riotously foul odor.

They prepared a sumptuous feast that evening; spit-roasted peccary, yuca, and pineapples gathered from the village gardens. Sorrentino was served first, a customary courtesy bestowed upon the provider of fresh meat from the forest. In fact, this was his first communal meal with the tribe; during his first weeks as their guest, he had eaten alone, his food brought to shelter by one of the children he'd befriended or sometimes by A'kunayaz. He sensed that his status among the A'kun had advanced a notch; adults were more willing to make eye contact with him (the children had always been less inhibited). He was more comfortable than he'd yet been among them.

The shaman was clearly the eldest of the tribe, somewhere around sixty years old, Sorrentino surmised. The chief, named Bayna'kun, was second oldest, perhaps in his late fifties. Bayna'kun remained aloof from Garwell, but his son interacted with him with an ever-increasing frequency.

Te'bayna'kun was extremely protective of his younger sister, De'bayna'kun, an attractive young woman in her early to mid-twenties. She was not married, nor seemed to be courted by any of the young men. De'bayna'kun had a five-year-old son who had become a favorite of Sorrentino's. She and her boy shared a house with her brother and his family. One day, alone with the chief's son at Sorrentino's hut, Gar asked him why De'bayna'kun was unmarried. Te'bayna'kun frowned and shook his head sadly. "<She

was walking alone in the forest gathering mushrooms and was raped by a man from another village>", he told Gar. "<We hunted him down and killed him, but none of the unmarried A'kun men would ever make her his wife>." He further recounted how the shaman tried to induce an abortion early in the pregnancy, but the remedy had failed. A'kunayaz then declared that the spirits wanted the child to live.

The boy had taken quite a shine to Gar, often bringing him breakfast in the morning, then sitting nearby while Sorrentino ate, as well as accompanying him into the forest to collect plant material. The boy's mother had noticed their bond and clearly approved in the absence of any other father figure. She greeted Gar more and more warmly every time they encountered each other, and Sorrentino found himself engineering at times that their paths would cross. If her brother noticed them making eyes at each other, he certainly did nothing to discourage the flirtation.

The rainy season had begun in earnest, but Garwell and the shaman could count on four or five hours of collecting in the morning if they left at dawn. Gar was rapidly filling his notebooks with identifications, at least to genus. Most of what he recorded were species new to science. Between his adventures with *ayahuasca*, which burned their insights into his memory, and the knowledge imparted to him by A'kunayaz, he was accumulating an ethnobotanical treasure house of forest medicine.

The overall health of the tribe was exemplary. The older generation showed none of the typical metabolic disorders of western humanity. Their shaman treated everything with confidence and acumen. Cuts, scrapes and insect bites were often enough that at least one family member was usually conversant in the parameters of treatment. A'kunayaz was called in for problems in pregnancy, high fevers—which were exceedingly rare—and any accidental poisonings. Gar served increasingly as assistant on the few serious interventions.

Gar found himself spending at least part of his day with De'bayna'kun, practicing his increasingly expressive conversational skills in the language of the A'kun. The chief's daughter was quick to laughter and had a radiant smile that he found enticing. About three months after his arrival, she would take his hand when out of view of the other tribe's people. Her son, whose name was K'naya (it meant "spirit child"), adored Sorrentino by then and sometimes hung his hammock in his hut. During long afternoons of rain, the two would play with a series of figurines that Gar had carved from various pieces of wood. The boy was respectful of Garwell's personal effects, but after K'naya's first visits, Sorrentino placed his handgun and remaining rounds into one of his last plastic bags and buried it at the foot of an ipé tree not far behind his shelter.

One ritual of tribal life had still not been given to Sorrentino. He had yet to be invited to the longhouse evening meetings of the tribe elders and other adult males. He knew that went hand-in-hand with the chief's aloofness from him. It bothered him, but he didn't bring up the issue with his mentor.

When a year had almost gone by, the shaman told Garwell that it was time for him to spend a day and night in the forest by himself, under the mediation of the *ayahuasca*. His "spirit quest" would take place a few miles away from the village. "You must shed the last shadows of the other world," A'kunayaz told him. And he must bring fresh meat back to the settlement; that would be his token of success.

The shaman accompanied him part of the way to the appointed site in the forest. "You will know when you arrive. There is a small stream with a giant kapok nearby." The old man handed Gar a bowl fashioned from the fruit of a Brazil nut relative, sealed with beeswax. "Drink when you arrive." He then pulled a short and narrow tube of palm stem, also sealed with beeswax at each end. "Take these at night." He removed the wax from one end, and poured out three small round pellets, dark brown in color. He placed them back in the tube and reworked the wax into a cap again. Sorrentino recognized the resin pellets as *cumala*, prepared from the inner bark of the *Virola* tree. He was surprised; use of the tree to prepare a snuff or pellets for ingestion were unknown in southwestern Peruvian Amazonas, or at least not reported. The use of *cumala* was much more widespread in the northeast, particularly in the Orinoco of Venezuela, where it was known as *epená*. When he had asked his mentor about the *cumala* on one of their frequent field trips, standing before a specimen of the tree, the shaman spoke only of the use of the leaves for straightforward medicinal purposes.

To Gar's surprise, A'kunayaz gripped him in a short but tight embrace, as if there was a possibility that he would not see him again. Then the shaman set off on his return to the village. Gar watched him retreat, then hoisted his bow, quiver, and small satchel and began the short trek to his appointed spot. He had little trouble finding the stream, and the kapok tree, beginning to flower, dominated the immediate landscape. Garwell was slightly hungry, but knew better than to eat anything before swallowing the *ayahuasca* brew. He spread out his cotton mat, drained the bitter potion, and waited. First, as always, came the tingling of his hands. He rose and walked in circles around his blanket, noting an ever-increasing vividness to his surroundings. Gar laid back down on his mat and welcomed the wave of forest communication which swept over him, forging new connections in his own brain. He had no doubt that the network of life had an objective reality; *ayahuasca* merely opened a door that allowed him access.

High above the treetops, he heard the keening of a harpy eagle. With the speed of thought, his consciousness shifted to that of the bird as it flew above the forest. Something wasn't right, he quickly determined. There was a thick haze of smoke above the treetops, and a horrendously acrid smell of burned wood infiltrated his nares. The forest below was a patchwork of green and brown, brown where the trees had been set on fire or cut. A network of dirt roads connected the cleared areas, and he could see trucks loaded with downed timber inching along some of the roads. In an instant, he knew that he was divining a grim future for southwestern Peruvian Amazonas. There was more: the celestial music of the forest's syncopated network was now like a scream of anguish in his ears. The realization stunned him and, with a jolt, he came back into his body, immobile on the cotton mat. There were tears in his eyes, and he experienced a deep and abiding sense of dread with a physicality that was as if his body was being throttled. The forest song bathed him, soothed him, dispelling the terror into which he had been submersed. He rose and wandered among the trees that whispered their secrets to him and brought him back to the now. He sensed that what he had witnessed so graphically was but one of a myriad of possibilities.

Gar walked back to his mat and lowered himself cross-legged upon it. He closed his eyes and listened for the harpy eagle's plaintiff call. In the instant of hearing it, it transported him back into the harpy eagle's consciousness. Knowing exactly what he had to do, the magnificent bird began its trip north.

Whether it took days, hours or minutes, Sorrentino could never judge afterwards. The eagle did not pause the flapping of its powerful wings, neither to hunt, drink water or sleep. It arrived in New York on a sultry summer day, and the few reported sightings of a harpy eagle in Central Park were summarily dismissed. It landed on the fire escape of the apartment where Nell and their kids lived. Nell was working on her computer while the kids, Loren, their son, and Rose, their daughter, worked on their homework. Nell suddenly looked up, and, by her expression, had seen his avatar. A swell of unconditional love for them all washed across his consciousness, and silently bade them farewell for what he suspected would be the last time. And with that mission accomplished, Sorrentino's totem animal took off, heading south, while he suddenly found himself back on his mat in the forest.

Gar walked to the stream and drank a copious amount of water using the *ayahuasca* bowl as a vessel. He was still abuzz from the drug, but it was wearing off slowly as it grew dark in the understory. The experience had left him with an abiding sadness, admixed with euphoria. He made a small fire with his wooden fire starter to provide light and discourage curious animals and coated himself with the A'kun's insect repellent. He pulled forth the small tube containing the pellets of *cumala*, and swallowed all of them, washing it down with water. And then he waited, unsure of what to expect beyond what he had read by his graduate school professor Richard Evans Schultes, the Harvard ethnobotanist who had explored the use of the "plants of the gods" across the Amazon region, always rather dispassionately.

Gar experienced a rising, almost manic energy; he got to his feet and paced, then ran in place as his nervousness peaked. He began shaking violently, and he momentarily experienced the worst headache pain of his life. It lasted only seconds. He lost control of his muscles, and dropped to his knees, then stretched out on his mat, slack-jawed, enervated, and involuntarily drooling. He was thoroughly stupefied.

And then they appeared. Little people that glowed with bioluminescence. They were all identical in appearance and appeared genderless. They surrounded his prone body, and in unison bade him upright with their palms upraised. Some part of him followed them into the darkness of the forest. The beings of light suddenly coalesced into a sphere, and they began picking up speed. Sorrentino's consciousness kept pace with them the entire way, never flying above the canopy but through the enormous cathedral of forest giants, lit by the radiance of the sphere. They finally came to a halt at a waterfall that thundered, even in the dry season, from a wall of rock. The sphere brightened, and it dawned on Gar that they were at the base of a lone isolated mountain surrounded by forest. They rose towards the canopy, but only Garwell's consciousness sailed above it. In the light of a full moon, he sped upward. The mountain rose to 4000 feet above the rainforest. Vegetation densely cloaked its breadth of a half mile; it was studded with waterfalls in its unsparingly vertical areas. He circumnavigated the strange formation and knew that his corporal self would have to return.

Far below, he could see the sphere. Its light pulsed once, and he sensed himself being drawn down. Rejoined with the radiant globe, he was spirited back to his encampment. Gar's immobile form stirred as the light of the sphere faded away. He knew from the literature that the entire experience had probably consumed only an hour or two of the nighttime. His fire was almost gone, and he replenished its fuel from a woodpile he'd collected before becoming incapacitated. Even this small task took extraordinary effort. He crawled away from his mat, lifted his loincloth, and relieved himself without standing. Gar expended his last energy returning to his mat and fell into a deep, drugged sleep. All night nightmarish dreams visited him; the only one he remembered afterwards involved Nell and their children, in which they were torn to pieces by a ravenous band of harpy eagles. It had filled him with a mournful sense of loss, until with a bone-shattering scream, he woke as the faintest light of morning and the earliest daylight birdsong infiltrated the forest. Gar was cold and shivering. He needed some food in a large way and easily found some comestible fruits in sufficient numbers to stave off the worst hunger pangs. He went to the creek and followed it upstream to a spot deep enough to bathe. Now moderately refreshed, Sorrentino returned to his camp, rolled and tied up his mat, fixing it to one shoulder, and hoisted his bow and quiver over the other. He had one last task to complete.

Gar began his trek back to the village, alert for any sound of game. It didn't take very long. He spied a red brocket deer browsing around the base of an immense fig. The deer was a skittish animal that usually fled as soon as alerted of a human presence. Sorrentino unburdened himself of his cotton mat and got his bow and an arrow readied. He stalked the deer soundlessly, drawing close and closer until he dared not lessen the distance between them any further. Gar drew, aimed and let the arrow fly. The tip entered the deer's ribcage, piercing its lungs and heart. It fell silently to the ground. "Thank you, little brother," he muttered in A'kun. It was considered bad luck not to acknowledge the sacrifice of successfully hunted prey. Gar retrieved his arrow, cleaning it with a wad of crushed leaves from a copal tree before placing it back into the quiver. With a deep breath, he slung the carcass over his shoulders and grew light-headed with the effort. He continued his return journey, his thoughts preoccupied with the mysterious massif of his *cumala* vision. He knew he would not rest until he found it in the forest.

A'kunayaz was waiting for him when Gar emerged from the forest into the settlement clearing. He was smiling broadly and congratulated Sorrentino on a successful hunt. "Did you see?" he asked. Gar nodded. The shaman grunted in satisfaction.

"Why have you never spoken about *cumala*?" Gar asked.

A'kunayaz signed. "It can be bad medicine. For some. No one knows who."

"What happens to them?"

"They die."

Gar was greeted with accolades and warm approval as he made his way into the village. De'bayna'kun and K'naya ran up to him, failing to hide their evident glee. Several young men unburdened him of the deer carcass and took it away for cleaning, skinning, and preparation for roasting as well as reserving some to be smoked for preservation. As per custom, the hunter would receive the hide after it was tanned. The chief's son embraced him. "After tonight you join us in council," Te'bayna'kun told him.

While the meat cooked, the chief called everyone to the longhouse, not only just the men. He stood at the front, while all the tribe members crowded in. Bayna'kun had on a resplendent headdress, adorned with feathers from the forest's most glorious avian residents. He motioned for Gar to come forward and stand next to him. When the longhouse had filled, Bayna'kun raised his arms, and the crowd grew silent.

"Today we welcome a new brother into our people. We have watched him for many sleeps. He is a great man of the forest and a skilled hunter. Our children love him. A'kunayaz had a true vision of this soul, who we now call A'kun: Gara'kun." For the first time, he embraced Sorrentino. The chief's wife came forward and placed a necklace around Gara'kun's neck. It was a collection of forest seeds strung on braided cotton twine, interspersed with small but iridescent blue and green hummingbird feathers.

"I wish to say something," Gara'kun suddenly spoke. The tribe turned to him as he turned towards the chief. "Bayna'kun, you have welcomed me today into the A'kun. Now, I ask you to welcome me into your family. Will you allow me to make De'bayna'kun my wife?"

For the second time that day, the chief embraced him. He was beaming as he answered Gara'kun with an affirmative nod of his head. A cheer erupted from the crowd, and the younger women besieged poor De'bayna'kun, who only wanted to enfold herself around Gara'kun. Gar raised his voice above the uproar again. "How about right now?" he asked the chief.

Bayna'kun looked at his wife, who was beaming, and then caught A'kunayaz's eye. "Shaman?"

The old man nodded sagely. "It's a good day for a wedding" was all he said.

It was a simple ceremony. A'kunayaz had disappeared quickly from the longhouse but returned not too much later with a collection of forest flowers. Several women arranged the floral bounty in various ways around the longhouse. Several others took De'bayna'kun away to bathe and otherwise ready her for the event. Bowls of *chicha* beer appeared inside, ferried from several of the village houses. Te'bayna'kun spirited Gara'kun away from the longhouse and did his level best to get him drunk on the *chicha*. In place of his soiled breechcloth, he was wrapped in a fresh bolt of woven cotton, dyed a brilliant blue. The chief's son put an arm around his shoulder. "Now we are true brothers," he told him, and the sincerity of his proclamation almost brought the inebriated gringo to tears.

The chief and shaman presided. His bride-to-be looked radiant; adorned with jungle flowers and scented with an intoxicating fragrance extracted from forest herbs. She never took her eyes off Gara'kun. Both elders made some brief statements that he only half understood, with his focus diminished by the fermented maize libation. He assumed the deed was done when everyone tossed flowers at the betrothed couple. He bent down, and for the first time kissed the young mother on her lips. A wild cheer rose around them.

It was a grand feast. The A'kun had a dry rub derived from various forest plants that gave the venison a delicious flavor. De'bayna'kun sat close to Gar through the meal, and at one point placed her arm around his waist. Several of her friends noticed and smiled with sidelong glances at each other.

Little K'naya was beside himself with joy, competing with his mother for Gara'kun's attention. At one point, after yet another round of beer, the three of them embraced and tumbled to a woven mat spread on the floor. The couple's lips found each other again over the youngster's head, and the kiss was deep and passionate.

Drums appeared, along with some flutes fashioned from hollowed out palm stems. Everyone danced in a circle around the newlyweds, who by this time were longing for the conjugal hammock. It would have been considered rude if they had disappeared before the party's end, so they contented themselves with frequent kisses and furtive pawing when they thought no one was looking. The dancers were now also singing to the rhythms and the piping of the flutes, a wedding song wishing the couple a bountiful life together and many additional blessings.

All the festivities seemed interminable, but bit by bit, couples withdrew to their private quarters, carrying their sleeping children. The foment of the dancers lessened, and the singing ended. K'naya would thankfully spend the night with his grandparents. The wedding couple strolled slowly hand in hand in the light of the full moon back to Gara'kun's home, which was now theirs. The interior had been transformed. A stack of new cotton mats had been placed on a woven palm fiber foundation. Flowers were arranged all around the room, and a newly woven large hammock, fit for two, hung from a post driven into the wall. A large basket of fresh fruit was positioned where it could be reached from the hammock. Several beeswax candles illuminated their nest with soft light, and a wooden bowl filled with fragrant oil sent waves of a sweet and pungent scent throughout the shelter. As Gara'kun took it all in, De'bayna'kun came up behind him and wrapped him in her arms, while she undid the cotton shroud that had been his wedding garment. Naked, he spun around and drew her body to his. They tumbled onto the cotton mats and made long and energetic love for hours until falling back languorously into the hammock to devour the fruit with as much zeal as they had consumed each other. Gara'kun experienced waves of deep and abiding love for his new wife, and before long he grew hard again. She lowered herself onto him and rocked them both to another orgasm. De'bayna'kun uttered fricative noises as she neared climax, bringing Gara'kun along. Their tongues danced in each other's mouth, and they fell asleep as if one body, drinking deep of each other's scent, admixed with the odor of sex. "My love," she whispered in A'kun, as he drew his wedding cloth over them, and he replied in kind, squeezing her in a tight embrace. He had fallen from the sky and found his true home at last.

"Their shaman?" Kovac exclaimed. "You're their fucking shaman?"

"I became A'kun one year after they found me. For twenty-five years, I have lived among them, one of them in every way. I built a new life, deeper than I ever thought possible—forgive me, Nell—than I could have ever constructed in the outside world. I am an insanely happy man."

"Or just insane!" Anton spat.

Sorrentino just looked at him with a withering glance. "You feel betrayed," he said.

Kovac got to his feet. "Yeah, well, my best friend disappears off the face of the earth, without so much as a … a sign; excuse me if I don't know who my best friend is anymore."

"It's Nell, Anton."

Anton strode over to Garwell, whose face was half in shadow. "Don't you fucking tell me who my friends are! I know who my friends aren't."

Gar stood and placed his hands on Anton's trembling shoulders. But he said nothing. He walked away and began conversing with Oscar in Spanish.

Kovac turned his wrath on Nell. "You sure stayed quiet during all that!"

Nell sighed and motioned for him to join her by the fire. "I had my meltdown, and I've moved on. Gar made a choice that while I may never understand why, I can still respect. You know, he told me he has a family. Two boys and a girl. They're all grown-up; they all have wives and a husband of their own; Gar's a grandpa!" She trailed off. "Imagine that."

"And a wife?"

"She died suddenly two years ago. Gar is convinced it was black magic. He thinks it was the family of the boy who raped her when she was a teenager. Her brother had tracked him down and murdered him."

"Black magic? Nell, he is insane."

"No, he's not," she stated matter-of-factly. "He left our world, our rules, a quarter century ago."

"I'm going to bed," Kovac declared. "Good night." He disappeared into his tent. When he woke some hours later to relieve his bladder, Gar and Crescente were still in muted conversation. What little he caught was about the gold miners that their band had encountered in the forest a few days ago. Sorrentino lost his composure at one point, and he raised his voice loud enough for Anton to hear the words "¡*Deberíamos matarlos a todos!*" — we should kill them all.

Kovac found it difficult to fall asleep. His mind raced hither and yon, but always came back to the same subject: what compels a man who had so much to give to the world, a giant in his field, to abandon it all for a clutch of people living in the stone age? It made little sense; had his friend truly lost his mind; was that ultimately the only explanation?

There was a rustling of his tent wall, and he heard Gar call his name.

"What?" he said gruffly.

"I brought you something to help you sleep." Kovac unzipped the front of his tent enough to accept a cup of a dark and fulsome tea. Inexplicably, it tasted much better than it smelled.

"Thanks," he replied, wondering how Gar knew that he was suffering from sleeplessness. "Hey, Gar?" he continued, not sure where he was going with this. Gar said nothing but was still standing outside the tent. "Look, uh, I'm sorry I've been such a dick."

His friend grunted and then laughed. He paused, as if to tell his old friend something more, but thought better of it. "Good night, Anton," he said, then walked off to sleep in a small lean-to that he'd constructed during daylight hours.

Gar was the first to wake. While he waited for everyone else to stir, he foraged from the nearby trees for edible fruit, which was plentiful enough to provide breakfast for them all. Sorrentino explained he would not be introducing them to his family or other members of the tribe for fear of transmitting disease. At a certain point, he drew Kovac away from the others. "I'd like you to stay after Oscar heads back with Nell. There is something I want to show you. When was your last flu shot?" Anton allayed his concerns. "I've built a small shelter for you in the village, big enough for your tent."

Kovac later told Nell that he would stay on for a short while, but that she should go back with Oscar the next day. She became angry and protested vigorously. Finally, Anton told her it was Gar's request, and that he had specifically mentioned that she would return with Oscar. Nell stormed off, muttering something about male pinheads.

They spent the rest of the day in relative leisure as Oscar prepared to head back to the Cincinnati Botanical Garden's research station, where the canoes would be waiting. He would leave the plant press, blotters and drying frame with Sorrentino and Kovac, by Gar's specific request. Alvaro and Isidro packed up the rest of their gear to load it on poor Blanca, the mule, in the morning. Sorrentino and Oscar disappeared among the trees, returning with several *pacas*, and a satchel of *abiu* fruit for dinner.

When Anton emerged from his tent, Blanca was packed, and there was coffee waiting. Nell was still unhappy and stood away from him and Gar. When the band was ready to depart, Garwell forced the issue. "Nell," he pleaded, "this is not about you. Don't let your memories of the past blind you." And then he asked, "Would you ever have agreed to take *ayahuasca* with me if I had said that you could come with us?" Gar knew the answer; she had never experimented with drugs her entire life. She relaxed and hugged her ex-husband, knowing that she would never see him again. Then she turned to Anton and held him for a long time. "Come back to me, Anton. I know you're in good hands but stay safe, anyway."

"What are you going to tell the kids?" he asked as Oscar signaled it was time to leave.

She shot an odd glance at him. "What else?" she replied. "The truth."

Kovac and Sorrentino watched silently until they disappeared among the trees. Then Anton broke down his tent and affixed it to his pack. "How far?" he asked Gar.

"Just a few miles. My people are expecting us."

Gar strode through the forest, Kovac doing his best to keep up. Sorrentino seemed to follow a trail which, for the life of him, Kovac found imperceptible. He had generously covered himself with A'kun insect repellent, but the day grew increasingly hot as they hiked.

Sorrentino paused beside a rubber tree and waited for Anton to catch up. "You know, I was sure Kevin hired someone to spy on me," Kovac declared. "The guy disappeared after Cusco."

Garwell laughed, shaking his head. "Anton, that was me."

Kovac stood transfixed. "What do you mean, that was you?"

Sorrentino grew serious. "I've become very adept with *ayahuasca*," was all he said.

As they neared the A'kun settlement, Anton heard voices and the laughter and yells of children. When they broke through the forest into the village clearing, a momentary silence enveloped the A'kun. "I am called Gara'kun here; just so you know." He pointed to a small hut on stilts just under the forest canopy. "Stow your crap in there." Two young men and a young woman came towards them. Gara'kun raised a hand to keep them at a reasonable distance. "These are my children," he said. "K'naya'kun is the oldest. He is my adopted son. Then there's Na'bayna'kun, my daughter. The youngest is Pa'bayna'kun, and he's 23. They are my biological kids." He said something to them in the A'kun language that made them laugh. A lithe, fit-looking middle-aged man walked across the village and halted near the children. He was dressed much like Gara'kun, in a loincloth, and with considerably more ornament around his neck. He stared forthrightly and unsmilingly at Kovac, who suspected that he was being read.

"Welcome, brother of Gara'kun from another life," he said, which Sorrentino translated.

"This is my brother-in-law, the chief, Te'bayna'kun," Gar explained. Anton awkwardly bowed, which brought new gales of laughter from Sorrentino's children. The grandchildren of Gara'kun seemed to materialize out of thin air; they gathered around their parents' legs (three spouses had joined the welcoming party) and peered at the stranger. Gara'kun said something, and the greeting ensemble broke up and walked back to their respective dwellings.

When they were alone again, Kovac told Gara'kun "I'm trying to get my head around all this."

The shaman of the A'kun nodded, his face unreadable. "Come, let me take you to the river to bathe."

12

Anton Kovac spent his boyhood in the borough of Queens. His lower middle-class neighborhood comprised apartments, single-family houses, and clusters of garden apartments, each built around a central courtyard with trees and turf. One such was his home. The management company employed his father as superintendent for the 25 single-story units, for which he received free rent and a modest salary, augmented by episodic odd jobs, primarily for local homeowners. He was what one would call handy.

The first-generation American-born son of Ukrainian immigrants, Leon Kovac grew up in another area of Queens, close to the 1964 World's Fair site. He had one sister, two years younger than himself, who developed leukemia that took her brief life at ten. Leon chafed at his father's Old World autocratic ways and enlisted in the army at eighteen to escape his old man's expectations. Leon saw combat in Korea and spent three years battling the Chinese and North Koreans. He returned, aged beyond his years, though barely twenty-one.

He met the woman who would become his wife a few years after he came back stateside. Her name was Fiona Bunting, and she worked as a secretary in the nearest USO office in Brooklyn. She greeted him with a dazzling smile on his visits, and he soon found reason to stop by frequently, with the purpose only to see Fiona. At last, he summoned enough courage to ask her to dinner. They agreed to meet in Queens, where Leon could introduce her to Ukrainian cuisine.

Kovac was waiting at the subway stop when she arrived. Her beauty spellbound him. As they walked to the restaurant, Fiona put her arm through his.

Fiona Bunting was wholly Irish on both sides, with only the faintest traces of a brogue, no doubt learned from her Belfast-born parents. She was 23, her birthday just a few weeks after his, and she lived in Brooklyn with her parents.

The restaurant owner was a friend of the Kovac family and waited on the couple personally, suggesting an accompanying wine.

As Leon and Fiona dawdled over cappuccinos, the bill paid, and most of the tables now empty, he took her hand in his own.

"That was a feast," she proclaimed. "It will be an Irish place in my neighborhood next time."

One year to the day, Leon Kovac and Fiona Bunting were married in her neighborhood Catholic church, and soon after moved into the superintendent's quarters at the garden apartments.

◆ ◆ ◆ ◆ ◆

Ten years passed without any children added to the Kovac family. Leon and Fiona visited a fertility specialist recommended by their neighborhood general practitioner. He determined the problem lay with Leon's sperm count, and he began a ritualized program of dietary regimens and nutritional supplements. To their surprise, Fiona became pregnant six months later, and Anton was born on Halloween day in 1965. Two years later, a baby sister followed, named Hannah after Leon's late sister, much to Fiona's disapproval.

"Why do you handicap your daughter with her dead aunt's name? I don't see any reason."

Anton Kovac was a small kid before puberty. Short and skinny, he was an easy target for bigger boys with a penchant for bullying. That Anton was the smartest kid in the class was just fuel for the fire.

Seeing his son come home bruised and sometimes bleeding, Leon was infuriated. His mother counseled that they should make an appointment to talk to the school, but Anton's father would have none of it. "I'm gonna teach the boy to fight."

In retrospect, Anton considered this the one genuine service he received from father to son.

Leon brought home boxing gloves for them both, and their ring was the postage stamp backyard of their apartment. The training went on for months. His father also taught him some dirty moves to be used only in an emergency. It paid off handsomely when Anton broke his worst tormentor's nose one afternoon in sixth grade, earning a three-day suspension.

Hannah was a quiet and introspective child. Anton was devoted to her, and she to him. He was her protector, her bodyguard. The depth of their sibling relationship was of great pride and joy to Fiona. And then, chillingly, like her namesake, she was diagnosed with leukemia at ten years of age. She became the family project, and for the duration of the year-long battle to save his sister's life, the Kovacs became as close as they ever would.

The death of Anton's sister was a cleaver to the heart of her family. There was a recess of his mother's mind that believed that naming her Hannah had been a curse. She would be condemned to revisit the end of her aunt's brief life. Fiona withdrew from her husband. Both parents started drinking; Leon, the Ukrainian vodka he preferred, and Fiona, whiskey sours. They rarely drank together. Leon sprawled in his lounge chair in front of the TV. His wife drank in the kitchen, reading one of her preferred trashy romance novels. Anton hid in his room, his companions only books about the natural world, seasoned with classic science fiction.

When Anton turned thirteen, a hormonal blitzkrieg overcame his body. He grew so quickly that he swore his bones hurt. The boy also filled out, developing a ravenous appetite. He reached six feet in height by his sixteenth year, exchanged his eyeglasses for contact lenses, and developed a burgeoning confidence. Young women paid him attention he'd never before experienced. His acumen for school work didn't abate, and he was thrilled when he received an acceptance letter from the Bronx High School of Science.

The natural world around him fascinated young Kovac. He combed the New York parks, learning the trees and observing the birds and the insects. His bible became Elizabeth Barlow's "The Forests and Wetlands of New York." In high school, he volunteered first at the American Museum of Natural History and, in his senior year, at the New York Botanical Garden.

Were his parents even remotely interested in what their son did in his free time? It hardly seemed so. Anton was aware of the dysfunction that was now the theme of his parents' marriage, but he refused to let it become his, too.

The barriers he constructed between himself and his forebears collapsed when his mother ingested a lethal amount of sleeping pills one cold early spring day in his junior year. Her hungover husband found her that morning when he woke. Anton was on a college tour and heard nothing until he arrived home.

"Your mother is gone," Leon told his son in an emotionless monotone. "She took her own life."

Anton embraced his father. He detected no acceptance of the gesture on the old man's part. At that moment, he realized that his family life was little more than a prison sentence. He had one more year to go.

They set the body of Fiona Kovac to eternal rest in the cemetery that adjoined the church where she and Leon had been married. Her son stood mutely during the ceremony, attended by a handful of friends and relatives of the deceased. Family connections in the old Brooklyn neighborhood that reached into city hall had managed to expunge suicide as the cause of death. The certificate read: "cardiac arrest."

Anton accumulated a tight circle of close friends during his final year of high school. They got together to smoke pot and talk about college, books, music, and girls, dropping the latter subject when young women were in attendance. Their homes became ersatz domiciles for Anton, who could no longer abide by his father's silence and turpitude. He drifted home twice or perhaps three times during the week, passing through like a ghost, unless he needed a parent's signature on a form related to his college applications. As far as he could tell, his father lived a compartmentalized life: he did his job, kept himself fed and clothed, and drank himself to sleep every night.

That New Year's Eve, he attended a party at one of their houses. He spent most of the time with a girl named Martina Darocy with whom he'd taken several classes and befriended. Martina was half-Peruvian, a Manhattanite, and very bright. She had long, dark hair that framed her pretty face, which she constantly drew back behind her ears. She wore large-framed glasses that gave her a slightly owlish look Anton found endearing. He loved talking to her.

The group dropped acid and rode the subway to Times Square to join the crowd and watch the ball drop. Anton lingered by Martina's side as they tripped through the crowd, and when the ball landed with an explosion of music and light, Anton and Martina kissed. Her lips were open, welcoming his tongue. He pulled her closer and grew hard in response. "Down, boy," she giggled, feeling his insistent boner even through her winter coat. "Come home with me. My folks are on Long Island, staying with my aunt and uncle."

Anton required little convincing. They left a trail of clothing to her bedroom and tumbled naked onto her bed, locked in an embrace. It soon became evident that Kovac was bereft of experience. Martina guided him gently through her body's intricacies, which he eagerly devoured. The effects of the LSD were still potent enough to enhance the occasion of his first sexual adventure. The taste, the fragrance, the sounds that she made, inspired by his ministrations, brought to him a sharp ecstasy, tinged by the acid.

In the afterglow, they lay entwined, sharing a post-coital cigarette. "Well, I guess we're a thing now."

"You think?" he replied with a smartass grin.

Their "thing" became the new year's theme for both of them. That, and the results of their college applications. Anton had gained admission to Cornell University. Anton applied through the public New York State College of Agriculture & Life Sciences, which lowered his tuition from the lofty height of the university's private colleges. Kovac calculated he would not have to assume too much debt to earn his degree between his Regents scholarship, a National Merit Scholar award, and a work-study appointment. He knew his degree would be in some aspect of biology. Martina would pursue a pre-med course of study at NYU, and Ithaca was just four hours away.

As graduation neared, he stopped by his father's house—he always thought of it as that, never his own, even on the rare occasion of staying over in his old room. He had never brought Martina to the place and doubted he would ever do so.

Anton told his father about his acceptance to Cornell. If his dad was in any way moved by this information, it wasn't particularly clear. But he told his son that he had something for him. He excused himself and shuffled into his bedroom to rummage through his top dresser drawer. Leon pulled out a savings account passbook and brought it to Anton. "It's not that much, but it should help you some. Your mother made me open the account years ago in trust until you turned 18." His son glanced at the ledger. There had been annual deposits since his year of birth. It was an unexpected but gracious gift, and for the second time in a decade, Anton Kovac embraced his father.

Martina helped him move into his dorm room in September. The trees were turning, and night temperatures dipped precipitously. "It's beautiful here!" she enthused. He showed her around the town's famous gorges and ate Italian food at the city's best. "My roommate's not due until tomorrow," Kovac said conspiratorially. "Your bus doesn't leave until 11. I'll drive you to the station in the morning."

They lay naked and spooning in Anton's narrow bed after a rousing session of lovemaking. It was tinged with melancholy, as it would be a span of time before it repeated itself. "I love you, Marti." She pulled his hand over her breast.

"I love you, too, Anton."

Kovac took his college career as seriously as he had high school, though he longed for Martina throughout the long, cold winter nights. She made two visits by bus that first semester and he drove to New York twice as many times.

As the end of the term drew closer, he had vivid and recurrent dreams about the Amazon rainforest. Though he sensed that he wasn't alone, he encountered no companions. Perhaps because of these dreamtime forays, he settled on botany as his degree focus.

For summer, he managed to get a paid internship at the New York Botanical Garden, laboring in the herbarium that housed millions of dried plant specimens. He wrangled student housing near the Garden, little more than a shared dorm-like habitation, but when

Martina told him her parents were spending the summer in Peru, he spent most of his time in Brooklyn, despite the long subway ride to the Bronx.

Anton moved into an apartment off-campus in Ithaca with two classmates in his second year. They each had their own rooms, which were a godsend after sharing a small space with someone else. He mainly subsisted on pizza. When she came up for the weekend, his girlfriend forced him to eat vegetables, chiding him good-naturedly about his unhealthy diet.

As his junior year neared its terminus, he began sending out feelers to master's degree programs in taxonomic botany at institutions across the country. He received a cordial reply from a professor at Duke who ran a well-regarded program in Amazonian botany. His dreams about the rainforest continued engaging him, and he viewed them as portents.

He noticed a subtle change in Martina when they began their final year of undergraduate study. It perplexed him, though he could find little reason for it. Anton characterized it as a slight distance between them. The reason came to light when she gingerly suggested that they start seeing other people when he was last with her in the city.

Kovac's first reaction was anger. "Why?" he exclaimed. "What have I done?"

She shook her head. "Nothing. You haven't done anything. I just," and here she paused, "I met somebody at college. We became friends. We've been helping each other with classwork. I really like him." She lowered her gaze, unable to meet his eyes any longer. "I'm attracted to him."

Anton became tongue-tied. He turned abruptly away from her and marched out of her apartment. He leaped down the stairs, hearing Martina calling behind him, and flew through the doors of the building and into his car. Enveloped by dark thoughts, he drove back to Ithaca immediately, locked himself in his room, and gave vent to his sorrow, ignoring her repeated phone messages. Eventually, his phone stopped ringing. Kovac and Martina Darocy never spoke again.

♦ ♦ ♦ ♦ ♦

Kovac moved to North Carolina a few weeks after graduation. He found a one-bedroom apartment close to campus, purchased a bike, and familiarized himself with the department and his major professor's lab. Bruce Stauber was an associate professor in his mid-forties, whom Kovac found immediately likable. Stauber had a sizable National Science Foundation grant that subsidized his students, Anton included. The project was a massive floristic survey of a region in Amazonian Peru, north of Iquitos. For his master's thesis, Kovac would set up plots using a new method, named after its originator, a young curator at the Cincinnati Botanical Garden. Stauber was effusively complimentary about the so-called Sorrentino method and assured Anton that he would garner sufficient data for two publications. Anton would join his supervisor and another student in Peru during the spring semester. Kovac had wrung the botany curriculum dry while at Cornell, and his chair didn't see much need for him to enroll in many courses beyond Stauber's own Field Biology Statistical Analysis.

Anton's first experience in the *terra firma* forests of northern Peru was as enthralling to him as his first night in Martina's arms. They worked out of a research camp forty miles up the Napo River, reached only by motorized canoe. The days were long and exhausting, the sampling laborious, and the meals primarily rice and beans, with the occasional catch out of the river, usually landed by Stauber himself. The rainforest slowly was transformed from a chaotic green blur into an ordered association of plants and animals that each fulfilled some role in the biome. Curiously, the Amazon of his dreams evaporated now that he was there in the flesh, or at least he had no memories of any nocturnal excursions. His dreams were mostly about Martina.

Kovac successfully defended his thesis at the midpoint of his third year at Duke. Over a celebratory lunch, Bruce asked about his future plans.

"I've been reading Garwell Sorrentino's papers," Anton told him. "And for my Ph.D., I'd like to do monographic work. I'm going to apply to Ohio State and see if I can work with Sorrentino."

A wry smile danced across Stauber's lips. "We support monographic work in my lab," he lamely protested.

"Bruce, the past three years have been like a compass point for me. Everything — the fieldwork, the ability to find patterns in the data and bring solid statistics to analysis; I'll always be in your debt for orienting me to where I wanted to go."

"I'll write you a peerless reference," Stauber promised, "but you know he's incredibly picky when it comes to grad students."

13

Penelope Henrietta Antonia de Souza placed her hand lens down on the dried plant specimen in front of her and rubbed her tired eyes. She was about halfway through the pile of mounted specimens of the genus *Faramea* in the coffee family. The genus was a rainforest understory jewel, often with showy blue flowers. She was finishing a postdoctoral fellowship at the Smithsonian and attending the Botanical Society annual meeting in Cincinnati. She would join the New York Botanical Garden as an assistant curator in two months.

Nell, as she preferred to be known, had noticed that the worst specimens were invariably collections by Garwell Sorrentino. The young assistant curator at the Cincinnati Botanical Garden had already achieved notoriety for the inferior quality of his specimens, many of which looked as if they had already wilted permanently before being placed into a herbarium press.

A shadow suddenly materialized from behind her. "Hello there," the person who had cast it said.

Nell turned and met the piercing glance of Dr. Gilbert Sorrentino. "You make the shittiest specimens, Dr. Sorrentino."

Gar laughed and sat down across from her in the guest workspace that she had been assigned. "My apologies," he replied, "it's so hard to be a saint in the jungle," paraphrasing Springsteen. He leaned back in his chair, appraising her from beneath half-hooded eyes. "You're Nell de Souza," he stated matter-of-factly.

She nodded, impressed that he recognized her.

"I like your work," he continued. "You have a fantastic eye for detail."

"Thank you, Dr. Sorrentino."

"It's Gar, please! This isn't a job interview," he said curtly.

"That's a relief," she countered. "I have a new job already."

"So I hear. I stop by there pretty often when I'm not in the field. New York."

"Well, then I'll see you around."

"Not if I see you first," he laughed.

Their conversation lagged for a moment. Sorrentino leaned forward in his seat and pitched a dinner invitation. She was taken aback at first, but figured, *what the hell*? "Tonight?" she asked. She was leaving tomorrow for DC.

Sorrentino shrugged. "Why not?"

Nell smiled. "You're on. I'm staying in the visitor's apartments."

Gar stood and stretched. "Pick you up at 6:30? I'll make reservations. There's a great Thai place we can walk to." He started to leave, then backpedaled. "Please bring that smile," he added, with a quick bow.

Garwell was punctual, arriving by 6:30 at her door. The restaurant was a few short blocks from the Garden's visitor quarters. The server staff appeared to know Sorrentino, and escorted them to a table for two near a large front window that faced the street.

Nell grew steadily more charmed as the evening ensued. Sorrentino asked about her history. She outlined her life while enjoying a panang curry, until she piped up, "What about you?"

"Me, I'm an Arkansas redneck. Folks were solid, country types. Good parents. I was a wild child, loved the woods, hunting, fishing. Dad grew Christmas trees; did well for many years until the mob began moving in on the independent sellers. He finally stuck to wholesale rather than get beat up or worse in the retail trade. Mom grew flowers for the city florists, which Dad delivered. We had an enormous vegetable garden, a small orchard, and ate off the bounty of the land well into winter with everything Mom put up after harvest."

"What drew you to botany?" she inquired.

Gar pushed his empty plate toward the center of the table and sipped his iced tea thoughtfully. "It was the lady slipper orchids," he finally answered decisively. "There are three in Missouri," he continued. "The small white is the rarest, known only from one population now." He frowned. "I think I was thirteen. I was hunting with my old man in the southern part of the Ozarks. We stumbled onto an enormous population of showy lady slippers, the pink and white one. I don't reckon I'd ever seen such a beautiful sight in all my life up to that point." He chuckled, remembering. "That was my baptism."

She nodded in appreciation.

"And you?" Gar asked. "What was your epiphany?"

Nell silently considered this before replying. "You know, there really wasn't one. I always knew since I was a child that I wanted to work with plants. My Brazilian grandmother probably had a lot to do with it. When we visited, she was always showing me some new plant that she'd collected. When I was ten, she took me to the most incredible place in the granite mountains north of Rio, around Petropolis. The walk up this steep inselberg seemed interminable; I could barely keep up with my Gran." Nell paused to finish the last of her Thai iced coffee. "We slipped and slid on the slick rock, getting wet from the fog. When we turned a bend on the torturous trail, we saw something we could never forget." She was back there in her mind's eye. "There were islands of moss on the slope above us, thick enough in some places to support a variety of plants that grew nowhere else: giant tank bromeliads six feet across, prostrate vellozias with brilliant red flowers. But the most magical of all were the four-foot-tall blue amaryllis plants, known in Brazil as *imperatriz* — the empress, that formed thick clumps all across the rock expanse, flowering in waves of amethyst and lilac." Nell laughed. "Maybe I was wrong. I guess that was my epiphany, after all."

"That is, without a doubt, one of the most beautiful plants in the world," Gar commented. "Brazil missed the boat; it should be the national flower."

Sorrentino accompanied her to the visitor apartments where he'd left his car. "That was nice, Gar," she said. "Thank you."

He smiled. "See you in New York."

◆ ◆ ◆ ◆ ◆

"Penelope!" her mother called. "It's pouring. Get inside now!" She turned to her husband, who had just cracked open a beer after coming home from work. "Ray, you gotta get her."

Nell's father sighed and forced himself to rise from the table in their small kitchen. Ray de Souza lumbered out the front door and swept his giggling seven-year-old daughter up into his arms. She was already sopping wet. "I didn't know you were home, Daddy," she squealed. Ray nuzzled his daughter in reply.

"C'mon let's get you dried up."

She breathed in her father's smell, a mix of sweat, tobacco, and the faint remnants of his aftershave. Ray was half Puerto Rican; the other side was Irish. The family's diverse roots led to holiday trips to Brazil, the Caribbean, and an upcoming trip to Ireland with her uncle's family for Easter. Nell's father was a subway operator on the D line, which was convenient to their home in a pleasant part of the Bronx, circled by verdant parks, and best of all for Nell, a short walk to the New York Botanical Garden.

Angela de Souza took note of her daughter's fondness for the place and ensured they made a visit each season, even during winter, when the stark beauty of the bare trees and shrubs, particularly after a snowfall, was captivating. Nell loved to gauge the progression of spring most of all, from the early ephemeral flowers that appeared before the trees leafed out, to the banks of redbud, dogwood, and mountain laurel that followed. The plants that came from other countries equally entranced her and she promised herself that she would see them one day in their native haunts.

She was outstanding academically, played girls' soccer with skill, and had a tight-knit group of friends. Boys started to pay her attention as she slipped into her teenage years. That was also when she sensed something had changed in her family dynamics.

It commenced with a few arguments between her parents that she blundered into unexpectedly. Their conversation ceased as soon as they saw her standing in the kitchen. "Is everything OK?" she asked the second time it happened. Her parents at first said nothing. Then her dad spoke up, "Nothing for you to worry about."

A pattern settled upon their household. It would start with her father coming home very late from work, and the altercations between her parents would then follow. Their fights would mount to crisis proportions until they reached an unspoken impasse; either her mother broke down in tears, or her father stormed out of the house. In the beginning, they would reach some sort of settlement in remorse, and things at least appeared to return to normal. Ray came home at his expected time, and they had dinners together again. Once, Nell witnessed a rare moment of affection from her father towards her mother when he placed his hand over hers at the table. That peaceable interval would last a few months, and then the signs of a deeply troubled marriage would re-assert themselves.

One night, in her sixteenth year, she came home to find her mother alone in the kitchen, drinking tea and drying tears from her eyes with a paper towel. "Mom, what's wrong?" she said in alarm.

Angela just looked at Nell and shook her head.

"No, Mom," she prodded. "This has gone on long enough. What the hell is going on?"

"You know."

"Is he cheating on you?"

"Yes." She sighed deeply. "Not all the time. They're usually married like him; he meets them in bars. He says it's just sex."

This revelation shattered the last vestige of her childhood concept of her father that night. In its place was a picture of a pig.

Her mother toyed with the rim of her teacup. "At least he comes home to us," she said, as if that should count for something.

Graduating from the Bronx High School of Science as valedictorian, Nell received a stellar financial aid package from Harvard, and took refuge in the vast holdings of the Gray Herbarium and jogs through the Arnold Arboretum. Four years later, she received her bachelor of science in botany. During those four years, she struck up with a classmate who turned into a boyfriend. He was smart and funny, but also a tender lover.

Nell chose the University of Michigan for her Ph.D. A professor she admired, who also held the position of herbarium director, was highly supportive of her research on the coffee family, as it aligned with his area of expertise. That summer, she bade farewell to her boyfriend, who would begin medical school in Florida. It was an amicable separation, though both claimed there were no closed doors to their relationship. She didn't love him, of that she was sure, and their career paths were widely divergent.

Two years into her program, Angela called her and announced that she was leaving Ray. The affairs had continued and lengthened in Nell's absence. This didn't come as a surprise, but it was not without sadness, along with a degree of cynicism about human pairing. The distance between her and her father grew steadily. She even wondered if he had ever really wanted children in his life.

Angela moved back to Brazil, and it was part of the reason that Nell chose a Brazilian group of plants to study. Nell saw her mother two or three times a year. Nell prospered in her doctoral program. She was well-liked and made a few lifelong friends among her fellow grad students.

The National Science Foundation awarded her a postdoctoral fellowship, and she selected the Smithsonian's National Museum as her headquarters. She applied for a job at the New York Botanical Garden when she saw the posting in January of her last fellowship year. The rest, as they say, was history.

♦ ♦ ♦ ♦ ♦

Nell hadn't been settled back in the Bronx for more than a month when she heard from Garwell Sorrentino. She found herself mildly elated that he called. "I'm coming to New York on Thursday," Gar announced. "Dinner? I've also got a proposition—uh, bad choice of words," he laughed. "A proposal for you to consider."

"Splendid," she replied. "See you at the Garden?"

"No, I get in around four. How about we meet at Umberto's on Allerton Avenue, say seven? It's my favorite place in the Bronx."

Nell smiled to herself. It was hers, too. "You're on," she said, perhaps over enthusiastically. "I look forward to it, Gar."

She came home early from the Garden that afternoon and spent nearly an hour deciding what to wear. "Good god," she muttered, "I'm acting like a fucking teenager." Nell rummaged through a cabinet and found a half full bottle of bourbon and knocked back a shot. "There," she said aloud to no one in particular, as the alcohol announced itself to her bloodstream.

Nell sprang for a cab to the restaurant, which was about a mile and a half from her apartment. She had chosen a slinky black dress that showed a little cleavage, and a string of opalescent pearls that her mother had given to her. Garwell had already secured a table and was nursing a cocktail. When she slipped into his field of view, he did a pantomime of shocked surprise. "Wow, you look stunning!" he exclaimed. He leaped to his feet and pulled out the chair opposite his own.

"Thank you," Nell said as she sat. Their server danced to the side of the table to take her drink order and drop off two menus. Sorrentino suggested they start with some oysters.

Garwell had on a light sport coat, a robin's egg blue shirt, and a black bowtie, which he wore rather unselfconsciously. He was, Nell had to admit, extremely charming, and unconventionally handsome.

They shared a tiramisu for dessert, and over cappuccino, Gar circled back to his proposal. "It's a major study of the Madre de Dios area in Peru," he explained. "We'll be blazing new ground. I'd love you to be a part of it." Sorrentino explained that he'd brought a draft of the actual National Science Foundation proposal he was planning to submit. Some preliminary work indicated that the area contained a lot of diversity for the coffee family. He reached under his seat and handed her a manila envelope. "We can talk about it at the Garden tomorrow after you review it."

To say Nell was interested in joining the project was an understatement. "Why me?"

Sorrentino shrugged. "It's like I told you in Cincinnati; you have a superb eye for detail." He smiled. "I think we'd make a great team."

Gar walked her back to her apartment building, and Nell contemplated inviting him upstairs. *Too fast*, she thought to herself. *Don't be a slut*. They lingered at the outside door. As she turned to fit the key to the lock, Sorrentino pulled her in close, and landed a kiss on her lips. She didn't resist. It was just the right duration and intensity. "Goodnight, Nell. Thank you for a second perfect night out on the town."

She watched him disappear into the long shadows of the nocturnal streets, half tempted to summon him back, wondering if he was feeling as discombobulated as she. Nell hurriedly climbed the two flights of stairs to her abode and changed into sweatpants and a t-shirt. She threw herself onto the couch and turned on the television. Nell lay supine for several hours, the TV affording the sole illumination in the room, and read the draft of Sorrentino's grant proposal from first to last page. Then she rolled off the sofa, extinguished the tube, brushed her teeth and disrobed in her bedroom, but not before burrowing through her underwear drawer for her vibrator.

♦ ♦ ♦ ♦ ♦

"It's certainly ambitious," Nell said.

She and Sorrentino were in her office in the herbarium, the proposal manuscript occupying a central position on her desk.

Garwell opened his eyes wide and absently scratched his head. "Well," he said, "that's certainly damning with faint praise."

"No, no, no!" Nell protested. "That's a compliment. I love it! I absolutely want to be a part of it. And it's so cool that it's a hotspot for Rubiaceae."

"I'd like you to be a co-lead on the grant."

"Wow, OK, I'm in. NYBG will love this."

"Excellent!" Gar declared. "You had some brilliant suggestions." He glanced at this watch. "But now we should decide where to dine tonight."

The choice was Nell's that night, and she picked a new Ethiopian restaurant that she'd heard good things about. "I'll pick you up at 7," Sorrentino suggested. He turned to leave, but stopped and looked back at Nell with a mischievous smile on his face. "Would you mind wearing that same black dress? I look forward to slowly peeling it off you later." She blushed imperceptibly, she hoped.

"I can do even better," she sang back.

Dinner was sumptuous and filled with wine, humor, a small bit of botanical gossip, but quantities of flirtations. Sorrentino had a way of always catching her eye just before delivering a thinly veiled double entendre. Nell had worn red, with an equal degree of bodice exposure as the black one. At one point, he slipped out of one shoe, and ran his toes up her calf to her upper thigh. Nell gasped, but the gesture aroused her. Garwell Sorrentino excited her; she had no residual doubts she would sleep with him that night.

They burst through her front door, their lips already locked. Nell was like a mad woman; she couldn't tear his clothes off fast enough. Half-undressed, she pulled him into the bedroom, where they quickly freed themselves of their remaining garments. Sorrentino held her at arms' length for a moment, as if drinking in her nakedness. "My god," he whispered, "you are a sight to behold, Nell de Souza."

Nell surrendered herself completely to her lust, taking Gar in her mouth, until he pulled away, lifted her onto the bed, and worked his mouth languorously down the length of her body, teasing the tips of her breasts until her nipples stood erect, then buried his face between her thighs. Her orgasm was intense, and she nearly howled. She wrapped her legs around him when he entered her, meeting his thrusts and pushing him down deep inside her as she built to a second climax. Gar found her lips, and their tongues touched again before he lifted his head and, with a deep moan, came simultaneously with her.

They lay naked on the bed in each other's arms for a long while. The rest of the night passed with intermittent bouts of repeated and equally ardent sex, but surprisingly little conversation. Nell could feel herself falling for Sorrentino already, and the realization brought her joy and dread in equal measure.

♦ ♦ ♦ ♦ ♦

The New York and Cincinnati Botanical Garden were no strangers to collaborative projects, and the newfound couple spent nearly equivalent time in both cities. The sex continued to be divine.

But there was something barely perceptible about her boyfriend that gave her pause. It was elusive and difficult to characterize.

Their grant proposal was successful, and Nell looked forward to what several hundred-thousand dollars would do for her nascent program at New York: a postdoc or a Ph.D. student, maybe even both.

Gar and Nell planned their first trip to Peru for the start of the rainy season. She was extremely excited; this would be her first venture into the *terra firma* forests of the Madre de Dios basin in southeast Peru. They would be joined by a young, native Peruvian that Garwell had befriended, a naturalist named Oscar Crescente. "Oscar is absolutely topnotch in the field for such a young guy," he told her. Crescente was 10 years younger than Sorrentino.

It was a breathtakingly beautiful forest where they set up their sampling plots. Among the emergent forest giants that formed the upper canopy were two members of the coffee family. Nell marveled at the capirona trees that shed their bark constantly, exposing the smooth green under bark. Similar in stature, but with smooth red inner bark, was a member of the true genus *Capirona*, which with binoculars, viewed from a tree fall a hundred yards away, was in bud. Within a week, she had filled her plant press with over a dozen representatives of her family of interest, of which half were new to her.

Nell took to Oscar immediately. He was as likable as he was knowledgeable. His prowess at identifying birds and insects left both

Gar and her in the dust, but had yet to surpass Sorrentino's botanical acumen.

One memorable day, Gar brought her to a waterfall that Oscar had discovered. Crescente stayed back at camp to hunt for dinner. They had energetic sex in the cool crystalline waters. And it was at that moment that she whispered in his ear, "I love you."

It startled Gar at first, who then seemed to perform some mental calculus, before replying, "Yeah, I do, too."

Thus, it came as a complete surprise to her when one year later Sorrentino asked her to be his wife, his grandmother's wedding ring in his hand. How else could she have responded but, "Yes."

They had a civil wedding in Cincinnati, and a party at the home of Kevin Hobart, director of the Garden. Her mother flew up from Brazil, but her father sent his regrets with a small check.

Nell and her new husband had previously accomplished the necessary discussion about children. Sorrentino had a strange reaction at first; Nell could have sworn that it hadn't even previously crossed his mind. "If that's what you want," was all he said. She held back from replying, *what do you want?*

They agreed to cease birth control in time for their wedding night, and let serendipity prevail. Nine months later, Loren Sorrentino was born, followed two years later by his sister, Rose. Nell would always remember those as the best years of their marriage, when Gar cut back on his fieldwork and made his family a priority in his life. It would not last long. She could never understand that unidentifiable and indecipherable shadow that seemed to reside at Garwell's core. She was fearful of peering too closely.

14

Garwell Sorrentino was conceived late in his parents' marriage, when his father was nearing forty and his mother, three years younger. Whether it was an intentional conception was an unresolved matter, but he sensed no lack of welcome on their part. Born prematurely, he spent his first few weeks in the hospital with nurses taking care of him, until the pediatrician gave permission for him to be discharged.

Gar had few friends as a child growing up in rural Arkansas. He got along well enough with his schoolmates, but formed no deep bonds with any of them. Even as a young boy, he drew the greatest satisfaction from his own company, and second, by accompanying his parents on their farm chores. He had a middling interest in his education, but maintained a decent academic record. His performance on standardized tests always belied his grade point average. Science was his favorite subject, and by the time he entered high school, he considered agriculture as a likely pursuit for college, which his parents were adamant he attend despite his lack of enthusiasm.

By his junior year, he had grown tall, dark, and tight muscled from farmwork. Gar was a good-looking adolescent, though most would not consider him handsome in any stereotypical way. Several girls in his class showed interest in him as potential boyfriend material, but he found them mostly frivolous and not anyone with whom he would wish to spend lots of time. Any budding attraction on their part was quickly abrogated by Gar's introverted silence that came off as indifference or arrogance.

A new teacher was hired just before the start of Garwell's senior year. Her name was Lydia Bellafonte, and she was a fresh graduate of the University of Arkansas, barely twenty-one years of age. They assigned her to teach all three flavors of biology: regular, honors, and advanced placement. Gar had already signed up for the latter, and the school expected her to also provide a senior elective of her own design. She chose botany, and Gar immediately added it to his first semester schedule.

Gar was not at all prepared for the effect that his first glimpse of Lydia had on him. As it was, he was late for the first meeting of the course, and, as he stammered his apology along with a string of excuses involving farm equipment mishaps, all of which in retrospect mostly sounded like fabrications, his eyes took in the dark-haired, green-eyed young woman before him. Gar was smitten instantly. Ms. Bellafonte smiled, and advised him to arrive on time in the future, then bade him sit down with the other students, ten including himself. He was the sole male in the class, he noted.

"Hi Gar," the girl next to him whispered sweetly. Sorrentino involuntarily rolled his eyes. They'd been in several other classes together but couldn't recall her name. Gar grunted in reply. Young Sorrentino had eyes only for Lydia Bellafonte.

The intricacies of botany drew him in almost as much as his teacher captivated him. He wondered if she knew the spell she cast on him; he searched painstakingly for signals on her part. Inwardly, he berated himself. *You're an idiot,* he thought darkly. Once, she let her hand rest on the back of his for the briefest of moments, and it inspired several bouts of orgiastic onanism that night.

He wrote a report on lady slipper orchids for extra credit. That spring, he invited her to visit the large population of *Cypripedium reginae* he had found in the Ozarks once before.

Lydia's face brightened. "Oh, wonderful! But I'll have to announce it to the class and see if any of the girls want to go." Gar was crestfallen.

Fortunately, not a single female student was willing to give up her Saturday. It would be only Gar and Ms. Bellafonte.

It was a three-hour drive south to where Gar had last encountered the showy lady slippers, followed by an equal duration of hiking. While in the car, the two talked about Gar's college applications. Gar figured he would end up at the University of Arkansas because of financial constraints and average grades, but he applied to Harvard and Duke on a whim.

Gar could tell that the glade of lady slipper orchids impressed his teacher. He'd timed their excursion for expectations of peak bloom, and they were not disappointed.

When they returned to her car, Lydia opened the trunk and took out a picnic basket. They walked into the woods and found a flat area between two old white oaks. She took out a blanket from her backpack and spread it across the clearing. Lydia sat down and patted the space next to her, smiling.

Sorrentino obeyed, and dizzily drank in her perfume, as he drew close to her. She next extracted a bottle of wine and two plastic cups.

Lydia poured them each some wine. "I brought sandwiches for us, too," she said.

Gar was fixated on her glistening lips, moist from the wine. "Have you ever kissed a girl before, Gar?" she asked.

He shrugged, and muttered, "Sort of. You know, at parties and stuff."

She emptied her glass and slid closer, draping one arm across his shoulder. Her green eyes locked with his. "Show me," she breathed, and pulled his head towards hers gently so that their lips met. Lydia's were open, and she parted his with the tip of her tongue. She reached over and touched his cock through his jeans, squeezing gently as it came to life.

Sorrentino was beside himself as Lydia pressed her lips tighter to his. Their tongues wrestled as she lowered his zipper and unfastened his belt. An involuntary moan rose from deep in his throat as he fumbled with the buttons of her shirt. He placed his hand over her breast, feeling her nipple harden through the soft fabric of her bra.

Lydia pushed him away briefly and reached behind herself, unhooking the brassiere to free her breasts. "I wanted to jump your bones the minute I laid eyes on you," she said sibilantly. She got on her knees, now half naked, and slid his pants down to his ankles, watching his erect member do its throbbing dance, then took it into her mouth. Garwell was completely overcome, despite his gallant efforts to slow his arousal.

"Oh my god," he exclaimed as he climaxed, then muttered his apologies for his lack of control.

"Mmmmm," she hummed as his penis grew flaccid again in her hand. "You'll last longer after a rest, hon." She poured each of them some more wine and distributed the sandwiches from her basket.

Lunch over, they put Lydia's hypothesis to the test, several times in blissful succession.

Ms. Bellafonte studiously managed their illicit affair for the rest of Gar's senior year. In class, they were all business, a counterpoint to the furious rutting that took place during their heated assignations. The workings of sex under the tutelage of Lydia Bellafonte were the subject of her unspoken second elective. And Sorrentino discovered he liked sex and was even good at it (or so she assured him).

"Can you keep a secret?" she asked him one Saturday afternoon. They were at a hotel near another species rich botanical site they'd visited that morning and lolled about in post-coital laziness.

"I think so," Sorrentino replied.

"I'm not returning to the school next fall," she continued. "I'm starting a graduate program in California."

Garwell said nothing. He wasn't sure how the news made him feel. As much as he was madly in lust with Lydia Bellafonte, he was not able to unearth any other passions that defined his relationship with his teacher. He wondered if there was something wrong with him, some beholden insufficiency of emotion. Lydia seemed unconcerned. If she sensed some wall inside Sorrentino, it didn't show. She was wild in bed, tender in the aftermath of their couplings, but never spoke about love. Lydia didn't seem to be looking for anything more profound from Gar's investment in her. He knew it was meager, but he, in turn, had nothing more to give her.

"I'll come out for a visit during winter break," he assured her.

"That would be nice," she said unconvincingly.

On one of their final outings, Lydia presented Gar with a National Geographic coffee-table book about the Amazon. The volume was filled with exquisite photographs that entranced him. He spent hours in his room at night poring over the pages. It ignited something in him, as if a compass bearing suddenly aligned with his true north, which actually led south.

A week later, Lydia moved to California. Gar never made it out there, and their communications gradually faded into silence.

◆ ◆ ◆ ◆ ◆

Sorrentino applied himself to university with a sharp focus the likes of which had never manifested in grade, middle or high school academics. He was on track to finish in three years. His only distraction was the plethora of young women that filled the campus and night spots in Fayetteville. Since Lydia Bellafonte, Garwell had an insatiable hunger for sex, for which he found no insufficiency of compliant partners. The relationships, if indeed they could be called as such, lasted a few weeks at best, typically ending when his partner discovered he'd been cheating. His few male friends called him a "chick magnet." His enemies preferred "male slut." Sorrentino was, self-admittedly, a dog.

Gar graduated with a 4.0 GPA and, as always with standardized tests, very high GRE scores. He was determined to get into Harvard for graduate school, and to work with the legendary explorer of Amazonian ethnobotany, Richard Evans Schultes. He went so far as to make a pilgrimage to Cambridge to meet the man and state his case for mentorship midway through his last year, and submitted a formal application to Harvard shortly thereafter. Evans Schultes took a shine to him, he thought, and was ecstatic when the professor wrote a letter of recommendation for his admission, agreeing to be Gar's major professor. Sorrentino received his acceptance letter a few months later, along with a graduate assistantship. Gar would be paid to work alongside Richard Evans Shultes!

Sorrentino would always claim that this was where his education truly began.

♦ ♦ ♦ ♦ ♦

"That's fucking incredible," Gar exclaimed.

"We call this one Yggdrasil," his companion said. They were amidst the Río Negro watershed, not far from the Venezuelan border. Gar was with two other students of Schultes, both far more experienced than him, and he was staring up the trunk of an immense *Ceiba*, the subject of his doctoral thesis. Its canopy was hidden from view by the second-story treetops.

"You gonna climb this guy?" one of the two challenged him.

Sorrentino eyed the light gray trunk that splayed below into a small fortress of buttressed roots. "I do so declare," he drawled. He swung his pack off his shoulders, kneeled, and began removing his climbing gear.

One year later, it was Sorrentino leading the newbies into the field, unless Schultes himself joined them.

In his final year of graduate school, Kevin Hobart, the young and dynamic new director of the Cincinnati Botanical Garden, paid a visit to Evans Schultes. His professor invited Sorrentino to join them for lunch. Gar was impressed by Hobart. He had been a well-established full professor of botany at the University of California before accepting the helm of the Garden five years previously and had already built a productive and well-funded research program there.

After their meal, Kevin pulled Garwell aside as their entourage traversed the restaurant's parking lot. "What are your plans after you finish?" Hobart asked him.

Gar shrugged. "I'm looking at a postdoc with the Smithsonian," he revealed.

Hobart handed him his card. "Forget that," he said. "Come to work with us."

Schultes encouraged him to take the offer. "You won't get rich, but you'll have an incredible research budget," he opined.

Sorrentino left Cambridge immediately after graduating, driving out to Arkansas to see his parents. On the way, he stopped in Cincinnati, and told Kevin Hobart that he'd take the job. "When do I start?" he asked.

"You're on the payroll as soon as you return from Arkansas," Kevin told him. "We'll set up a temporary residence at the Garden while you look for a place to live."

Two years later, he bought a fixer-upper with potential in a leafy neighborhood not too far from the Garden. His father flew in to help with the renovations.

Women continued to move in and out of his life with abandon. While some were content with whatever they received from Sorrentino, there were always a few who waited around to plumb some expected but unrequited depth of feeling from him, abandoning their efforts in due course when patience ran out.

All of this came to an end when he met Penelope de Souza in the herbarium five years later. Garwell Sorrentino fell head-over-heels in love, something of which he'd thought of himself as incapable.

As children entered his life, Gar struggled to embrace them with an expansion of that love. He was close to failure when it came to the parental tasks of infancy, and the duration of his field work in the Amazon lengthened perceptibly in that period of their young lives. As they became toddlers, his interactions with his kids improved, but a degree of remoteness instilled itself in his dealings with them. He was pleased when his mother-in-law returned from Brazil and moved into their house; her patience was extraordinary and brought a certain stability to family life, in stark contrast to the benign chaos of the Sorrentinos' parenting style.

The infidelities began when Loren was seven and Rose, five years old. They were occasional and discrete at first, but grew more frequent as the next few years passed, as did his carelessness.

When he was finally confronted by his wife, he was struck dumb, neither denying his behavior nor begging forgiveness. Gar may have experienced some vague intimations of guilt, but he knew that he could not help himself, and stared at her mutely when Nell announced that she and their children were moving to New York permanently. Inside was only a hollowness that was halfway comforting in its familiarity, accompanied by a sense of relief.

15

Of course, it was from the lips of Anton Kovac that Nell first heard of Sorrentino's missing ultralight. It was an inappropriate time of year to receive such news, for New York City was in the throes of mid-spring, its most glorious time of the year.

Nell became weak-limbed, and she lowered herself to a couch seat. "Lost," she said flatly, "what do they mean … lost?"

Anton sat down next to her and took her hand. "He was flying by himself. And he never returned to the landing strip."

"What are they doing this minute?" Nell stridently asked.

"It's the height of the rainy season right now," Anton replied. "Crescente says they can't even get a helicopter in there just to survey the forest and look for the crash site. He's got one on standby if there's a break in the weather."

Nell lowered her face to her hands. Kovac heard one plaintive sob, and then Nell shivered and composed herself. "You should stay here tonight. I'll make up the couch. The kids will be glad to see you when they come home from school."

"I'll charge dinner to Kevin," Kovac grinned.

Oscar's rented copter, paid for by the Botanical Garden, finally managed to lock in the coordinates of the crash site, but to no avail when the ground team could find no trace of a human being. Garwell Sorrentino was pronounced dead seven years later.

At that time, Nell was embroiled in a complex project involving gaining access to Myanmar's tropical forests. Permits were looking increasingly doubtful, and she absolutely needed a plan B. Rose and

Loren were doing well in their respective junior and senior high schools. Loren was the serious, brooding one; he harbored a deep onus against his father. Rose took time to enjoy life more than her brother; she was cognizant of her dad's shortcomings but somehow also found a measure of forgiveness.

Even after a decade had passed, Nell kept Gar's surname, perhaps as a measure of honor for the man, no matter his serious peccadillos. Nell had watched her mother do the same, burying each infidelity beneath a mountain of suppressed betrayal. Everyone, she concluded, no matter how smart, revealed a mushy core of stupidity under the right conditions.

Nell was an attractive woman in her forties, with a unique mix of Brazilian, Jamaican, and Irish heritage. She had the opportunity to meet many appealing men among her colleagues, who were mostly botanists. Her most enduring romance was with a Brazilian zoology postdoc, working with someone at the American Museum of Natural History. They met at a party in the Garden. He was a sweet lover and a brilliant scientist. Loren greatly liked him as his nascent interest in zoology developed in high school. Nell and Paulo talked about living together briefly after the second year of their three years together. The failure of that to happen was like the tolling bells of the end. Paulo finished his postdoc and moved on. Nell hardly mourned.

It surprised her how much Gar still infiltrated her thoughts ten years after his disappearance. She only had to gaze upon her children, particularly Loren, who had so many of Gar's features and build. But there was one memory that she couldn't let go. As she remembered, it took place a year after the crash. She was working at her desk, the children quietly laboring on homework in their bedrooms. Something caused her to turn towards the window. What she saw stunned her, burning into the core of her forever memories. Impossibly, a harpy eagle stood outside on the window's brick ledge and met her gaze with ferocious intensity and then was gone. In the wake of the brief visitation, she doubted that the bird could have been what she thought it to be; it must have been some other raptor, bewildered by the urban jungle. She never told either of her offspring about the incident.

The constant in her small constellation of friends was Anton. She had tried successively to introduce him to some of her single colleagues, but the encounters led nowhere. Kovac was a hard nut to crack. But she doubted there was anyone else on earth whom she trusted more. After his appointment at the Cincinnati Botanical Garden came crashing down, five years after Gar was reported lost, she nursed him back from a deep spell of depression, comforted him when his father died suddenly from a massive stroke, and helped him secure a teaching post at the college in Queens. It was the least she could do for him. But their relationship never violated an unspoken boundary between them, drawn half-consciously by silent accord.

As the second decade since Gar's unsettled oblivion transpired, Nell shifted her studies back to South America, focusing on Brazil. She developed a fruitful collaboration with a group at the State University of Campinas. When the kids were in college, she spent several months a year exploring the remnants of the Atlantic Rainforest. She tracked down Paulo and found him tenured and married, with two kids, living in Minas Gerais. A growing "dad bod" was in full effect. One night, they met for an awkward dinner when circumstances brought her to Belo Horizonte. Paulo's wife was a botanist, and she and Nell compared notes and discussed their projects. Paulo said little.

A year before Kovac told her Gar might be alive, the New York Botanical Garden offered the more senior scientists a retirement buyout. She did the math and decided to take it. She spent two, sometimes three, days every week in her old office, though her emeritus status made her feel like a botanical crone. Maintaining a coterie of graduate students, the majority from other countries, kept her sane and even enthusiastic at times. To her surprise, she received the Asa Gray Award from the American Society of Plant Taxonomists, its highest honor. Anton was more excited about it than she was, but she enjoyed the celebratory dinner with her children and best friend, despite feeling like a fossil. She watched the kids blossom into wondrous adults. Loren was finishing a Ph.D. in ornithology from Columbia University via a collaborative program with the American Museum of Natural History, and Rose would soon graduate medical school from Yale. She would begin her internship in New York that fall. Her daughter was deeply concerned about medical inequities between the developed West and the Third World, and she spent several months each year volunteering with Paul Farmer's Partners in Health, traveling to whichever of the dozen or so target countries was deemed critically in need. Loren and Rose filled her with pride, and she secretly wished that Garwell had witnessed their flowering into committed, energetic adults.

Now, she sat on the Cincinnati Botanical Garden's research station veranda, facing the little river that would soon take her back to the Río Las Piedras and Puerto Maldonado. She watched Oscar and his right-hand men prepare the canoes for a morning departure. During the trek back to the station, she had withdrawn into silence, attempting to reconcile her reunion with her former husband with something that made sense. It was difficult to countenance the fact that her life with Sorrentino had never been enough for him, a "fiction" he had called it. She envied Kovac for the fact that he would get the opportunity to peer below the surface of Gar's rebirth, but she understood why she had been excluded.

Oscar and Nell had pored over the specimens that he, Alvaro, and Isidro had collected. These would be left at the research station, and a set of duplicates would eventually find their way to the Cincinnati Botanical Garden. She was sure that two of the *Faramea* specimens represented unnamed species. More treasures would be brought in time to the attention of specialists in their particular groups for either identification or recognition as something new. Crescente told her that Gar would be ferrying specimens regularly to the research station. "Why suddenly now?" she exclaimed. "He's had twenty-five years!"

Oscar shrugged. "He hasn't been idle. Anton will bring back dozens of completed notebooks."

Luis and two botany graduate students, a young man and a woman, joined them for dinner. The young woman was beside herself, sitting next to the famous Dr. Nell Sorrentino. Afterwards, Luis took Nell aside. "He is alive," he said, less a question than a statement of fact. She nodded. Luis smiled tightly, and his eyes clouded with tears.

"But he doesn't live in our world anymore," she replied.

16

Gara'kun and Debayna'kun's first child was born nine months after their wedding day. Na'bayna'kun was a healthy baby girl, blessed into life by A'kunayaz and her father. Gara'kun thought his wife looked radiant, her new daughter glued to her breast. K'naya'kun was as good an older brother as one could wish for, solicitous of his mother and new sister. Gara'kun could not have loved him more if he was his biological son. As for himself, he knew a peace that had eluded him for over forty years. He didn't look back in shame or anger, only with a stoic empathy for the half-man he had once been.

A'kunayaz met him one day about a year after Debayna'kun gave birth. "It is time to take you there, Gara'kun. That place you saw with the little people." As usual, the shaman was direct and to the point. "We leave tomorrow."

When Gara'kun broached the subject with De'bayna'kun, she wasn't pleased. "How many sleeps?"

He shrugged. "A'kunayaz tells me little."

She sighed and handed the baby to him. "I'll kill him if you don't come home," she said with narrowed eyes.

At dawn, Gara'kun woke and, as was customary, discovered the shaman standing just outside their habitation. He carried a woven palm fiber basket on his back, held in place by two straps of hide. Gara'kun had packed his old backpack with everything that he thought he needed. The old man had told him to bring the deerskin he had earned; as an afterthought, he also packed his mylar blanket.

Gara'kun added a notebook, indelible pen, and GPS. The latter he wrestled with internally for a few moments, weighing whether the mountain should remain in geographical anonymity. The scientist in him, little more than two years in the past, won the day. A'kunayaz handed him bolts of cotton weave. "To wrap your legs if it gets cold," he informed him.

His wife silently watched them disappear into the forest, the sleeping Na'bayna cradled in her arms. "De'bayna my love," he called out over his shoulder. K'naya took his mother's hands, and they walked home together.

The passage through the forest took three days. They would appear as an indigenous father and son to anyone espying them, except the younger one carried a pack of modern design on his back. A'kunayaz seldom paused, except to collect fruits for immediate consumption. Gara'kun had never walked in the forest before without frequent momentary pauses when the shaman would point out plants with medicinal value. On the last day, the low relief gave way to a gradual elevation gain, and Gara'kun noticed how the secondary canopy and understory plants changed. They heard the rush of falling water in the distance in the late afternoon, somewhat restrained in the dry season. An hour later, they stood before the monolith of stone that rose like a temple into the clouds.

"This is the most sacred place of our people," the shaman explained. "All our young men must complete their spirit quest here."

"Why didn't I?" Gara'kun asked.

The old man smiled. "You did. You went the hard way. I told you, the *cumala* collected in this forest can be dangerous."

A'kunayaz walked around the sheer base of the mountain. After a half mile, he stopped and pointed to what looked like the start of a trail. "Now, we climb."

♦ ♦ ♦ ♦ ♦

Kovac had only the faintest idea where they were headed, he and Gar. He hummed the main theme from Sondheim's "Into the Woods." Of that much, he was sure; into the woods they went. "I want to show you something," was all Sorrentino had told him.

As they marched across the forest primeval, Anton couldn't help but reminisce about the many times he had spent in the field with Garwell. He remembered a trip in Colombia when he was in graduate school. An exquisite cerise-colored vining hydrangea grew on the slopes that frame the Cauca Valley. He never forgot how beautiful it was. Gar was shamelessly hitting on Anton's girlfriend, and it pissed him off. Further down the hill, a member of the African violet family, *Alloplectus*, was in flower. When Gar and Kovac's girlfriend caught up with him, Sorrentino said, "Nice *Kohleria*."

"It's not a *Kohleria*, Gar; it's an *Alloplectus*," Kovac replied flatly.

A tight smile marched across Gar's face. "Pretty sure you're wrong there, Anton."

"Pretty sure I'm right," Kovac muttered under his breath. He had worked at a botanical garden before graduate school with a massive collection of that family from the American tropics.

"It was an *Alloplectus*; you were right," Gar suddenly said.

158

Anton froze. "How… how did you do that?"

"Practice," Gara'kun replied.

The twenty-mile first day was a slog for Anton, and he welcomed Gar's calling it a day at that point. While Kovac set up his tent and built a fire, Gara'kun disappeared into the forest with his bow and arrow, returning an hour or two later with two birds, a species of guan. Anton hoped they tasted as good as their relatives, the curassows. They did, roasted on the fire with a dry rub procured from Gar's pack.

On the second day, they stopped for a rest alongside a moderately sized river, the current steady, the banks separated by about thirty feet. "That river originates from where we are going," Gar announced. They pushed on through the forest for a while longer, which was changing subtly as the relief gained elevation. Kovac found himself immersed in the same awe that had placed him on this path over thirty years ago, nature untrammeled, the largest unbroken rainforest in the world.

Gar pulled two striped bass from the river for dinner, while Kovac gathered *abiu* fruits from a tree near their camp. Around the fire that night, Gar suddenly asked him about his fall from grace two decades ago. Anton sighed and didn't answer immediately. "She made me feel wanted, I suppose," he lamely declared. "And I was furious at Kevin when you disappeared. The way he pushed everyone at the Garden—do more, do more. 'Be like Garwell,' he always said. Meanwhile, he posed for magazine covers, and next to activist movie stars, dressed to the nines. I guess I wanted to humiliate him."

His friend was shaking his head. "He always stayed on message, at least as long as I've known him. You can't blame Kevin, Anton. I was right where I wanted to be when that ultralight came down. The accident freed me. I'm sorry that my subsequent choices have made you so angry. In my own way, I was incomplete until the A'kun found me."

Kovac eyed his friend, trying hard not to appear disbelieving. But he was no longer angry. "A collapsed marriage is one thing. I just don't understand how you could walk away from Loren and Rose."

Gar silently peeled an *abiu* fruit while he considered his reply. "I don't think I can give you a satisfactory answer. My abandoning them may have been a gift."

Anton snorted derisively. "Oh c'mon, man!" he replied. "What kind of rationalization is that?"

Garwell tossed a piece of wood on the fire. "You stepped up, Anton. I will always love you for that."

Kovac said nothing. He wondered if he had ever heard his friend use the word "love" before. Oscar was correct; Sorrentino was a complicated man. Or had been. He wasn't sure who this Gara'kun was anymore. Can someone shed a life, a persona, like a snake tosses off its skin? Had Gar found redemption among the A'kun? Or had he merely traded one broken self for another, equally in disrepair?

"*Ayahuasca* has taught me so much, Anton. It's been the one true teacher in my life; A'kunayaz was just a guide along this trail of learning." He leaned forward, his gaze fixed on Kovac's eyes. The reflection of the flames danced in the dark irises of his own. "Terrible things are going to happen in this world, Anton. It's no longer just one of infinite possibilities. Terrible things."

Kovac shivered as an icy chill suddenly enveloped him. In some core part of him, he knew what his friend just told him was true. He looked upward and towards the river, where the break in the forest revealed a slice of the Milky Way. "So, what do we do?" he said.

Gar leaned back. "We do what we've always done. We live. We love. And sometimes we fight."

♦ ♦ ♦ ♦ ♦

A'kunayaz led the way up the mountain. Someone, and who knew how long ago, had sculpted stairs from the rock in some places; Gara'kun wasn't sure that they made the ascent any easier. A good share of the way was a climb over rock-face and tree roots. Many of the steep surfaces had ancient hand- and footholds carved into the stone; Sorrentino tried to imagine how many had made this same journey over the millennia of human existence in these forests. After several hundred feet of rise, they broke above the canopy's expansive rooftop. Periodically a promontory jutted out from the main track, forming a small terrace. They took rest stops on these platforms, replenishing the wads of coca leaf and ground shell in their cheeks to fuel the next phase of their climb. The forest stretched to the horizon, broken only by the occasional river cutting its meandering way across the green expanse.

Nearing 3000 feet, the air was cool, and Gara'kun draped the deerskin over his shoulders. There was a visible trail that they followed; it wrapped itself around the face of the mountain, slowing their ascent, and cloud banks collided with the pinnacle of rock, droplets settling upon their hair and skin. Tree ferns clung precariously from the steep inclines, interspersed with evergreen shrubs, plants whose closest relatives lay hundreds of miles to the west in the cloud forests of the lower eastern Andean slopes.

Above 3000 feet, rounding a turn on the sinuous path, they were greeted by a flat expanse of stone, a massive terrace the size of a football field that could only have been formed by a sizable portion of the slope above giving way many years in the past. Soil had even accumulated in the more sheltered places, and several trees had colonized such pockets, including a thirty-foot-tall *Ficus* whose roots snaked across the rock surfaces. Gara'kun couldn't believe his eyes. He had never seen so many plants in flower at once in any one place in the tropics. The gentler slopes above the terrace had offered opportune conditions for a profusion of shrubs, herbs, and vines representing more than a dozen plant families.

A'kunayaz smiled. "The Garden," he said. "We will sleep here tonight."

♦ ♦ ♦ ♦ ♦

By the afternoon of the third day of traversing the forest, Anton could hear what sounded like falling water in the distance. It grew louder as they progressed until the wall of rock from where the river that they had been following emanated came into view. Its appearance was so incongruous to Anton, that his brain perceived it as a side of a castle hewn from stone. A waterfall cascaded down from a height he could not see. On either side of the river's now much narrower channel, tall trees grew close to the rock-face, and lianas as thick as his arm snaked upwards along the rough surface of the wall. "Holy shit!" was all he could say. "How high does this thing go?"

"About 4000 feet," Garwell answers. Kovac whistled in amazement. Gar continued, "The exposure makes it cooler than a similar elevation would be in the Andes. The relatives of many of these plants would occur there at higher elevations."

Gar foraged for fruits and edible seeds. Anton found a flat spot to set up his tent and then looked for any relatively dry wood. Gar came back with an assortment of fruits and nuts, plus two *pacas*.

After dinner, Kovac and Sorrentino sat quietly; the varied sounds of night in the forest and the crackle of the fire lulled them into silence. It was Gar who broke it. "Why did we become botanists?" he blurted. "Think about that."

Anton's answer was immediate. "We had no choice."

"Exactly. And that is also why I became A'kun."

The next morning, Gar led Anton to the entry point of the ascent. "People have been visiting this mountain for thousands of years. But we'll have to do some scrambling. It's worth it, believe me."

The climb put Kovac to the test. But when they stopped to rest at a rocky terrace that afforded a view 2000 feet above the tallest trees, miles of unbroken forest as far as the eye could see, he felt privileged to be there with his old friend. They sat in silence and watched the torrents of bird life that flew above the treetops. *I could die right now with a smile on my face*, Anton thought suddenly.

Gar jerked his head up, smiling. "Not yet," he said. "Come on, let's keep going."

To Kovac's relief, they were on a genuine trail, albeit a narrow one, that switch-backed across the mountain slope. The trail led inexorably upward, through tree ferns dripping with water from condensation. They had left lowland forest far below them, but to Kovac's wonder, Gar found edible fruits even up here. Anton recognized them as a member of the blueberry family, and they were a welcome repast.

Sorrentino had disappeared around a bend in the trail. Anton hurried his pace. As he rounded the same curve, he almost collided with his friend. Then his jaw dropped as he took in the courtyard that opened to his tired feet, stretching out before him for yards. A sixty-foot-tall *Ficus* occupied one corner of the massive terrace. It bore a large crop of figs, many of them ripe and quite tasty, it turned out. But what drew him forward was the riotous profusion of flowers that covered the rocky overhang that jutted out from the continuing slope behind it, sheltering a portion of the flat expanse that formed the terrace. An assortment of hummingbirds worked many of the flowers, the different species showing fidelity to certain plants. Kovac identified two different species of *Bomarea*, twining lilies of the alstroemeria family, one with brilliant red and yellow flowers, and another pink and white. Three unique members of the blueberry family were in full bloom, their display of lavishly colored waxy flowers like clarion calls to the iridescent hummers. An amethyst-hued Andean bell flower was abundant along the width of the escarpment. "This is like a garden," Kovac said, wonderment in his voice. "I've never seen anything like it."

"When A'kunayaz brought me here for the first time, that's what he called it. 'The Garden.' Even Oscar knows nothing of this place."

The edge of the escarpment harbored a profusion of plants in the African violet family, all in bloom. Kovac recognized most of the genera, but the species were new to him. From Anton's vantage point, the slope beyond the garden appeared much gentler than what they had encountered on their ascent, and an open dwarf cloud forest had established itself all the way to the top. "That's for tomorrow," Gar told him.

In the last hours of the day, the clouds momentarily dispersed, and the sun, low in the western sky, provided some welcome heat. Steam rose from Anton's sodden field clothes, and he hoped they would soon build a fire.

The logical place to camp was under the overhang, and Kovac threw his pack down and set up his tent. Gar hung his hammock from two hefty branches of the *Ficus*. Anton scoured the terrace for anything that appeared burnable, while Gar dug some *Bomarea* root tubers to roast from plants that clambered across shrubs at the edge of the cloud forest. They tasted like potatoes. "No protein tonight, I guess," Anton declared when Sorrentino returned. Wordlessly, Gar picked up his bow and arrow, and headed into the cloud forest, appearing a short time later with two plump birds.

A full moon reached its zenith while they ate, bathing the stone plateau with an unearthly light. Cloud banks came and went all night, sometimes enveloping them in fog for a few minutes before hurrying on. The night air was cool and humid. "So, what's the plan?" Kovac asked.

"Tomorrow, we'll explore the cloud forest on our way to the top."

"And then?"

"We'll collect specimens from the garden to press when we get back to my village. They should stay in decent shape. The next morning, we start back down."

Anton was sitting naked, wrapped in a mylar blanket, hoping that the fire would dry his clothes. "How many times have you been here?"

"Every two or three years," Gar replied, "in the flesh. After A'kunayaz died, I took responsibility for the *m'kunaya* harvest."

"Versus?"

"In my spirit animal, with *ayahuasca*, I have visited hundreds of times."

"And what is your spirit animal?"

Sorrentino took a silent measure of his next words. "I'm sorry, but I would rather not say."

Kovac shrugged. "Suit yourself. Does everyone have a spirit animal?"

Gar shook his head. "Only the true *ayahuasqueros*." he said.

◆ ◆ ◆ ◆ ◆

The shaman and Gara'kun woke with the first light of morning in the east. The hummingbirds were already hard at work in the garden. From his basket, A'kunayz withdrew two small vessels containing the *ayahuasca*. He handed one to Gara'kun. "Drink," he commanded.

They then set off across the undulating gentle grade into the cloud forest that never exceeded twenty feet in height. One of the most beautiful trees was a species of *Meriania* in the melastome family, with almost fluorescent orange flowers and strange bladder-like appendages on the pollen-bearing stamens, interspersed with a purple-blossomed *Clusia*. Terrestrial orchids dotted the edges of the elfin woodland.

They pushed on, alternately warm when the sun appeared, then cool when a cloud bank enveloped the mountain. There was something different about the *ayahuasca* to Gara'kun; he wondered if the old man had used a different recipe for the decoction. The usual hand-tingling sensation had persisted and spread throughout his body. If he closed his eyes, the music of all the life on the mountain came to him in waves.

The shaman paused in their path. "Here is where the *m'kunaya* starts to grow," he said. He pointed to a fairly nondescript tree with alternate leaves. It was also flowering. The flowers were pink and about an inch in diameter. Other trees were in fruit. As they continued up the slope, it became a dominant species, with several over fifteen feet tall.

"This is the most important healing plant of our people," A'kunayaz said. "Close your eyes and touch the trunk so you may hear the *m'kunaya* speak."

Gara'kun kneeled before one of the larger specimens and placed his hand on the tree, with his eyes closed. He almost recoiled; the sensation he experienced was incredibly powerful. Through the network of life, Gara'kun instantly gained knowledge of the plant's healing capabilities, a key that only ayahuasca could provide.

M'kunaya was the most effective immune system boosting agent nature had stumbled upon through the serendipitous precision of evolution. No wonder the A'kun enjoyed such robust health throughout their lives.

♦ ♦ ♦ ♦ ♦

There were abundant ripe tropical blueberries available, but Gar told him to eat nothing and only drink water in moderation. Kovac had pulled two energy bars from his pack, one of which he had proffered to Sorrentino (Gar refused with a grimace). He placed the bars back into his pack. From his ancient backpack, Gar withdrew two 6" tubes fashioned from almost hollowed-out palm stems; the lowest half inch was retained as a plug. The open end was sealed with beeswax and pitch, Anton recognized, from a *Clusia* species. "I'd like you to take *ayahuasca* with me."

It was Anton's turn to grimace. "I don't know, Gar," he protested. His friend made a dismissive gesture with his free hand.

"It's time for you to understand who you are, what all of this is," Gar replied, waving his arm across the wilderness that spread

168

around them, a carpet of green seemingly without end. "It is time for you to put your fear to rest. The fear that prevents you from truly living." He paused briefly. "You will never have a better guide." Kovac wasn't sure if his friend was referring to the *ayahuasca* or to himself. Gar removed the beeswax cap from both tubes and handed one of them to Kovac. "*L'chaim*," Sorrentino toasted, swallowing his draft quickly. Anton did the same. "I want to show you a very special plant." He stood and pointed to the slope above the garden that continued up to the peak.

As A'kunayaz had done that first time with him, Gar had not added the ingredients that lessen if not forestall the digestive purge effect of the drug; most *ayahuasqueros* believed that this was an important part of the ritual. Gar told Anton to disrobe. "It will be easier to clean you up afterwards," he said, and Kovac couldn't tell if he was joking. He did as he was told, just as the first of several convulsions gripped his guts, and he expelled lustily from both orifices. "There's a creek over by the end of the garden; you can wash up there."

"My hands are tingling!" Kovac exclaimed with slight alarm. And then he stiffened, his jaw agape. "The colors ... around everything. My god!" He grabbed his clothes and took a circuitous route to the creek. He cleaned himself as best he could and drank some water from upstream of his bath spot. It was warm in the sun; the heat and light entered his body as he dressed. Anton saw Gar already above the garden, waiting for him. He had to pause once before The Garden's bounty of floral diversity, and that was when he heard the music, weaving through the ringing of hummingbird wings. *Life's song*, he thought.

He set off, pleased by the gentleness of the slope, and soon joined his friend. Gar appeared less than pleased. "This is the *m'kunaya* tree," he said, waving his arm across the elfin forest that crept up the slope. "It is the most powerful healer of the A'kun. Listen."

Kovac closed his eyes and detected a dissonance in the meshing of so many musical threads, one that he had not noted in the garden. "Something is wrong," Gar said. He walked over to what appeared to be the largest *m'kunaya* tree in the vicinity. "This is one of the mother trees," he said. He kneeled and placed a hand flat on the trunk, closing his eyes. He shivered, and his eyes suddenly opened wide with an intake of breath that through pursed lips sounded like a hiss. Tears flowed down both cheeks. "They're dying," he whispered, and as if in reply, a gust of wind swirled around the slope, causing a rustling across the low forest dominated by *m'kunaya* trees of various size and age. "This environment is changing," Gar continued. "It's getting warmer, drier. The *m'kunaya* trees are the first to feel it."

They continued up the slope. Some trees bore leaves with desiccated tips or margins. Anton drew near one of the *m'kunaya* that was flowering. He studied the flowers, which the *ayahuasca* enveloped in a fluorescent pink glow. The flower had eight to twelve petals and sepals that were indistinguishable from each other. The pollen-bearing anthers were held on the tips of petal-like but smaller structures. At the center of the flower were a cluster of eight to ten carpels[13]. He noticed that each developed into an elongated, fleshy, red fruit enclosing a single seed. "What family is this in?" Kovac asked.

Gar smiled tightly. "I was hoping you could tell me," he said. "Come, there is more to see." They continued upward towards the peak of the strange mountain. The terminus was a rock wall that rose to the highest point in the formation. A flat face, protected by a short escarpment, was a gallery of carved drawings and handprints. "As I told you, people have come here for millennia."

The tableau of drawings depicted birds, jaguars, and what Anton surmised were *m'kuyuna* trees and other plants. The illustrated wall exuded a strange power that Anton palpably felt in his body. He turned towards his friend, only to discover him gone. A sudden keening reached his ears, and he looked up to see a harpy eagle riding the thermals that rose from the dense forests below. "Gar?" he ventured timidly, but heard no comforting reply.

A great weariness suddenly overcame Kovac. He sank to his knees, then lay supine on the rocks at the base of the gallery. Anton closed his eyes and sunk into the ground. Kovac discovered he was in a cave that he knew immediately was inside the mountain. Though he should have been enshrouded by darkness, Kovac could somehow see the cave walls. He grew afraid; it was a formless fear that grew from deep inside of himself. In an instant, Kovac sensed he was not alone. He turned and saw himself. Or something like himself. The

---

[13] Carpel: female reproductive structure in a flower.

apparition was almost a caricature; it stared back at him with a dull look on its face and then whimpered. The whimpering became hysterical; it edged the fear inside himself to a fever pitch. His doppelgänger suddenly loped around the cavern on all fours, moving faster than any human should be able to manage. Other figures materialized; they were in some way reminiscent of himself, but different from the first. Several had faces that could only be described as demonic. A few ran at him, then leaped over his body. Soon, the cave was filled with more ersatz Kovacs than could comfortably fit inside the small space; Anton was drowning in a sea of himself. The Antons morphed into manifestations of Leon Kovac. Several of the creatures wearing his father's face sat on him and sniffed his face, arms, and legs. The fear was now insufferable; he wept as hysterically as the banshee maelstrom surrounding him ascended to a fevered pitch. A brilliant light caught his attention. It was a vision of his mother. She looked directly at him, a peaceful expression on her face. In an instant, she disappeared, and Kovac was engulfed again by chaos. Finally, the insurmountable fear could no longer contain itself inside him, and he screamed with a ferocity that he never knew he could achieve. The cave grew silent, and Kovac fell into a serene and senseless blackness.

◆ ◆ ◆ ◆ ◆

The shaman collected stems, leaves, and fruits from the *m'kuyuna* trees, placing them carefully into the basket he had carried on his back for the entire ascent. "The medicine of the *m'kuyuna* is very strong and lives in every part of the plant. We will extract in water, boiling for hours over a fire to concentrate it. We strain it with woven cotton. You must learn how to do this. All the A'kun are given one pellet each moon. What we collect here today will make enough for several years." A'kunayaz pointed to Gara'kun's backpack. "You have something in there to gather with?" the old man asked. Gara'kun nodded and pulled a collecting bag from the depths of his pack. He filled it with branches of the trees, taking care not to break off too much from a single plant. Gar carefully studied one flowering branch and realized he had no idea to which family the *m'kuyuna* belonged. He suspected it was something ancient based on the floral morphology. But where it fell precisely on the tree of life, he could not tell.

"Leave the *m'kunaya* collection in the shade of this mother tree," A'kunayaz said. "There is more to see."

As they walked the rest of the way, Gara'kun experienced a curious buzzing in his body. It differed from the hand tingling with which *ayahuasca* announced itself; this was coming from somewhere outside. It intensified as they neared the large rock wall at the base of the mountain's stone peak.

Gara'kun was struck speechless by the tableau before him. How many generations of A'kun, or whatever people they had branched off from, had created the thousands of carvings and handprints that flung along the expanse of the wall? "This is a place of power," the shaman intoned. "That is what you feel in your body. Now let's go into our animal spirits before the *ayahuasca* wears off." A'kunayaz lay down on the ground in front of the rock wall gallery. Gara'kun did the same. Before he closed his eyes, he had a vision of a black jaguar bounding up the final precipice of the mountain peak. He heard the call of a harpy eagle summoning him, and seamlessly joined with it as it soared above the mountain top.

♦ ♦ ♦ ♦ ♦

Kovac woke from what he thought was a dreamless sleep, but which in actuality had been visited by strange visions that left no memories behind. Sorrentino sat nearby, his arms around his knees, studying Anton intently. Wordlessly, he handed Kovac a canteen that he had pulled from Anton's backpack. "Drink," he said. Two woven cotton sacks filled with pieces of the *m'kunaya* trees were next to him. "How do you feel?"

"Drained, but … but different," he replied and shrugged. "I don't know…" He trailed off.

"It takes the brain a day or two to process the experience," Gar told him. "But I sense the purpose was met." He stood. "There is one more thing to show you. It's on the other side of the rock. It's kind of a scramble."

Gar helped Kovac to his feet, and they set out across the creek, following it along the peak until they reached a small waterfall that tumbled from a large crack in the granite precipice of the mountain. The stone walls rose almost straight up, but they were draped with clumps of the most exquisite orchid that Kovac had ever seen. It was a species of tropical lady slipper orchid, of a brilliant red hue that was uncannily luminous. The flowers themselves were three to four inches across; most bore two flowers on the stem, a few had three.

They reminded Anton of the famous purple flowered slipper orchid in the Andes to the northwest that roiled the orchid and botanical worlds with the scent of scandal in the early years of the new millennium. The first population found of that species was quickly stripped of all but the most inaccessible plants to feed the obsessive acquisitiveness of orchid fanciers in the developed world. Anton hauled his pack from his shoulders and pulled out his camera. Gar reached out his hand and grabbed Kovac's wrist. "Let this one go," he said. "Keep the pictures in your head." Reluctantly, Anton slipped the camera back into its pocket. "Let's take a bath, and then head back to the garden for the night," Gar told him.

The water was cold but not bone-chilling. When he'd stripped, Gar handed him a small cake of soap. They stood under the waterfall to rinse. "This trip has been good for you, Anton. You've lost some of that fat around your gut."

"That's just what I lost during the *ayahuasca* purge," Kovac joked. "So, tell me, what's so amazing about the *m'kunaya* tree?"

Gar sighed, still saddened by the decline he sensed had begun in the sacred trees. "It is filled with some alkaloid that is undoubtedly the most powerful immune system booster ever discovered in a plant. We cook all parts of the plant for half a day. It forms a thick slurry that we form into pellets that are given to all our people once a month. The A'kun are rarely ill, except by accidental or deliberate poisoning, and, of course, black magic."

"About that," Kovac interjected. "Do you really expect me to believe that there's such a thing as black magic?"

Sorrentino looked annoyed at first, but shrugged off Anton's trivializing tone. "You can call it whatever you please. But a true *ayahuasquero* can tap into a source of power that you can't imagine."

As they made their way down from the pinnacle and through the elfin forest, Anton mused about the possible relationship of the *m'kuyuna* tree to all other flowering plants. Kovac sensed that the tree was an element in the group known as the "basal angiosperms,"[14] which constituted the first branches on the flowering plant tree of life. Modern DNA technology had resolved a plant found only on the island of New Caledonia as the first branch in the phylogeny of the flowering plants. Perhaps the *m'kuyuna* resided somewhere near the base of the tree as well.

When they reached the flat expanse of the plateau below the garden, Kovac set about collecting wood for a fire, while Gar took his bow and arrows and went off to hunt. He once more returned with two birds that looked similar to the Andean guans that lived in the cloud forests that lay miles to the west. Sorrentino expertly cleaned the game and set them to roast over the fire with the remaining lily tubers that he'd stored near their camp. The bounteous supply of tropical blueberries provided dessert.

Kovac pulled a small flask from his pack. He offered it to Gar, who declined with a customary grimace. Anton shrugged and took a long draught of the pisco inside, a final gift from Oscar. He eyed his friend, who, he had to admit, seemed curiously at peace with his life

---

[14] Angiosperms: group encompassing all the flowering plants.

and the choices that he had fashioned it from, and finally confessed to himself that maybe it was a good thing after all. "Thank you for bringing me here," he said. "It is the most unforgettable place I've ever been."

"My grandchildren may be the witnesses to its end," Gar said. "If the *m'kuyuna* starts to die, the garden won't be far behind. And the slipper orchid at the top." He grew angry. "The way you live in the world has consequences even here." He shook off his bad temper with a vigorous head motion. "We've got about two hours before it gets dark. Let's do some work." They set about gathering specimens of whatever was flowering in the garden as the shadows lengthened. Kovac exhausted his camera battery, photographing the diversity of flowers.

A light rain fell for part of the night; the patter of drops against Kovac's rain fly was a comforting sound, though he knew it would make the descent of the mountain treacherous. It was cool that night and Anton had recourse to drape himself with his mylar blanket. He drifted off to sleep, his mind awhirl with bits and pieces of his *ayahuasca* visions. He woke refreshed but famished and was pleased to see that his friend had foraged a passable breakfast of fruit from the abundant tropical blueberries.

They started down the mountain, now encumbered by bags of specimens and *m'kuyuna* for processing. "We'll probably have to camp at the base tonight," Gar said. "The rocks are slippery; we'll have to go slow." When they came to the most difficult spot, the rock face with the hand and foot holds likely centuries old, Gar pulled his nylon cord and grappling hook from his backpack. He inspected the immediate area and settled on a fig that clung tenaciously to the rocks. He flung the hook over a stout branch and had Anton test the line with his weight. All looked well.

Kovac rappelled down with two of the sacks. Sorrentino tossed the other two down to him. He unhooked his rope and hooks and placed them back in his pack. He tossed it down to Anton, who waited below. Then, to Kovac's astonishment, he scrambled down the rock wall like a spider, making use of the ancient grab and foot holds chipped into the rock.

As they descended, Anton was shocked by how the light diminished when they dropped below the canopy. It was late afternoon when they reached the base of the mountain. Kovac was exhausted and with his last iota of energy set up his tent. He realized that Gar likely expected him to make a fire as usual; his friend had wordlessly headed into the forest with his bow and arrow. He returned an hour later with a young white-lipped peccary, which he dressed as Kovac dealt with the fire.

They ate in silence except for the crackle of the fire and the sounds of forest night. Nell had identified a number of the night birds by their call, and Anton had remembered a few. Most were various species of potoos. He missed Nell suddenly and deeply. He'd be home in a week.

They began their return to the village at daybreak the next morning. Traversing the forest was a cakewalk compared to the Magic Mountain (as he had christened it). Gar's pace was unremitting, and their trek was as silent as the previous night's supper. "Is there something wrong?" Kovac asked.

"I'm not sure," Sorrentino replies, and quickened his pace even more. "Something feels … off."

"Gar, it's still gonna take three days to reach your village."

"I'm shooting for two."

Anton cursed. "We'll see."

They celebrated completing between thirty and forty miles that first day with a fish dinner plucked from the river, and clusters of both *abiu* and *ñejilla* fruits. Kovac fell into a deep slumber and didn't stir until the first light. Gar had already gathered breakfast when he emerged from the tent.

After morning ablutions, Gar handed Kovac a pouch of coca leaves and a tube of crushed shell. "You'll need this today," he said. They broke camp and pushed on, stopping only once to have a brief rest. Sorrentino remained withdrawn. As darkness infiltrated the forest understory, it became obvious that to reach the settlement in just two days was wishful thinking. About fifteen miles remained. Gar bagged a large guan for their dinner, and Anton gathered *abiu* fruits from a nearby tree before starting a fire.

Kovac broke the silence that of late had become the feature of their evenings. Anton considered it as much an artifact of his *ayahuasca* experience, but he also sensed just below his conscious mind that he'd begun saying farewell to his old friend for the last time. "Are you still sensing something amiss?" he asked.

"We'll find out tomorrow," Gar replied. Then silence reasserted itself.

The next morning, when they drew near to the village, they could hear what sounded like angry voices. "Wait here," Gar commanded. He dropped all but his bow and arrow at Anton's feet and ran towards the edge of the forest that surrounded his home.

The voices stopped as he bounded into the large clearing of the settlement. There were eight men, half of them armed. Several of the men swiveled their automatic rifles to point them at Gar. Te'bayna'kun and the most seasoned warriors of the A'kun stood opposite them, weapons brandished. All eyes were on Gara'kun.

"*¿Qué carajo está pasando aquí?*" he said — What the fuck is going on here?

17

Nell arrived home ten days after leaving Gar and Kovac and didn't even call the kids for a day and a half. She needed to process everything that had transpired in Peru. Despite her words about "getting over it," there was a hollow ache deep inside her, along with a profound and abiding sense of rejection. She could rationalize about it, but she could not make it disappear. She remembered the last words that Oscar had said to her when he dropped her off at the airport.

"Never make this about you, Nellita. It just took him forty years to find his place on the planet." He sighed. "And that I wouldn't wish on anyone."

She opened a bottle of wine as she went through her mail. Except for "The New Yorker," it was all junk. She grabbed her laptop and winnowed through hundreds of emails. Her botanist friends in Brazil were coming to the New York Botanical Garden next month. A depressing missive from her last graduate student, bemoaning the dearth of positions for her skills, which these days had grown large by necessity and required training in DNA data acquisition and analysis, as well as field studies. She had both, but the competition was strenuous.

Nell shoved the computer to the other side of the couch. All right, she'd put it off long enough. She reached for her phone, dialing first Rose, then Loren.

"Mom!" Rose exclaimed. "How was it?"

"I have a lot to tell you. Dinner tomorrow? Here."

"Sure. I'll bring a salad." She paused. "Mom, you sound a little weird. Is everything OK?"

"Everything's fine," Nell lied. "See you at six tomorrow. I'm calling your brother next. Love you!"

Loren didn't step lightly when he answered his phone. "Did you find him?" he said flatly.

Always perceptive, her son; he had seen through the ruse of the "field trip with your uncle." His mother ignored the question. "Dinner at six with Rose and me at my place," she said. "Bring something good to drink." She paused. "All will be revealed."

"I take that as a yes," her son replied. "OK, tomorrow at six."

The next day, Nell went out shopping for dinner. She chose one of her favorites to make: roast duck with a peach and cranberry sauce. It was bizarre to be inside a Bronx supermarket; it was as if she had slipped through the space-time continuum. The price for duck was alarming, but she inwardly shrugged and placed it in her cart. Peach preserves, and a can of whole cranberry sauce. Fresh asparagus. At the bakery next door, she bought a *tres leches* cake.

When she got home, she found a message from Anton sent from the Cincinnati Botanical Garden Research Station. "Too much to tell you. But I'll be home soon. Love, A." Curiously, the brief email warmed her heart. There was a photo attached, an astounding one. It was a shot of a rock ledge, literally swarming with hummingbirds. In flower was a literal garden of what she thought of as Andean plants: gesneriads, tropical blueberries with luminescent flowers, brilliant twining lilies. She had no idea where in southeastern Peru one could witness a scene like that, reminiscent of cliff sides along one-track roads above the great rivers of the eastern Andes that ultimately fed the Amazon.

By 5:30 in the afternoon, the odor of the duck filled the kitchen of her small apartment. Rose was the first to arrive and early at that, as was her habit. Loren, who was usually late, was uncharacteristically punctual. They sat around the dining room table, making small talk as they ate. Both expressed surprise that Kovac was absent from the dinner table. Nell told them that he was still in Peru.

"Mom, this is heavenly!" Rose exulted over the duck. Loren announced he would be defending his Ph.D. dissertation the following month. He already had a funded post-doc awaiting him at UC Berkeley in the fall. Rose would remain in New York for her internship after graduation, at Montefiore Hospital in the Bronx. "Any apartments opening up in your building?" she asked. Nell promised to inquire of the superintendent.

Loren, who always ate quickly, finished first and laid his cutlery across his empty plate. "Time to let the elephant out, Mother," he said. "The elephant in the room." Rose grew still and turned her eyes towards Nell.

"We found your father," she began slowly, "or rather, he found us." Nell carefully considered her next words. "He … is a changed man. He has created a new life in the forest for himself. You would scarcely recognize him. He says that he's their shaman, the people, the A'kun they call themselves. They call him Gara'kun." She stopped, allowing her overture to settle across the minds of her children. "He is a full member of their tribe."

"How full?" Loren asked, his dark eyes locking with his mother's.

"He's a grandfather."

Her son let out a profanity. "You've got to be kidding me!" he exclaimed angrily. "The son-of-a-bitch!"

Rose laid a hand over her brother's. "No, Loren. He left us long ago. That was a preamble. I... I don't hate him, I really don't." The room grew silent, and Nell took the opportunity to bring dessert and coffee to the table.

When she returned, the two siblings were arguing. Loren had always been the one with the chip on his shoulder; his father's desertion was a betrayal that he could never reconcile with his preconception of what a father should be. "So, Mom, how many children does he have down there?'

"Three. The oldest was adopted."

"And a wife?" Rose inquired.

"She died two years ago. Your father says someone from another tribe murdered her." She omitted the part about black magic. That news drained the anger from Loren. Nell poured herself a cup of coffee. "Let me tell you his story," she ventured.

When she finished, both of her children were silent. They had turned inwards, assembling the parts of this new reality of a father transformed, consumed, and then spat out as different clay, molded by circumstance, madness or predestination; who could say?

Nell's daughter exhaled a breath that she hadn't even realized had been held. "I think it's amazing," she said. "One, that he lived. And two, that he found his Eden. I guess I'm a little sad that it wasn't with us."

"Me too," Nell muttered. "But he did have words for you both." She stood. "I wrote them down." She disappeared into her office and came back with the notebook that had accompanied her to Peru. "Can I read them aloud?" Both children nodded in assent. She sat back down and began:

"'To Rose, the healer. Why am I not surprised that you chose this path? The spirits have shown me the depth of your soul, my sweet child, and the world will have need of it in the years to come. Be as good to your mother, your brother, and your true father.'"

A single tear ran down Rose's cheek. "I will," she whispered, a promise.

Nell continued. "'To Loren, who is fire and ice. Both your weakness and your strength, my first son. If this means anything to you, when I look at my blood A'kun son, I don't see me; I see you. It is a good vision. I didn't walk away from science; I fell from its precipice, but into something that completed me in ways I still don't fully understand. I was a terrible father to you, but at least I had the foresight to leave a good proxy behind.'" Loren nodded, his eyes glistening.

A pregnant silence settled over them as Nell filled everyone's wineglass. Nell wondered if her children could resolve the wounds left behind by their father's abandonment or if they would continue to fester insidiously inside them, leaving behind scars for which there could be no absolution.

Loren was the first to raise his glass. "To Anton," he toasted, as if in reply to his mother's darker thoughts. With sudden clarity, Nell at last saw Kovac in a new light, one that shone brightly, illuminating her inner thoughts. *I've wasted so much time*, she thought to herself.

"To Anton!" Nell and Loren repeated in unison.

18

When Gara'kun and A'kunayaz returned from the magic mountain, the shaman immediately set to work chopping up the *m'kunaya* branches and placing them into a large cooking vessel of water. "It needs to boil for half a day," he told Gara'kun. "Go see your family."

De'bayna'kun leaped into his arms when he walked into their hut and met his lips longingly. The children were out playing. She reached below his loincloth and stroked his cock. "I want you," she hissed.

"Let's sneak into the woods," he said, grabbing a woven cotton blanket. They found a spot below a kapok tree, spread the mat and threw off their breechcloths. Their lips found each other's again, quickly moving across each other's bodies with wanton abandon. "De'bayna," he moaned as he sucked at her breasts, massaging her dark nipples with his lips and tongue. She slid down against him and took his engorged member into her mouth. He almost lost it after a few minutes, but pulled free. "Let me," he said as he got on his knees, parted her legs and kissed his way to her almost hairless vagina, which parted like a lotus flower for his tongue. De'bayna writhed and moaned as he became intoxicated with her musk.

Gara'kun entered his wife slowly. She squeezed her muscles around his tumescence and moved with him. They held each other's hands as he thrust inside her. Their gaze met and locked. De'bayna grabbed his buttocks, pulling him deeper as she neared orgasm. They came at the same time, a tantric moment that seemed to last forever, and left them spent and entwined in each other's embrace.

And that was the moment of conception for their son, Pa'bayna'kun.

The years passed with a paradoxical timelessness for Gara'kun and his growing family. Three years later, one more son was born to De'bayna'kun and him, but the baby stopped breathing, and no amount of forest medicine could restore his brief life. De'bayna mourned for weeks, and something in her had changed. She began taking the A'kun birth control formula again, a tincture derived from several plants with contraceptive activity. "Three is enough," she told Gara'kun one night after they made love.

Gara'kun took an additional pleasure in watching his children learn and grow. His son, Pa'bayna'kun, showed the most interest in learning about plants and often joined his father and the shaman on field trips to gather healing agents. He also loved tending the village garden and had established a small flower bed at the periphery in which he cultivated ornamental foliage and flowers from the forest with his sister.

And so, the years continued their timeless procession. Days, weeks and months lost their outside world imperative, and the life clock of Garwell Sorrentino was now that of Gara'kun. He watched his hair turn gray, and sons and daughter morph into each stage of their young and then not so young lives. Gara'kun loved his wife furiously. He imagined them aging in their paradise, surrounded by children and grandchildren, and the joy that this evoked in his heart brought tears to his eyes, with an emotional intensity that was just a shade away from painful.

And in the otherworld, that of the *ayahuasquero*, he continued his apprenticeship with A'kunayaz, his knowledge of the forest continuously expanding under the shaman's tutelage. This life transpired side-by-side with that of his family; they accepted it with almost solemn deference, acknowledging what it would ultimately mean for their husband and father. At least he was seldom very far away.

Despite their close relationship, he realized that he knew very little about the A'kun shaman, and absolutely nothing regarding his past. Whenever Gara'kun attempted to wrest some tidbit of his life from the old man, A'kunayaz gently but firmly diverted their conversation, usually by pointing out a particular plant.

Gara'kun noticed that the old shaman was no longer as spry as he used to be in the forest; they paused more often than usual, but this time A'kunayaz was silent and withdrawn. "What troubles you, my friend?" Gara'kun asked.

"Soon, it will be your time, Gara'kun. I think you are ready."

"Ready? For what?"

A'kunayaz dark eyes held Gara'kun's gaze. "To become shaman of the A'kun."

On one of the last *ayahuasca* ceremonies with his mentor, A'kunayaz turned towards his pupil and said, "I have one more thing to teach you." They were up on the Mountain, in front of the wall of ancestors as Gar thought of it, the petroglyph-rich site that bespoke the power of time and mystery. They were in their corporal bodies while the plant medicine enveloped them in music and light, and both let the hum of the embellished wall wash over them. "This last thing is perhaps the most powerful tool of the true *ayahuasquero*, right alongside your spirit animal in importance," the shaman continued. "You have divined the future before as an infinite possibility. Today, you will learn how to bend time." The old man swept the space on the ground in front of them, and using a stick, drew a diagram that Gara'kun recognized as one that was repeated frequently on the wall. "This sacred sigil is the purest representation of the time-stream that we know. Have you ever seen it in your *ayahuasca* visions?"

Gar thought long and hard, but reluctantly had to answer, "No, only on the wall."

A'kunayaz smiled. "That is because it must be summoned. Then it is with you forever. It is the key to bending time."

The younger man had to admit that he still had no clue as to what "bending time" entailed.

A'kunayaz continued his instruction. "The act of bending time allows us to act without the constraints of its dimension."

"Then why is it not called 'stopping time?'" Gara'kun asked.

The shaman shook his head and smiled. "No one can stop time, Gara'kun," he said. "You can only bend it, and escape the moment in your spirit body. That allows the *ayahuasquero* to step outside of where time flows. Both he and his spirit animal. It is exhausting in the long term and should be used with discretion. You must bring the sigil to life inside your spirit. There is a song that helps the process."

The shaman started chanting, at first not invoking words, just inflected sound with his voice. He bid his student to join in. Gar encountered no difficulty taking up the wordless chant, and when it transformed into the A'kun language, he seamlessly switched in synchronicity with the shaman. The sigil formed in his mind's eye, burning with a perceived numinousness. No sooner had the pictograph become fully featured in his internal vision, then he found himself in his spirit body. "You have bent time," A'kunayaz stated matter-of-factly. Indeed, there was a stillness to the world. Clouds stopped moving in the restive sky, and all manner of birdsong had ceased.

"The sigil is now a part of you," A'kunayaz told him. "To return to the time-stream, you need only will it." Gara'kun watched the birds come to life as order was restored to the universe.

Three years to that day, the old man weakened, and the semi-daily collecting trips came to a halt. Gara'kun tended his teacher with De'bayna'kun and their daughter's assistance. At A'kunayaz's insistence, the only medicines he received were for pain. On the fourth day of his sudden decline, he called for the *ayahuasca*. "Today I leave you, my son. The *ayahuasca* vision was true. You will be a fine shaman in my place. Of that I have no doubt. I bequeath my spirit animal to you when I leave this world. This will give you special power." Gara'kun helped his teacher drink the cup of *ayahuasca*. It was a special blend, one known only to every shaman, one concocted by every *ayahuasquero* late in life, to be only prepared and administered on the day of his death. A'kunayaz would make this trip alone, as would Gara'kun one day.

Gara'kun was with him at the hour of his departure. There was a long final breath, and then A'kunayaz was silent. Gara'kun suddenly looked towards the entrance to the old man's shelter. A black jaguar stood there, as noiseless as a shadow, its golden eyes locking onto Gara'kun's. Then, with a swipe of its muzzle with his long pink tongue, it vanished into the forest.

The body of A'kunayaz, wrapped in cotton cloth, was cremated on a funeral pyre constructed in a small clearing cut from the forest. The wood used was from a copiously resinous tree that would burn at high temperature, and the withered body of the former shaman of the A'kun was soon consumed by the flames. Gara'kun stood by to make sure that the flames didn't grow out of control. Te'bayna'kun, now chief of the A'kun on the passing of his father one year previously, joined him in vigil. "You were a son to him. A bond that was beyond blood," he told him.

That was the second loss to strike the heart of Gara'kun after that of his and De'bayna's infant son. The third, arriving five years hence, would nearly shatter it beyond repair.

It began innocently enough, one day in the middle of the rainy season that had begun with a brilliant blue sky and a spate of dryness for a change. He and De'bayna'kun had walked to the river to bathe. She still excited him, even as she advanced through middle age, and she giggled when he cupped her breasts from behind as they stood midstream. She called him the A'kun equivalent of an "old goat," referencing instead the tapirs that sometimes culminated a successful hunt. He made grunting noises in response, growing hard against her smooth, wet buttocks. She cast him a sloe-eyed smile, and led him by his member to an old, fallen tree trunk over which she bent, waving her behind seductively. Gara'kun slipped inside her, heard her moan several times as he thrust, and then suddenly realized, when she grew silent, that she'd fainted. Her husband quickly withdrew and cradled his limp wife, lowering her body, which had grown hot to the touch, into the cool water. He chanted her name as he dripped water over her flushed cheeks until her eyes fluttered open. "What happened?" she asked weakly. He told her and asked how she felt. Her skin had at least cooled, and her cheeks regained their usual color. He helped her to her feet, and they walked to the riverbank. She was slightly unsteady and sat down heavily on the sandy beach. Her husband was already anticipating which medicinal herbs he would prepare for her when they returned to the village.

As they came into the settlement clearing, their children dropped what they were doing and came running to their parents' side when they saw how weak their mother appeared. Pa'bayna'kun, now a strapping youth of 20 years, asked his father what to prepare, and set to work manufacturing the elixir Gara'kun barked out to him, as he disappeared into their house. He lowered his wife into their hammock. "This is foolish," De'bayna opined. "I'm fine." Her mate would hear none of it, and gently massaged her arms, legs and head until their son returned with a wooden bowl of steaming broth.

"Small sips," he told her. "Be careful; it's very hot." Their daughter brought a basket of assorted fruits from the village gardens. De'bayna picked at them absently, mostly using them to chase the sips of the bitter and astringent, healing brew. Gara'kun lay down beside her in the hammock while she dozed.

She slept straight through the night. The fever returned a few hours after she woke and had attacked breakfast with alacrity, but this time it failed to abate, even with continued ministration of powerful medicine. Her husband supposed like he was being toyed with by these abrupt reversals in her condition. Gara'kun frantically ransacked his pharmacopeia for anything that could stem the tide of this inexplicable affliction. He called his children to their mother's bedside. "I must take the *cumala*," he told them. "It's the only way I can try to see what this is." From a shelf in Akunayaz's old house, which he maintained as a shamanic sanctuary, he plucked a short tube of palm stem, and peeled the wax seal at the open end, and poured four pellets of the resin into his hand. A strong dose, one more than he had taken that first time many years ago. He swallowed the *cumala* with some water and walked back to his family's house.

Gara'kun's heart sank when he saw how ashen De'bayna'kun looked. He touched her forehead; she was burning with fever, and he instructed Pa'bayna'kun to prepare the fever remedy with fresh leaves from the forest. He told his older son to just keep his father from hurting himself. "Most of the time, I will seem insensate on the ground. Just leave me alone."

Just as before, the onset of the *cumala* was a period of almost crazed nervous energy, followed by complete loss of his senses, at least regarding his body, which lay on a woven mat of cotton, twitching occasionally but otherwise still. His awareness was elsewhere, transfixed by what he saw surrounding his ailing wife. Wraiths were what you would have to call them, though he could not determine if it was one entity or three. They were dark, smoke-like, perpetually shifting opacity, shape, and luster. Gara'kun knew immediately that black magic had been employed against his wife. And he was completely helpless. A'kunayaz had never prepared him for this.

He shifted his perspective as if he was charging the spirits, but hit some sort of psychic barrier. He could get no closer to his wife in this strange other dimension. And this time, there were no little blue people to show him the way. Gara'kun suddenly found himself staring at the maw of a titanic hopelessness that shredded his heart. He fell back into his body and into an unnatural sleep, visited by nightmares that clawed at him emotionally even though he remembered not a one.

Gara'kun rose unsteadily, gasping for water. He drank and turned to his wife, who looked peaceably asleep in the hammock. "De'bayna?" he called out in alarm. The shaman lay two fingers on her neck for a pulse; her skin was cold to his touch. Gara'kun fell to his knees and wailed.

19

The presumable leader of the gold miners stepped forward. *"Por lo que es verdad. El gringo de los indios existe. ¿También es cierto lo que dicen sobre cocho indio?"*[15] He grinned but remained steely eyed. A few of the men laughed.

Gara'kun stared back. *"¿Qué quiere aquí?"* —What do you want here?

The man waved his hand in the direction of the A'kun's river. *"Estamos interesados en ese pequeño río a medio kilómetro de esa dirección."*[16]

"Esta es la tierra A'kun por ley. El río es nuestro suministro de agua. Ustedes deberían irse,"[17] Gara'kun said.

The *jefe* grimaced. *"No queremos ningún problema. Pero usted debe saber que mis jefes no son el tipo de personas que desea cruzar."*[18]

Oscar Crescente had told Gara'kun that the drug cartels were increasingly getting involved in timber poaching and gold extraction in the indigenous and conservation reserves, going so far as to bulldoze their own roads into pristine forest, and he didn't view this as an idle threat.

---

[15] So, it's true. The Indian's gringo exists. Is it also true what they say about Indian pussy?

[16] We are interested in that little river about a half kilometer in that direction.

[17] This is A'kun land by law. The river is our water supply. You should just leave.

[18] We don't want any trouble. But you should know that my bosses aren't the type of guys you want to cross.

The leader asked if his men could gather some fruit from the A'kun's orchards, which Chief Te'bayna'kun agreed to, as long as they moved on right after harvesting. Several of the A'kun men followed alongside, their blow guns in hand. As the men filed away, Te'bayna'kun pulled Gara'kun aside. "Four of those men are from the tribe of my sister's rapist," he told him. "I recognize their tattoos." The tribe was an acculturated settlement down the river from the Cincinnati Botanical Garden's research station. "Their village is probably the reason my sister — your wife — is dead."

Gara'kun rushed back to where he'd instructed Kovac to stay put. "What's going on?" Anton asked.

Gar shook his head. "Gold miners."

"What are you going to do about them?" Anton asked innocently enough.

"I don't know yet," Gar replied.

They got back to the village and hurriedly prepared their specimens in plant presses and set them to drying. The *m'kunaya* was chopped into small bits by Gara'kun's daughter and set to cooking over a fire.

At the council meeting in the longhouse that night, the men discussed what to do with the interlopers. The chief was the most outspoken. "They must all die," he declared solemnly.

Gara'kun spoke up. "Let me use *ayahuasca* to spy on them in the morning. And then we can decide what to do."

The next morning, Gara'kun stopped at his friend's shelter at the periphery of the settlement. He told him what he would be doing that day, asking for his forbearance before disappearing into the forest.

Gara'kun spread his cotton mat near a kapok tree and swallowed the *ayahuasca* that he'd brought with him. He attentively awaited entry to the spirit dimension that, especially since De'bayna'kun's death, had become the authentic world for him. It enveloped him, always with the combination of music and light. He listened for the shrill keening of a harpy eagle, which soon rose above the forest song. The shaman took the inward leap into his daytime spirit animal and soared above the forest, eyeing the river, where he could immediately spot the miners' encampment. They were panning for gold at various places in the stream. Gara'kun knew what would follow next if gold was discovered — the slow poisoning of the river with mercury, used to separate the gold from the local soil. He noticed several large and valuable timber species marked with fluorescent red flagging tape. The rape of this area of forest was two-pronged; clearly, they intended to fell the flagged trees and float them down the river. The mercury contamination would spread quickly through the web of life that even now sang to him. This could not be allowed to transpire.

His brother-in-law's succinct solution was tempting. But he had another idea; it came to him, a vision through the *ayahuasca*, albeit a botanical one. He saw one tree before him, a member of the tomato family, that was not uncommon in the forests of A'kun territory. Every part of the tree was loaded with scopolamine, which when combined properly with other forest herbal ingredients into a potent concentrate, a tiny quantity would induce an almost zombie-like state, but without loss of motor function. Moreover, in this curious state of stupefaction, one became very suggestible. No one had to die. Gara'kun couldn't bear the thought of another spiral of tit-for-tat death matches that had begun with the rape of De'bayna'kun thirty years in the past. Even here in paradise, "the human stain," as Philip Roth called it. He sighed, deeper than perhaps he ever had before. *Not true*, he admonished himself; those first nights without De'bayna by his side were the darkest he'd ever experienced. There were plenty of sighs as profound in those days. Though life hadn't spared him sadness, he had learned to grieve and then move on, making his own life a testament to those he had lost. There was a symmetry to that he found appealing.

Gara'kun entered the chief's house and told him of what he proposed to do. Darts coated with the powerful poison could deliver the drug; it would require two darts per victim. Four men would go along with Gara'kun, armed with bow and arrows as well as blow guns. Te'bayna'kun agreed to this, but added an admonishing caveat. "If anything goes wrong," he said, "put them to death."

Gara'kun found Kovac sitting at the entrance to the small shelter where he kept his tent. His friend looked up expectantly. Gar knew he'd be disappointed. "I have to leave tonight," he told his friend. "I should be back by the morning, and then we'll head over to the research station. If…" and here he paused for a moment, "if our plans go awry, my son will escort you."

Kovac eyed him warily. "Does it have to do with those gold miners?" he asked. Gara'kun nodded. "Are they going to die?" Anton continued. Gar said nothing at first, surprised by the directness of Kovac's inquiry. He squatted in front of his friend, his long silver hair cloaking his face from inspection. *How does he do that?* Kovac thought extraneously. *I'm 10 years younger and my haunches would be screaming after one minute.* It was perhaps at that moment, more so than any other since their tense reunion, that Anton understood the degree to which their lives had diverged.

"I have a plan," Gar said, "that will hopefully avoid bloodshed." He sighed. "But I am not the A'kun chief; I am only their shaman. I can advise, but all decisions ultimately are those of Te'bayna'kun." He stood.

"Let me come with you," Kovac beseeched him.

"Absolutely not," Gara'kun countered. "Your presence would be a distraction to me, and probably our warriors as well. I can't countenance increasing our risks." He glanced over his shoulder, as if tuning into an inchoate summons. "I must go, Anton. One of my kids will bring you supper. Check our specimens in the dryer; we'll take them with us to the research station tomorrow." He turned and moved off into the lengthening shadows.

◆ ◆ ◆ ◆ ◆

Tebayna'kun picked the four warriors to accompany Gara'kun in the maneuver. All four were heralded among the tribe for their stealth and skill with blowguns. All, including Gara'kun, were armed with bow and arrows as well. Just before they departed, Tebayna'kun pulled the shaman aside and walked with him some distance away from the other men. "I will be behind you; the men do not know this." Gara'kun said nothing. He had half expected as much from his chief. "But there is one task that remains," he continued. "The shaman of that village on the river, the one whose spawn raped and then murdered my sister — your wife — must die. It is your shaman's duty. And that of a husband." With that, he turned and disappeared into his hut.

Gara'kun followed his companions into the forest. They walked in silence, in staggered single file, alert for any sounds that were foreign to the afternoon melange of birdsong and insect mutterings that echoed beneath the grand trees. In a short time they came to the embankment below which the small river, swollen by recent rains, careened through its main channel. With a hand signal from the leader, a distant relative of the chief's family, they arrayed themselves along the shrubs that aggregated at the edge where brighter light prevailed. Gara'kun could see the four armed cartel operatives gathered below on a white sand beach, while the four indigenous men from the acculturated river village labored on dinner or gathered additional firewood. Gara'kun worried that the distance between the A'kun and their encampment would strain the range of even the most skilled blow dartsman. He voiced his concern to the lead warrior, a strapping 25-year-old named Pe'cunya'kun. "The light of their fire should allow us to get closer after nightfall," he told Gara'kun. Full darkness was two hours away. The A'kun pulled back into the forest, and they ate their dinner, brocket deer jerky and fruits scavenged from trees further back in the closed canopy. Gara'kun pensively eyed the forest in the direction by which they'd come. His brother-in-law, the chief, was somewhere in that darkness. He didn't understand why the chief was hiding from his own warriors. The possibility that he was the target of Te'bayna'kun's scrutiny didn't even occur to him.

Pe'cunya'kun signaled that it was time to act. The cartel's men were spaced around the fire, facing away from them, handing around a bottle of pisco. The men from the enemy village sat together some 30 yards away, around a smaller fire that would doubtfully illuminate the band of A'kun. With caution, the tribesmen advanced until they were confident their blowguns could bridge the distance to the cartel gang. Individually, they studied their targets, examining them for exposed areas of skin. Gara'kun would provide back-up in case one of the necessary two darts went astray. With barely a sound, the A'kun loaded the first dart into their guns, raised the hollowed palm stems to their lips, and sent the darts successfully to the necks and arms of their adversaries. With extraordinary speed, they loaded the second darts into their guns and struck yet again.

The cartel crew, all half drunk, treated the faint sting of the darts' penetrations as insect bites, which they hardly allowed to distract themselves from the pisco. It became obvious when the alkaloid hit their bloodstreams as they entered a semi-stupefied state. The guns slipped from their laps to the ground.

It was Gara'kun's turn in the proceedings of his plan. He went to each of the four men and murmured in their ears in Spanish. "Pick up your gun and a full canteen of water." The four stood up and went about the commandeered tasks like zombies. "Now walk away, in the direction you are facing. Do not stop walking." He set each one off in a different direction, away from both the river and the village. The drug would last for about six hours, long enough for each of the four to become hopelessly lost in the immense wilderness. They would need their wits to survive. *At least I left them their guns and water*, he thought, though he had limited them to the single clip of bullets in the guns. He watched them disappear into the forest.

Gara'kun suddenly realized that the rest of his team was no longer in sight, nor were the four men from the hated river village. A full moon rose in the night sky above the treetops, illuminating a gathering some thirty yards down the river. There stood the four warriors and their chief, the four men from the river tribe, dead at their feet. Gara'kun quickened his pace. A fury was building inside him that his brother-in-law seemed to anticipate, as he was hurrying towards his shaman in order to keep their confrontation away from the other tribesmen. "Why?" was all Gara'kun said when the chief and he stood but inches away from each other.

"Gara'kun, do not question me. The people of that village made themselves our enemies. Think of only De'Bayna'kun, her two times suffering."

The shaman shook his head. "They would have gone home, and we would have demanded that they tell their elders that the price of their lives is the end of bloodshed between our two villages."

Te'Bayna'kun smiled tightly. "That is your old world talking, not the A'kun. We should have killed the other four as well. Enough." He turned back to the four braves and instructed them to strip the clothing from the corpses and burn it with the rest of the cartel men's supplies. "Take the bodies away from the river into the trees where they will feed the forest." He reached out a hand and clasped Gara'kun's shoulder. "Remember what I told you earlier." His brother-in-law nodded and began the short trek back to their village and Kovac.

♦ ♦ ♦ ♦ ♦

Anton was in his shelter but outside of his tent when Gar returned. He'd occupied himself by curating the specimens brought back from the mountain, assigning numbers to the collections, writing details about the plants in a field book, and preparing the specimens for transport. His electronic means of data recording had long ago become silent, silicon monoliths. "I won't ask you for details," he said to his friend as he burst into the shelter.

Gara'kun ignored the riposte. "It could have gone better," was all he said. He surveyed the obvious efforts of his former student's labor and nodded approvingly. "We'll leave tomorrow morning," he informed Kovac. "I can get us to the research station in two days."

"And then?" Kovac said.

"And then, what?" Gar rejoined.

"That's it?" Anton spat. "What happened to the goldminers?"

"The cartel hirelings were stupefied with scopolamine and set off in different directions."

204

"Jesus, Gar!"

"I let them keep their guns and some water." Gar sighed. "And then the chief gave the order to kill the indigenous men from the river village. This was not what I had planned."

Kovac looked stunned. It was at that point that he realized that he no longer knew who his friend was, and he was suddenly adrift. He shook his head, as if to dispel the abyss he felt opening beneath him. Anton thought suddenly of the gibbering caricature of himself that had tormented him during his *ayahuasca* vision. He willed it away, which was easier than he expected.

Gar was studying him closely. "Are you O.K, Anton?"

"Fine," Kovac replied flatly. "Go. I'll see you in the morning."

Kovac slept fitfully in the darkness. It was a particularly warm night and the heavily humid air hung like a saturated shroud around his tent. Anton wished he had asked Gar for the same plant medicine for sleep as before. He thrashed about on his sleeping pad and finally drifted off.

Kovac woke just as the forest was erupting with a morning chorus of bird calls, and the redolent tang of breakfast seeped into his tent. Gar stood outside the shelter when he emerged, and wordlessly proffered a large wooden bowl of fruit and manioc porridge, which Kovac dove into with voracity. When he finished, Anton excused himself for his morning call and moved into the trees behind his shelter. Upon his return, he discovered that Gar had been joined by his son. "We have too much shit for just the two of us; Pa'bayna'kun will be of enormous help."

Parcels of specimens were compressed and fastened with palm fiber straps that also served to sling the load onto their shoulders. Gar had a lidded woven basket, also equipped with shoulder straps. To this, he also fastened a sandwich of dried specimens. So encumbered, they set off into the forest.

Kovac labored to keep up with Gara'kun and his son. Gar would pause and wait for him to catch up. He would then impart an impromptu plant medicine lesson, as much to Anton as to the young man.

As always, the forest provided everything to remain refreshed during their two-day trek. Pa'bayna'kun was almost as good as his father at spotting some edible fruit in the forest. He could also climb trees marginally better than the shaman himself. Anton noted that his friend's mood was improving as they followed gentle rises and falls through the boundless rainforest.

The specimens that Kovac carried, affixed to his pack and tent, added perhaps fifteen pounds to his load. He partook of the coca leaf more than his companions did. Gar knew exactly where they were going, and never hesitated for a moment, leading them through what, for Kovac, provided no bearings whatsoever. Still, he was immensely grateful when Gar called for an extended lunch break. Anton freed his shoulders of their double burden and stood rotating his upper arms. He took a languorous swig from his canteen. "We'll hit a spring-fed stream at day's end," Gar told him, "and camp there for the night."

They sat about for an hour, feasting on *abiu*, ice cream bean, several palm fruits, and some *cupuaçu*, all collected by Pa'bayna'kun. "You know," Gar began, breaking the silence, "Pa'bayna speaks Spanish."

"*¡En serio!*" Kovac exclaimed. — No kidding.

"*Si*," Pa'bayna'kun replied somewhat shyly.

"He begged me for years to teach him," Gar explained. "I always dissuaded him … until I finally gave in."

"*¿Por qué quisiste aprender español?*"[19] Kovac asked him.

The young man, perhaps 22 or 23 years old, a parent already Anton reminded himself, glanced at his father. "*Para conocer mejor a mi padre,*"[20] he answered. "*Es un tipo complicado.*" — He's a complicated guy."

"That he is," Kovac replied in both languages. This got a laugh out of Gar's son.

"*¿Pero, por qué no aprender inglés primero?*"[21] Anton asked.

"*Eso es lo siguiente,*" Pa'bayna'kun replied. "*Pero el español es una opción más práctica aquí.*"[22]

"*¡Vamonos!*" Gara'kun announced, already with his load strapped in. His companions did the same, and they recommenced their journey.

---

[19] Why did you want to learn Spanish?

[20] In order to know my father better."

[21] But why not learn English first?

[22] That's next. But Spanish is a more practical choice here.

There were a number of trees in flower, and the forest floor was a mosaic of fallen blooms: kapok, ipé, among many others which defied Kovac's powers of identification, but for which Gar had no such difficulty. "The forest changes here, very subtly," Gar said. "The area is percolated with springs," he continued; "the substrate is predominantly limestone."

At last, they came to the low dip in the relief where the springs broke ground and fed a small stream. Gar signaled that the day's hike was over, and they set to work preparing camp. Pa'bayna'kun made a shelter to keep the specimens dry in case of rain, while Anton gathered wood for a fire. Gar disappeared into the forest and returned shortly with two plump guan. With the shelter complete, Gar's son foraged the forest for fruits to accompany the roasted fowl. A spiny *Bactris* palm yielded several bunches of sweet *ñejilla*. Gar plucked and cleaned the birds and applied the fragrant dry rub that he always carried with him on jaunts into the forest, while Anton built a roasting spit above the flames. The tangy smell of the cooking meat made Kovac realize how hungry he was.

After dinner, Gar passed around the A'kun insect repellent, with which Anton liberally anointed himself. He was still in awe of how well it worked. A brief shower made the fire sizzle, but quickly moved on from their camp. Gar and his son were murmuring in A'kun to each other. One or the other periodically laughed. Kovac took advantage of a pause in their conversation.

"Tell me about the spirit world," Anton said. "Do those *ayahuasca* visions have any palpable reality or are they biochemically induced hallucinations?"

Gara'kun smiled. "*Ayahuasca* shows us reality unmasked. It is the gatekeeper to the unbridled complexity and multi-levels of existence. It harmonizes with our DNA in the same way the ancients understood. The medicine frees our minds from the shackles of the corporeal self."

"You sound like a cultist," Kovac complained.

"Do I?" Gar replied. "Well then, it is the oldest cult in the world." He paused briefly. "You know, I met Terrence McKenna once. It was a few years before he died, at Schultes' house in Cambridge. I found him a little arrogant, I suppose, albeit very glib. He was on the right track, but he didn't really have as much direct experience with *ayahuasca* as people believed." He shrugged. "His brother Dennis, whom I never met, was really more of a scientist in his approach."

"So, do you understand how the universe works?"

Gar laughed. "No, but I understand the measure of its intricacy a little better." He waved his hands in the air, as if dismissing the discussion. "The important thing is: what do you believe, Anton?"

Kovac stood; he needed to pee. "It definitely showed me something about myself," he said as he moved to the periphery of their encampment. "I'm still processing exactly what."

In the morning, the trio continued their journey to the research station. Even Anton noted the change in the forest composition as they traversed the limestone spring area. It also began their gentle descent towards the river that would delimit their separation, most likely for the rest of their lives.

Kovac spent a good share of the remaining hours conversing in Spanish with Pa'bayna'kun. Gar's son was attentive, and garrulous once they broke the ice, and the young man pointed out numerous healing plants they passed on the way. Gar left them alone and remained ahead of them. *¿"Alguna vez has tomado ayahuasca?"*[23] Anton abruptly asked.

Pa'bayna laughed. *"Sí, pero no tantas veces como mi padre,"*[24] he replied.

"¿Y qué te enseña?"[25] Kovac probed further.

The answer came without any hesitations. *"Me muestra cómo vivir en el mundo y me revela quién soy realmente. Y también me enseña la medicina vegetal."*[26]

Kovac had little doubt that his friend had chosen his eventual successor wisely.

Pa'bayna'kun told Anton about his children, a boy and a girl in that order of age, three and one, and his wife, Sacha'kun. Anton had an inkling of why Gar had surrendered to this other world.

They had departed early enough and made sufficient pace that they could see the roof of the station ahead from the crest of the final

---

[23] Have you ever taken ayahuasca?

[24] Yes, but not as many times as my father.

[25] And what does it teach you?

[26] It shows me how to live in the world and and reveals who I really am. And it also teaches me the plant medicine.

descent to the river. Luis was beside himself when they materialized out of the forest. "Dr. Sorrentino!" he exclaimed. "You can't imagine what an honor this is for me."

"Just Gar … please. This is my son Pa'bayna, He speaks Spanish." He reverted to A'kun. "Give Luis a hand, Pa'bayna." Luis and Gar's son deposited the bundles of specimens into a large chest freezer hoping to kill any residual insects on the material. They would remain in the deep freeze for a month before being set upon their way to the Cincinnati Botanical Garden.

A cry of "For you is cheap!" rang across the breadth of the station's long veranda. Oscar Crescente came skipping across the wood surface, a gigantic smile across his face. Both Gar and Kovac embraced their old friend.

"How the hell did you know we'd show up today?" Anton exclaimed. Oscar kept silent, but passed a sidelong glance at Gar.

"He'll figure it out in a minute," Gar assured all present. A look of revelation crept across Kovac's face. "Of course," he muttered, remembering his own periodic instances of mind-reading and visitations by his friend, the shaman of the A'kun. He slunk off to charge his various electronic devices.

When Luis returned with Pa'bayna, Gar explained he would be delivering new specimens monthly for the foreseeable future. Without a moment's hesitation, Luis offered Blanca in service, to which Gar agreed and appeared grateful. Anton took advantage of an opening to speak to his former student in private. "Luis, please keep Gar our secret."

Luis nodded gravely. "Understood," he said.

It was a raucous dinner of river fish and plantains, and abundant beer that Oscar had brought upriver in the canoe. Only Isidoro was crew on this trip, Kovac noted and greeted the man warmly to a returned smile. Anton also observed that neither Gar nor his son imbibed the hops. After dinner, Gar pulled Kovac aside. "There's one more thing to give you." He walked over to the lidded basket that he'd carried from the village on his back. He opened the lid and withdrew one of several sturdy plastic bags. Each was filled with a half dozen or so notebooks. "Most of this information is unvouchered, but it will help you curate the specimens to come, which will serve as vouchers. Lots of medicinal notes in these, too." The shaman narrowed his eyes, and a quick grin danced across his lips. "Go make a name for yourself." His grin widened. "Again."

It was raining in the morning, fierce momentary downpours interspersed with intermittent drizzle. Isidro made haste to get everything stowed under tarps. The river rose with rain, generally a good thing; one needed to only be vigilant for snags far enough below the surface to be invisible but still a potential hazard to their motor's integrity. As before, Oscar would be pole man, but also armed with an electronic fish finder that would show any looming large objects in the water.

At last, the two old friends stood before each other. "I guess this is it," Anton said sadly.

Gar placed his hands on Anton's shoulders and pulled him into a tight embrace. "It's never it, *hermano*. Look to your dreams, the waking ones." He continued gazing into his friend's eyes. "Take care of each other," he whispered, with no further elaboration.

Kovac turned to Pa'bayna'kun. "*Serás un excelente chamán,*"[27] he told him. Pa'bayna bowed his head, a sign of respect he remembered Gar telling him. Anton took his place in the canoe and turned with a last wave. The boat's motor sprung into life, and they entered the primary downstream current.

Gara'kun placed his arm over his son's shoulder. "There is one final thing I must do, but by myself. You will take the mule and start back on your own. I will probably be able to catch up to you before you reach the village."

His son nodded. At some level he knew this had something to do with his mother. "Be safe, *a'kunda* [father]," was all he said, as Gar turned and began walking down river through the forest.

---

[27] You will make a fine shaman.

20

Nell woke from the dream, her heart threatening to burst through her ribcage. She worked to keep the pieces of the dream in the forefront of her mind, but they remained just fragments. She remembered Anton was in it; they were together but could neither see nor hear each other. This failure, this inability to cross some sort of interloping barrier, was a source of anxious agony because she knew that they were within inches of each other. She heard her phone chirp, and her spirits rose as she saw it was a message from Kovac.

"Back at the research station," Anton had typed. "Oscar is here, heading to Puerto Maldonado tomorrow morning. All is well. Love, Anton."

The message lifted her mood. Dawn was just breaking over the cityscape. She rose and traipsed into the kitchen to start a pot of coffee. She fried an egg, prepared some toast and jam, and moved into the living room, grabbing the tv remote and turning to the news. Fires out west, the further advances of a horrific candidate for president against the female former secretary of state. Her mood darkened again; *the country's becoming a parody of itself,* she thought. She briefly watched the man perform at one of his interminable rallies, everything staged, down to the Black man, visible off center behind the candidate, in a supporting t-shirt.

With a sigh, she switched off the idiot box and re-positioned herself in front of the window. She could see the turrets of the George Washington Bridge far to the south. Rose and she were getting together for lunch later at some new discovery of her daughter's in Brooklyn.

Her phone rang. She was slightly shocked to see the caller's name: Kevin Hobart. "Kevin?" she said, with the slight upturn at the end, a questioning note.

"Hello Nell. I've not heard from Kovac in some time. I thought perhaps you had."

"As a matter of fact, I just got a message from him. He's been without any electronic means of communication for days. I'm sure you'll hear from him soon."

Their conversation hit a lull rather immediately. She sensed Hobart wanted to ask her more questions, not least of which the 64-million-dollar one concerning Garwell Sorrentino's fate. "Kevin, I'm sorry, but I have to run. Send Anton a text; he should be in Maldonado tomorrow." She quickly said goodbye and promptly hung up on the most famous botanist in the world. It felt surprisingly good. The story had to come from Anton; of that, there was no doubt. She picked up her phone and typed a reply to Kovac. "So glad to hear. I miss you very much. Kevin just called me; he's rather impatient. At least send him a short note without revealing anything. Give Oscar and Daniela my best. I love you." She paused and back-spaced through the last declaration. "Love, Nell" she typed in its place.

She killed time processing emails until it was time to shower and get ready to meet her daughter in Brooklyn. They planned to spend a few hours after lunch walking around the Brooklyn Botanic Garden.

Nell took the subway to Brooklyn, something she hadn't done in some time. She passed the long ride by studying a few photos Anton had taken just before his departure. The one that captured her attention longest was one of Gar and his son, Pa'bayna'kun. Both men were smiling widely, and Nell experienced a catch in her throat. She zoomed into the picture and studied the two faces. Gar had been correct; when she gazed at the younger man's face, she saw her own son, Loren.

When her mother arrived, Rose was already seated at the restaurant. Nell's daughter suddenly appeared startled as she glanced at her mother. "Mom, were you crying?" she asked.

Wordlessly, Nell retrieved her phone from her small purse, and showed Rose Anton's photo. "Oh, my God!" she exclaimed, and stood to enfold her mother in her arms. "I never…" she stammered. Her eyes were now glistening as well.

"His name is Pa'bayna'kun. Your half-brother." Her voice broke. "Anton says that Gar taught him to speak Spanish." She giggled. "At his son's request."

The conversation paused, and the women composed themselves. A server swooped in and took their order. The food lived up to Rose's vociferous endorsement, and their talk remained light until Rose asked after Kovac.

"You'll see him soon," Nell told her. "He's had quite an experience, from what I understand, *ayahuasca* and all."

The Garden was at the peak of late-summer efflorescence. Nell steered them towards the beds of various surprise lilies, always one of her favorite late season bulbs. She had planted many at the house in Cincinnati, which she still owned and currently rented, and she hoped they were still in good shape. There were still a few late lilies in bloom as well, and numerous asters a few weeks from their peak as they moved into the shade of the woodland garden. "I hope you won't think me disloyal," Loren said, "but I've always liked this garden more than yours," by which she meant the New York Botanical Garden. "The scale of it, I think. New York always seemed so… imposing."

"But you grew up there!" Nell exclaimed.

"True, but I think that for me it was always 'Mom's work.' That was my chief competition for your attention." She paused. "You know, it was Anton that brought me here first." She paused again. "And half-a-million times afterwards. He'd always pick a time when something was at its peak."

Nell caught the sidelong glance that her daughter dealt her and said nothing. Anton had been the primary male role model in both of her children's lives, of that she would never contest, and she loved him for his presence in it.

And then the strangest thing happened. They were alone in the woodland, when a chipmunk started following them, soon accompanied by another, then another, until there were at least four dozen of the diminutive rodents trailing just behind them as they strolled. When Nell and Rose stopped, the chipmunk parade halted, too. At that moment, they assembled with seeming intent, working as if with one mind as a curious sigil took shape before the startled women. Rose, meantime, had been snapping away like a madwoman. After a brief stay once the icon had been formed, the chipmunk assembly explosively dissolved, as the winsome creatures dispersed in dozens of directions.

"Holy shit," Rose exclaimed. "Tell me we didn't see that." Nell had spied a bench along the path and was hurrying towards it as quickly as her trembling legs would deliver her. Rose soon caught up and sat down next to her mother. "Mom! You look so beatific all of a sudden."

"That was your father reaching out," she said softly. "I know it was."

21

Gara'kun moved swiftly but stealthily through the forest, his senses alert for any other human presence. He slowed at about the halfway point. With daylight still ahead, he needed to reconnoiter, and there was only one way. He would later need the cover of darkness for the task at hand. And of course, *ayahuasca*.

He began his preparations for the endeavor, spreading a cotton mat on the forest floor. From his satchel, he withdrew a vial of *ayahuasca*, swallowed it in one draught, and then lay down to wait for the customary effects as the plant medicine came on. He was all business on this trip. When he experienced the familiar sense of connectedness to the forest bio-network, he silently called to his diurnal spirit animal, and soon heard the keening reply. In a process as automatic to Gara'kun as breathing, he merged with the harpy eagle's consciousness, and skimmed the tops of the trees, following the river. The trail from the river to the settlement was obvious. A rope bridge joined the two banks of the river nearby, and a single dugout canoe was pulled up onto a short sandy beach. He turned from the river and instead followed the track. The eagle rode a draft upwards until he could see the clearing of the village ahead. He dropped his altitude and began a lazy circle of the clearing.

There were about twenty structures scattered across the opening in the forest. The people that the eagle saw mostly wore cheap shorts, worn t-shirts and flip-flops. About 100 yards from the periphery of the settlement was another but smaller clearing. This was the collective garbage dump of the community, circled by vultures, stinking of perdition, a growing mountain of glass, plastic, and metal, the refuse of acculturation. There was no longhouse at the center of the village. Instead, in its place was an obvious chapel adorned with a cross carved from mahogany. He silently descended, using his sharp vision to assess the inhabitants of each hastily built shelter.

He isolated the shaman's house by the smell, redolent as it was with a hundred different plant aromas. Yet even this structure had a noticeable aura of deterioration about it, as if the inhabitant had surrendered to sloth. And said inhabitant was sprawled across a hammock, snoring loudly, a nearly empty bottle of pisco in his hand.

The eagle climbed another updraft, and spiraled downward once again, when the shot rang out. He felt the moving air part his feathers as the bullet whizzed by, and he banked quickly, leaving the decrepit village and its drunken shaman behind.

Gara'kun came back to his own body. He drank some water and foraged in the forest for nearby wild fruits, to which the *ayahuasca* led him unerringly. He swallowed several pellets of a dried plant mixture that would assuage the lingering aftereffects of the potion. The shaman needed to have his wits about him after nightfall, when he would potentially be taking the drug again. This was something he had never done before, two sessions in one day. He realized he should sleep in the interim and found a place to sling his hammock. Gara'kun lay back and gave himself over to the rest of the plant medicine that was coursing through his bloodstream. He felt enveloped by the forest's spirit; it was an indescribable sensation.

Song and light surged across the biological network, and he had only to follow it wherever he wished to explore.

Gar woke sometime after sunset. Aside from being exceedingly thirsty, he felt energized and refreshed. He emptied his waterskin and navigated in the darkness to the river to refill it. He was not at all sure how best to complete the task that Te'Bayna'kun had bestowed upon him. That was the dilemma for which he needed the *ayahuasca* to provide guidance.

When he returned, he took the second dose of *ayahuasca* immediately. This mixture was slightly different than the first. It contained additional adjuvants that would intensify the effects of both the N-dimethyltryptamine (DMT) and the monoamine oxidase inhibitor β-carboline, each contributed by the two main constituents. The predicted result would be greater ease in telepathic communications, and greater control of his nocturnal spirit animal.

This time, he struck a meditative pose on his cotton mat, awaiting the plant teacher's enablement. To Gar's surprise, his spirit animal came to him. It was a beautiful black jaguar that he had seen a handful of times before, when his shaman A'kunayaz was still alive. The panther locked eyes with him as he closed his, but not before the luminescent yellow stare imprinted in his mind's eye. And then he was inside, looking out at himself on the mat. He turned away and started down to the river, his superb feline night vision making the way as clear as daylight. He plunged into the river, felt the cool waters wash over him, and the quickening of the current as he passed the halfway point, leaping up the bank as soon as his front paws touched the dry slope.

Gara'kun felt no barrier between him and his host. He was bonded to this magnificent creature that ruled the forest to large measure, the apex predator of tropical America's vast forests and savannahs. It was quite possibly the most exhilarating sensation he had ever experienced.

He loped along the well-worn track that led to the village. He was soundless in his approach, as if he were composed of air alone. The settlement was quiet when he neared. As he rambled past shelters, he heard mostly snoring, an occasional baby's cry. He found the degenerate shaman's house as before; the prone body of the unconscious fallen medicine man in his hammock, his breath labored, the dusky nearness of death hovering throughout the hut. He sensed that there would be no requirement for murder that night.

"No, Gara'kun. Not tonight." He heard, but inside the jaguar's head. Sensing a presence, the cat quickly turned, peering into the shadows. The panther suddenly made itself supine before the intruder. "He will be dead by morning," the internal voice said. A'kunayaz stepped out from the darkness into a beam of moonlight that was projected through an unrepaired hole in the roof. "I have bent time for us."

"A'kunayaz, why are you here? For sleep after sleep, I have waited to feel some kind of contact. Nothing."

His departed teacher shrugged. "I am not here for you, shaman. We completed our work together a long time ago."

"Then why are you here?" Gara'kun thought.

The vision of the old man pointed to the dying man in the hammock. "For him. My twin brother." The jaguar leaped to its feet.

"Twin brother?"

"Yes, Gara'kun. This was once my village, my people. My brother and I began training with the fine shaman of our village. He took us in when our parents died after the missionaries came. Our language is very much like A'kun, and we were probably once one people. The missionaries brought disease, and when my brother got sick, our shaman sent me away. 'You will come to another village,' he told me. 'Follow the river upstream; the fourth branch will take you where you need to go. Remember everything I have taught you.' I did as I was told. I made my way, and the forest took care of me. Four sleeps later, I arrived at the settlement of the A'kun. Their shaman met me at the periphery of the clearing where the forest ended. 'I have been expecting you,' was all he said. He became my teacher and my father."

"But your brother survived," Gara'kun thought.

"Yes. I was already shaman when I found out."

"Did your brother take De'bayna'kun from me?"

The shade of his shaman shook his head. "No. My brother refused the request from the rapist's family."

"Then who did?"

"I don't know. The family probably paid someone in another village. There is no one still alive from the rapist's family," the shamanic spirit said. "Te'bayna'kun made sure of that."

A terrible sadness swept across the disembodied mind of Gara'kun. "Could I have done … anything?" he thought.

"No. Te'bayna'kun has struck the last blow in this foolish war. And so, it ends."

"I am sorry, A'kunayaz."

"For what? You have been a powerful shaman for our people. They thrive because of you. And you have surpassed me in one way. I never was a father in blood." The voice in Gar's mind paused. "Pa'bayna'kun will be a fine shaman one day in his time." A'kunayaz stood. "And now you must go." As if timed, the decrepit figure in the hammock emitted a forlorn moan. "Your story continues to unfold, Gara'kun." The shaman began to sing; it was a chant of passing. The song pierced Gar's mind and instantly transported him back into his own body. He felt lighter, unburdened, even while the bio-network whispered to him via the *ayahuasca,* and his exhausted body fell into a healing sleep. Gar woke as the light began at last to creep under the forest. He drank half of his water and began the trek back to his village.

Nell met Anton at the airport in the early hours of the morning. They lingered in embrace for a while, and when they at last disentangled, loaded Kovac's bags into her car. "Where to?" she asked. Do you want to go home, come over for breakfast …"

"How about you come to my place," he replied. "We pick up bagels and I get to unload my bags. After a shower, I'll be ready to go uptown." He paused for a deep breath. "Wow, I've got a lot to tell you."

Nell was agreeable, and they headed across Queens to Kovac's bachelor abode. Nell wrinkled her nose when he opened the door, and the peculiar smell of inoccupation greeted her olfactory sense. "Sorry," Anton muttered, getting a whiff himself. "Hey, why don't you go get breakfast while I shower? Here, take my keys." He started opening windows.

When Nell returned with fresh bagels, cream cheese and sliced salmon, Anton was clean and dressed, and the small apartment smelled much better. Coffee was brewing. "Loren and Rose would love to see you. Would you stay for dinner tonight? I'll have them over."

"I'd love that," Kovac agreed enthusiastically.

"In fact," Nell continued, "why don't you hold the stories until then? That way, you'll only be telling them once."

They tucked into breakfast, and Anton allowed himself one reveal. "I took *ayahuasca* with Gar. Up on the mountain, the Magic Mountain we began calling it. I sent you a photo of 'The Garden.'"

"Ah, yes. The place with all the Andean flowers. O.K, so what did you learn?" she added mordantly.

Kovac flashed her an arch look. "Not if you're going to be that way about it."

Nell was slightly taken aback by Anton's sharp retort. Clearly, he took the experience seriously. "I'll behave," she promised, taking a sip of coffee.

Kovac took another bite of his bagel, lending him a short pause to frame his insights from the plant teacher with as much brevity as he could muster. "I confronted some monsters that looked like bizarre cartoons of myself and my father. They were somewhat demonic. That happened at the end of the trip. I remember emitting a scream that rose from the depths of my sense of self, and then I was unconscious." He poured another cup of coffee. "When I awoke, I felt at peace." Nell was silent. She could sense a change in him; it was subtle but apparent. "Before that, I experienced the bio-network that runs throughout all life. I could tune into different wavelengths, guided by the color of every organism's aura, which would give me knowledge about that form of life. Some of the plant revelations I remember, but I've forgotten many. I'm sure *ayahuasca* is partly how Gar absorbed his shamanic lore. You have to consider that the man's brain has been transformed by DMT.

"People of the forest have been coming to the Mountain for millennia. At the top is a rock wall covered with handprints, drawings of plants and animals, and abstract symbols. It hummed with an incredible energy."

Nell suddenly grew animated. "Oh, that reminds me," she exclaimed, and ran off to fetch her phone. "Have you ever seen anything like this?" she asked, showing him one of Rose's photographs of the sign that the chipmunks had given them that day in the Brooklyn Botanic Garden.

Kovac reached for his phone and wordlessly swiped through photos until he found the one for which he was looking. He held it up for Nell to see. It had been a frequent occurrence among the petroglyphs on the Magic Mountain's terminal wall, and it was an exact match for the sigil in Rose's photograph, the icon that could bend time. "Maybe it's a blessing of sorts," he mused.

Nell called each of her children and was pleased by how enthusiastically they accepted the invitation. Both demanded a few words with Anton and even though she couldn't hear what the kids were saying, she was happy to hear both conversations dissolve into laughter.

Nell and Kovac arrived in the Bronx in the early afternoon. They expected Rose and Loren in a few hours. When Rose texted that she was on her way, they worked together in the kitchen, preparing a large beef and broccoli stir-fry. Anton found it strange to be occupied with the tasks of everyday living; part of him was still deep in the southwestern Amazon of Peru. It caused him to pause several times, as if to remind himself that he had departed that world for one with less magic, fewer intangibles. He kept his own counsel on this mild schizophrenia; he knew Nell could not understand, and he doubted he could adequately describe it without alienating her. She could sense something was slightly off-kilter with him, but when she asked him how he was feeling, he merely smiled and shook his head. "Nothing is amiss," he told her. "I'm just happy to be here with you." Her face brightened, and just then the doorbell rang; it was Rose, ever punctual.

Nell's daughter grabbed Anton in a tight embrace that penetrated his heart. He framed her face between his palms and looked deep into her eyes. They were glistening, and in his mind's eye he saw her visage transform to that of a young girl, and then, like a flipbook animation, pass through the stages of growth into the confident, joyful, competent woman that stood before him. "I love you, Anton. I'm so glad you're back with us again," she said. That was when he felt his own eyes moisten. He didn't need to respond; Rose knew what she meant to him.

A similar scene ensued when Loren arrived, bearing a dessert box and a bottle of wine. "You look great!" he exclaimed, placing an arm around Kovac's shoulders. "Welcome home."

Throughout dinner, Anton told them almost everything. He didn't wish to burden them with the ugliness of the gold miners' fate. Kovac told them about their half-brother and showed them the photo of Pa'bayna'kun and their father, shoulder to shoulder, smiling at the camera. "He does look like you, Loren," Rose declared. Kovac spun the tale of the Magic Mountain, passing his phone around with the pictures.

"There's an amazing plant, a small tree, that grows only in the upper reaches of the mountain. The A'kun call it *m'kunaya,* and it's the most important plant in their vast pharmacopeia. It's very unusual; it seems to be something ancient and very basal in the flowering plant tree of life. Your father claims it is the most powerful immune system booster ever discovered. It's prepared into pellets after a day of cooking, and every A'kun takes one every month. They are incredibly healthy, the A'kun; they never get sick." He thought suddenly of De'Bayna'kun. "Well, almost never," he corrected himself.

The evening drew to its close, with hugs all around. Rose would drop Loren off on her way to Brooklyn. When they had departed, Anton said, "Well, I'll hail an Uber."

Nell fixed him with a small smile and said, "What for? You can stay here tonight."

Kovac glanced at the living room. "Sure, I can sleep on the couch."

Her smile widened. "No, you can sleep with me." She reached out her hand and took his, giving it a good squeeze. "This should have happened a long time ago." They strolled into the bedroom and embraced. Their lips met; their tongues danced in each other's mouths. Anton took off his shirt, while Nell eyed him appraisingly. "Mmm, you lost weight, and even tightened up a little." Anton removed her shirt and bra, bending down to shower her breasts with kisses while she undid his belt and freed his erect cock. Anton kicked off his pants, then slipped off Nell's.

They tumbled onto the bed, naked and trembling in embrace. Moving slowly against each other, they exchanged small sounds of pleasure. Kovac felt transported out of his body as he explored Nell's. He self-consciously berated himself for having stood apart from this moment for too many years, out of fear, and other complex emotions that had blinded him again and again to the love that he had harbored mutely for half his lifetime. *What a fool I've been,* Anton scolded himself, then swept all remonstrative thoughts away with an ease that he'd never before been capable of, as she welcomed him into her body with a deep kiss and a responsive moan.

Sex was only slightly awkward, at least until they discovered their rhythm, their respective likes and dislikes in lovemaking, which arrived sooner than expected, enough to inspire several repeats of the act, before falling asleep in each other's arms.

23

"So, there you have it," Kovac said. He was seated across an expansive desk opposite Kevin Hobart, Director and President of the Cincinnati Botanical Garden. Hobart looked almost slightly stricken by the news. He took off his glasses and rubbed his eyes.

"He's their … shaman?" Kevin said.

Kovac laughed. "That was exactly my first reaction. But it's genuine; the Gar Sorrentino that you once knew has…," and here he paused, "… transitioned, so to speak."

"To what?" Hobart exclaimed.

Kovac shrugged. "He is A'kun. Thoroughly. He has lived a life that we can barely imagine. And he is a full-fledged *ayahuasquero*."

Hobart shook his head. "You know, the Brits had a term for this back in the day. 'He's gone troppo,' they used to say."

Kovac nodded. "Yeah, I guess you could say that." He retrieved his phone and loaded the photograph of Gar and Pa'bayna'kun. "Here are Gar and his son."

Kevin Hobart stared at the photograph for a long time. "And he's going to make collections for us?"

"That's the plan. Once a month, he will bring specimens to the research station. The first ones we collected together will probably reach here in a couple of months. Beyond that, he would prefer that we maintain the fiction of his death."

Hobart stood up abruptly. "I need a drink; how about you?"

"It's a little early for me," Anton demurred, then added, "but what the hell?" Kevin poured two bourbons, neat, depositing one in front of Kovac.

Hobart raised his glass. "To our friend gone troppo," he toasted, as their small glasses clinked. He took a sip, and then sat back down. From his desk drawer, he withdrew an envelope and tossed it across the desk to Kovac.

Anton picked up the envelope and asked, "What's this?"

"A proposal," Hobart replied.

"For what?"

The older man sighed theatrically. "Just read it!" he declaimed.

Kovac sat forward in his chair and opened the envelope. The heading at the top of the page stated in all caps with boldface: "**THE GARWELL SORRENTINO SENIOR CURATOR OF AMAZONIAN BOTANY**." It was a position description. Anton took a long slug of bourbon.

"I already have an endowment for it," Kevin commented. His frustration at Kovac's silence got the better of him. "Are you being coy, Anton, or are you just dense?"

"It's just a little unexpected," Kovac finally spoke. "All things considered."

Hobart made a sweeping motion with his hands. "That's all water under the bridge. Look, think about it; you don't have to give me an answer today."

"Yes," Anton mumbled. He cleared his throat and said it again, this time more loudly. "Yes, I accept." Kevin leaped to his feet, his hand outstretched.

"Welcome home, Dr. Kovac."

◆ ◆ ◆ ◆ ◆

"He offered you a job?" Nell exclaimed.

"I know. Can you believe it?"

"Are you going to accept?"

"I already have."

They were eating Thai food at a favorite restaurant not far from Nell's apartment building, the sort of place where they were recognized from their customary visits. They were so well known that the wait staff rarely had to ask them for their meal choices.

Anton had been to his apartment only one more time since returning from Peru, just to collect several changes of clothing. He'd spent every night since with Nell. She took his hand across the table. "I'm really, really happy for you, Anton." He was expected in Cincinnati in the fall and had already informed his college that he would not be taking up his teaching position again. "You know, I still own the house there," she reminded him. Kovac nodded. "I can tell the tenants that I won't be renewing their lease. I'm sure you could get one of the Garden's apartments in the interim."

Kovac covered her clasping hand with his other. "Nell, what would it take to convince you to move back there with me?" he asked. She didn't seem surprised; her smile grew luminous.

"Not very much," she replied softly. "I'm very portable in retirement."

Anton lifted her hand and kissed it gently. "One other thing," he said. He let loose of her hands and stood, fishing in his pocket for a small black box. He placed it in front of her and got down on one knee. "Nell Sorrentino, would you join me in late-stage matrimony?"

Nell gasped, beginning to tear up. "Anton, honey, that's not necessary, really." She opened the box and withdrew a beautiful gold ring topped with a gleaming ruby, her birthstone. A small sticker fastened to the velvet inside the lid proclaimed *"hecho en Perú."* She slipped it onto the ring finger of her left hand. "But how could I ever say no?" she whispered. She stood, and they kissed passionately, uninhibited before a suddenly attentive crowd of other diners. The restaurant owners and staff had gathered near them and cheered, while the other customers showered them with applause.

At the end of the meal, their server brought out a big slice of mango cake adorned with a sparkler. Nell showed off the ring to her, and she wished them "forever happiness." *That sounds about right,* Kovac thought. While Nell visited the restroom, Kovac went over to the register to pay the dinner bill. "No charge," one of the owners, a married couple, declared. "It is our gift to you." Anton protested, but she was adamant, and he finally resigned himself to accepting their generosity, but left an equally generous tip on the table.

As he stood by the front of the restaurant, a man came in, ostensibly to pick up some takeout. He smiled and nodded to Kovac, who immediately felt a chill crawl up his spine. Anton recognized the man immediately as the same he'd encountered three times before. Gar's avatar noted his expression of familiarity and broke into a wide smile. "*Buena suerte hermano,*" he said. "*Que solo conozcas la felicidad en los años venideros.*"[28] Kovac briefly turned away to acknowledge Nell's return to his side, and when he glanced back, the man was gone.

♦ ♦ ♦ ♦ ♦

The wedding was just the right size; notable for the fact that none of the guests were Kovac's friends or family, since he really had none. Loren was the best man and Rose, the maid of honor. They held the ceremony and reception at the New York Botanical Garden, catered by a friend of Rose's whose chef's prowess had turned into a profitable business.

Nell was resplendent in an apricot-colored gown; Anton wore a white suit. A Unitarian minister presided over their vows. It was a crisp day, presaging the arrival of fall in short order. A band of gold now perched above the ruby engagement ring, matched by the one on Kovac's left hand. Both were etched with a braid of twining branches. She felt lighter than air, and spun her husband across the dance floor, passing him off to her daughter, when the master of ceremonies (Nell's oldest and dearest colleague during her career) called for a proxy father/daughter dance to Paul Simon's "Father And Daughter:"

---

[28] Good luck, brother. May you know only happiness in the years ahead.

"I am touched to the bottom of my heart, my sweet Rose," Anton told her.

"Silly man," she chided him gently. "Who else would it be?"

Loren led the toasts, speaking at length about how much Anton Kovac had hovered in his and Rose's life, like a guardian angel. "When I think of all the many firsts in my early years, it was always Anton who was there, beside our mother. Now, in the bond of their wedlock, we also find a sort of closure, lest we ever think that we were lacking something during that time." He nodded to the master of ceremonies who queued up Dylan's "Shelter From The Storm," his mother's favorite, undanceable, but a cogent testimony to their history. Substitute the "she" of the song for the masculine pronoun, and it became the story of their biological father.

Kovac found himself at the bar next to a senior curator from the New York Botanical Garden named Heinrichs who worked on the palm family. He was not someone that Anton knew very well, and he harbored a vague memory that he'd been rather judgmental regarding Kovac's indiscretion at Cincinnati many years ago. "I'm happy for you, Kovac. So, I hear Hobart has hired you again." Anton confirmed this with a nod. "I also hear that you and Nell were recently in Peru."

Kovac nodded again. "We have a project going with Oscar Crescente."

"Ah," his interrogator continued. "How is Oscar?"

"Doing very well," Anton replied. "Open for business."

"Yeah, I heard he's riding the ecotourism racket quite successfully. Give him my best the next time you talk to him." The bartender brought him his drink, and he moved back towards his table. Not a dancer, this one. He stopped and turned back to Kovac. "You know, for what it's worth, I never believed Sorrentino was dead," he added. "Funny, that. I still don't." Their eyes met, and Anton maintained his gaze until Heinrich averted his. "Well, congratulations."

Kovac let out his breath as he rejoined Nell at their appointed seats. "What did Johann want with you?" she asked.

"Botanical conspiracy theories," he muttered, leaning in and kissing his wife. "I never liked that guy."

"Fuck him," Nell rejoined with uncharacteristic color. "Let's dance."

A honeymoon was out of the question, as they faced the herculean task of emptying two apartments and sending it all to The Queen City. The Botanical Garden provided a healthy relocation subsidy. Rose was going to take over her mother's apartment, and at least half of the furnishings would stay behind. "Peru was our honeymoon," Nell suggested.

"Minus the sex!" he retorted, and was surprised to see her blush, even through her café au lait complexion.

The movers soon were fait accompli, and both Loren and Rose saw them off from the now half bare Bronx apartment. "Christmas?" their mother suggested hopefully.

"Maybe Thanksgiving, too," Loren said, glancing at his sister for compliance. "Drive safely," he added. Rose leaned into the window and whispered something in Nell's ear, which made her mother laugh.

"I'll try," she replied. "Keep fucking his brains out," her daughter had told her.

24

The specimens began rolling in, less a set deposited with the National Museum in Lima. The first included specimens collected by Oscar while they were together in Peru, along with the Magic Mountain material. Crescente had included his field notes.

So much was clearly undescribed. Nell swept all the coffee family specimens off to her work desk in a large office she shared with Kovac. Kovac curated the rest, deciding which specialists would receive duplicates in exchange for an identification, or "determination" in the parlance of the trade. The *m'kunaya* occupied a particular focus of interest. Rose had a friend, a MD who had also gotten a Ph.D. in natural product biochemistry, and he agreed to investigate the purported properties of the plant. The Garden had its own molecular lab, and a suite of nearly 400 nuclear genes would be sequenced, the DNA extracted from the best green leaves on the specimens. Meanwhile, Kovac worked long and hard on painstakingly describing the plant while waiting for the longer-term results. He emailed all his photos, notes and sketches of important details to his favorite botanical artist, a Brazilian with extraordinary ability to fashion an accurate drawing, even when confronted with a daunting lack of first-class material. If, in fact, *m'kunaya* turned out to be a genus new to science, he had already chosen a name: *Sorrentinoa*.

A few weeks later, the head of the molecular lab called him on the phone. "Anton, can you swing by the lab today?" she asked. "I want to show you something." The lab was located in the newest building in the Garden's research park, The Gillespie Plant Science

Center, named for the retired industrialist who had paid for the lion's share of it. Kevin Hobart was second-to-none at massaging immense donations out of the Cincinnati upper crust.

The trees were wearing their fall colors as Kovac traversed the grounds from the herbarium to the Center. A cool breeze presaged the near onset of winter. He swiped his ID card at the entrance to the facility and nodded to the receptionist behind a curved desk. The head scientist met him as the elevator door opened. "You're gonna love this, Anton." He followed her into her office. On the computer monitor was a tree of life, a representation of the evolutionary relationships resolved by gigabases of DNA sequence. She rolled a second chair next to hers in front of the screen. "Now, mind you, this is just a preliminary tree," she cautioned, "but the support values are perfect." With her mouse, she zoomed into one portion of the phylogeny. A consensus had grown in the community of systematic botanists that the genus *Amborella*, consisting of a single species known only from the island of New Caledonia, was the first branch on the flowering plant tree of life. The very next ramification of the tree terminated with the name *m'kunaya*.

"Wow," was all he could say.

When he got back to the herbarium, Nell was seated at her desk, intently studying the flowers of what she suspected was a new genus in the coffee family. Kovac sat down heavily in his desk chair. She looked up in concern. "What?"

He smiled and took her hand; his own was shaking. "It's a new branch on the tree," he said softly. "After *Amborella*! The *m'kunaya* is the fucking sister to all the rest of the angiosperms!" He exclaimed, growing animated. He enveloped his wife in a bear hug. "This is just so cool beans!"

"We need to celebrate," Nell declared. "Come on, you've been here since 7 am."

Kovac still appeared slightly shocked as they headed home, with a brief stop to procure some champagne. In truth, it was an unexpected discovery, one that would potentially re-write biogeographic scenarios for decades. *Sorrentinoa anomala*, he thought to himself. *Perfect.*

♦ ♦ ♦ ♦ ♦

Every month, new specimens arrived at the herbarium, always accompanied by a field notebook, rich with details of the plant biodiversity found in Gar's plots. Even after 25 years, the A'kun shaman hadn't forgotten the Sorrentino method, and applied it assiduously to the forests that stretched unbroken in every direction from the village.

The field books were alone, an incredible contribution to Peruvian biodiversity science. Page after page in Gar's careful script, multitudes of simple yet deliberate sketches of botanical details. And of course, notes on medicinal uses and preparation.

Aside from the collections, neither Kovac nor Nell had any sign from Gar, real or imagined. He phoned Oscar, who had the same to report. "Honestly, Anton, I always figure that anytime I do see him, it's probably for the last time. Oh, and I've got a story for you. About two weeks after you left, four guys showed up at your Garden's research station. According to Luis, they wandered in one at a time, looking very bedraggled. Two of them were infested with bot flies, and one had a broken arm. They were all armed, but were out of ammunition, thank goodness.

"They claimed that they woke up deep in the forest, with no clue how they arrived there. They were very vague about what they had been doing in the first place. Luis suspected that they had been prospecting for gold. It so happened that I'd sent Alvaro to deliver supplies to the station, and he took them downriver to the Río Las Piedras. He lost track of them; they weren't on the *Ana Cariniña* to Puerto Maldonado."

So, they lived, and loved, and of course, worked. The manuscript came together in the ensuing months as winter settled in upon the southern Midwest. "A new branch on the angiosperm tree of life" was the title. Kovac told Nell that he wanted her to be an author on the paper, which he planned to submit to *Science*, arguably the pinnacle of scientific journals. She protested at first, but then finally agreed, as Penelope de Souza.

On most days, Kevin Hobart left him to his own devices, but one afternoon in December, Kevin strode into the herbarium and knocked on his office door. Anton was by himself, comparing some of his specimens to related species from the herbarium's collections. "Hey, Kevin! Come on in. I could have swung by if you'd texted that you wanted to see me."

His boss perused the specimens. "No, no big deal; I like to get out from behind the desk now and again."

"Great. Hey, I'll have a manuscript later this week that I'd love you to review."

Hobart nodded. "Excellent. Look, there's a project with which I could use your help. I've been asked to address the U.N. General Assembly in the spring. It's a special session on biodiversity, with a focus on the Amazon. I am going to propose a global tax on petrochemical profits that would be managed by the U.N., with board representation from the countries targeted. In addition, the money would be used to start strategically buying up land in the region as mitigation for climate change. I know it sounds like fantasy, but I have some strong allies. Zach Coville, CEO of the Anapurna Company — you know, the high-end outdoor clothing and gear provider — has agreed to appear with me and has promised a sizable seed contribution to the fund." Coville was known for his commitment to ecosystem preservation and had established a number of private reserves in the southern Andes with his immense personal fortune. "I'm also working on the CEO of Ford. At the very least, he can add impetus." There was a lull in the conversation. "This may be the last really meaningful task of my professional career," said the man who had accumulated so many victories, large and small, aimed at the crisis of extinction. "I'm 78, Anton. I'm slowing down, while time runs along faster and faster every year." He laughed. "You've got twenty years to get here."

"Whatever I can do to help," Kovac said softly.

"I want to make Gar the inspiration for this proposal," Kevin continued. "With that in mind, who else should present him to the world other than the Sorrentino Curator of Tropical Botany?"

25

There occurs a time in the tropical forest when all noises are still. This is the moment of transition, when all the sounds of day cease, just before the night voices take over. In most instances, it would be barely perceptible. Under the influence of *ayahuasca*, it was purely extraordinary.

Gara'kun and his son, Pa'bayna'kun, were deep in the forest, two days out of the village. They had with them a pair of sizable baskets affixed with lids and several burlap sacks that Luis had given them the last time they dropped material off at the research station. But it wasn't them burdened with the containers, and much more, including two herbarium presses loaded with sandwiches of newspaper and aluminum corrugates, and the drying frame, but Blanca, the ever-uncomplaining mule. Pa'bayna'kun had grown fond of her, and always slipped her a fruit or two when they stumbled upon a cache and rationed the handfuls of oats from the bag Luis had given them. The station director had been very generous, providing waterproof tags, pens, and multiple field books, which would be depleted on this trip. He had even handed off an expensive and powerful GPS that would capture a signal under a thick canopy. Gar and his son would make the final Sorrentino plot in the forests that surrounded the Magic Mountain.

When they traveled together, father and son used a pastiche of Spanish and A'kun. It became their quixotic lingua franca, constantly changing in composition. Gar quizzed Pa'bayna from time to time about the names and properties of certain plants they passed on their trail. Nine times out of ten, the young man answered correctly. Gara'kun was pleased with the acumen his son had shown walking the plant medicine path. "All I want to do when we get there is set up the plot points and lines," Gar announced. "We'll begin sampling in the morning." Pa'bayna'kun was already an old hand at the process. He had been up to the strange, isolated inselberg twice, once with his father, and the other time alone. The latter occurred on the sacred instance of his coming of age, when he took *ayahuasca*, and was introduced to his spirit animal for the first time: an Amazon coral snake, as deadly as it was beautiful. One day, his father's nocturnal jaguar avatar would become his own.

It took them much of the remaining daylight to accomplish the task. When they finished, Pa'bayna'kun pulled three striped bass from a calmer eddy along the small river fed by the mountain's cascades. They hung their hammocks while the fish roasted over an open fire. In the last light, Gar hurriedly gathered an assortment of fruit from the forest edge above the stream to round out their meal.

Gar loved working beside his son. If there was any penance to be paid for having been a less than mediocre father in his old world, he had more than achieved parity with the successes of his three A'kun children, all now fine adults, loving husbands and wife, stalwart tribe members, and equally strong parents themselves. But the connection between shaman and apprentice was only with Pa'bayna.

"*A'kunda*, you never talk about the other world," he suddenly stated flatly.

Gara'kun shrugged. "I'm done with it, *a'kundin* [son]. It is a place boiling with strife and destruction."

"Then why are we doing this?"

"I am doing this for Anton, the only friend I ever truly loved in the world I left behind. And I suppose in some way, for the children I had there, too, and their mother." He gazed at this son's face. "The *ayahuasca* teaches us many things, but never suggests that the ties we bind in life can be fully discarded. Any life. There is always a legacy." He used the Spanish *el legado* for the last word.

"Would I like my half-brother and sister?" Pa'bayna'kun asked.

"I think so," his father replied. "There are aspects you share. I hope those same threads will guide them the same way they do you."

The next morning, they began the onerous job of collecting samples of all the woody plants, trees, shrubs, and lianas that grew in each of the plots. The young man had become as capable a tree climber as his father. Canopy giants were recorded by Gar in the field book, with an estimate of diameter at breast height but not sampled because it would take up too much time for one of them to ascend the lower bare trunks of the forest's aristocracy.

At the midday break, Pa'bayna'kun explored away from where the plots had been laid out. His father advised him not to stay away too long; there was abundant work ahead of them. "*Si, jefe*" — yes, boss — he called out, knowing it would annoy the old man.

Pa'bayna'kun walked determinedly beneath the penumbra of the forest, letting his intuition lead him. He was drawn to a spot where the sun had penetrated the closed canopy. As he neared, his curiosity mounted; this was no mere tree fall. He was about to burst through the thick herbaceous vegetation that formed an edge, much like that which would be encountered along a river break in the forest. But it was much more than that.

At first, he didn't believe his eyes. Certainly, nothing seen in his twenty-three years could match what stretched before him. Call it a crack in the earth, for "sinkhole" wouldn't do it justice.

The entire open expanse covered several hectares, and the depression itself looked to be at least close to 3000 feet deep, though, of course, that meant nothing to him. That it was huge and abyssal was obvious. The bottom was densely vegetated, and he caught the glint of water through the scant opening among the trees. The sides were irregularly studded with rock outcrops, more lightly colonized mostly by shrubs, and a very colorful bromeliad in full flower.

He called to his father, unsure if he would be heard. A barely audible reply did reach his keen ears. "Follow my voice, *a'kunda*," he shouted. Every few moments, he emitted another call, and Gar's answering hoots grew louder each time as his own unerring sense of direction led him nearer.

Just as he appeared before his son, he muttered, "I hope this is good."

"Oh, I think so," was Pa'bayna's reply.

Gara'kun was stunned when he took in the tableau before them. "I knew nothing of this," he exclaimed. "A'kunayaz never said a word. I don't think this would be visible unless you were on the other side of the mountain." There was no approach known to ascend the strange pinnacle from that face, which appeared sheer for a good share of its last 2000 feet. He rested a hand on his son's shoulder. "We have work to finish, *a'kundin*. This mystery will have to wait for another time." His son looked disappointed. "We can visit here first on *ayahuasca* with our spirit animals. After we're done with the plots."

They completed the sampling on the third day of their encampment. Plant presses were brimming with collections as they placed them on the drying frame, situated under a rain shelter Pa'bayna'kun had constructed, all numbered, all documented in the field books with immaculate detail.

The next morning, they rose early and loaded Blanca with their gear. "We'll head to the research center from here and deliver Blanca and her burden to Luis," Gar told Pa'bayna. "I know a shortcut that will get us there in two days."

Te'bayna'kun had interrogated him no sooner had Gar returned from the river village on what was supposed to have been a mission of vengeance. "The job is done," he informed the chief. "It's over." He provided no details, nor mentioned his vision of his shaman master, the curious relationship A'kunayaz had revealed to him, and that in fact, it had been a redemptive experience.

Te'bayna'kun's visage softened. "You should marry again, brother. It would do you good."

Gara'kun smiled. "As long as De'bayna'kun lives in my heart, I am married still." The chief considered this for a moment, but then nodded sagely.

That was all months ago. As they tracked their way through the forest, he considered what good fortune had been given him, the richness of his life invested in the well-being of his family and his tribe, even after his wife was taken away. He was grateful for the opportunity to reconcile his former life with that of the eternal forest.

They arrived late on the second day. Two ornithologists from a Peruvian university were in residence. They happily assisted in getting the specimens situated in the freezer, and Pa'bayna'kun amused himself conversing with them in Spanish. Neither had any inkling of the identity of the gray-haired indigenous man to whom Luis seemed to show the most extraordinary deference.

"Why don't you stay for dinner," the station director entreated. Pa'bayna glanced at his old man, who assented with a curt nod. "You can also hang your hammocks under our roof," Luis bid them.

Over their meal, Luis told Gar and Pa'bayna that Anton was back at the Garden, in an endowed position named for Garwell Sorrentino. His son seemed startled by the news; it wasn't often that he heard uttered his father's name from the other world, but he recognized it. Gara'kun just nodded intently, giving Luis the eerie sense that he knew all this already. "And Nell and Anton are married." A broad smile enveloped Gar's face.

"As it should be," was all he said.

In the morning, Gara'kun and his son melted back into the forest. After walking a few hours, Gar called a short stop, pulled two palm stem tubes sealed with beeswax at the top, and handed one over to

Pa'bayna'kun. They peeled off the wax and threw the bitter *ayahuasca* to the back of their throats.

As always with *ayahuasca*, the forest welcomed them with a cathedral of music and light. Both were long past the time where the plant medicine could bring them fear or terror. They allowed themselves a period to just bathe in it, because it brought with it such an abiding feeling of joy. Gara'kun looked over at his son, who was bathed in a vivid aura of golden light. He sat down upon his cotton mat in a meditative pose, as did Pa'bayna'kun, and called for his harpy eagle avatar. Gar heard the keening growing louder above the forest treetops, and with an *ayahuasquero*'s ease slipped into the bird's consciousness. He circled above the canopy, waiting to hear from his son through the biological network that *ayahuasca* unlocked for them.

"*A'kunda…*" came the thought, wearing the voice of Pa'bayna. "You must pick me up for the journey. Look for a tree fall not far from our bodies. I will crawl into the clearing. Look for my colors." The eagle descended in a slow arcing spiral, then evened out at about three hundred feet above the trees. He spied the tree fall below him, and dropped still further, his acute vision picking out the coral snake exposed and waiting. He dove and adroitly lowered himself to the trunk of the fallen tree, his feathered legs extended out below him as his talons gently enveloped the serpent. "Ow!" he heard inside his head, and his heart skipped a beat until a laugh followed.

"You're a monster, Pa'bayna," Gar answered back as he rose, the coral snake hanging limply in his talons. His wings beat powerfully and silently as he sped towards the mountain.

After some unknown passage of time, he could see the mountain in the distance, rising out of the forest. When he neared the inselberg, he banked sharply in order to approach the other side of the formation, and as he did, the fracture in the landscape became immediately apparent. A random aspect of geology had hidden it from view for decades, perhaps centuries or even millennia.

The harpy eagle began a descending spiral into the cavity, first depositing Pa'bayna'kun's avatar on a rock that protruded upright from the floor of the deep canyon. He then flew upward towards a protruding terrace of stone laden with the bromeliad that he'd spotted from up above. It was considerably cooler inside the canyon than the forest that surrounded the mountain. This situated him approximately at the canopy level of the elfin forest that filled much of the basin. A single species dominated, one that bore a certain familiarity. He opened himself to the forest's song, and his mind filled with it, accompanied by a radiance so familiar, it was startling. He sensed his son's similar reaction.

The dwarf forest was composed entirely of *m'kunaya*.

26

No one was quite prepared for the rash of popular interest generated by the publication of "A new branch on the angiosperm tree of life" when it appeared in *Science*. The paper included descriptions of the family Sorrentinoaceae, and the only known species *Sorrentinoa anomala*, as well as the tree of life based on the genomic DNA sequences that revealed the evolutionary relationships of the plant. The Garden employed a skilled plant anatomist, who determined that *Sorrentinoa*, like *Amborella*, had only the type of water-conducting tissue known as tracheids versus the more common vessel elements of most flowering plants. There was a parade of authors on the paper, including Kevin Hobart, a colleague from the Peruvian National Museum, the anatomist, the head of the molecular lab, Oscar Crescente, and Anton's former student Luis Rodriguez who had provided such sterling assistance. But only the first two authors were the naming authorities of the new family and the new species *Sorrentinoa anomala* Kovac & de Souza. He had been careful to muddy the exact locality of the *m'kunaya*. "An isolated inselberg amid *terra firma* tropical forest in the Madre de Dios watershed," Kovac wrote. "The exact coordinates are withheld for conservation and cultural preservation reasons."

"Deceased botanical Indiana Jones honored with a new branch on the tree of life" was the New York Times' headline on the Science section front page. Kovac was interviewed on one of the network news shows, and most of their affiliates used the footage; he was a guest on NPR's Science Friday. Several late-night television hosts used the discovery as fodder for jokes in their monologues, one of which was actually funny. The social media were predominantly congratulatory, with only the fringe element claiming "science colonialism." The Garden Museum created an exhibit on the plant and on the legacy of its namesake.

"It's a little creepy," he told Nell one night in their new favorite Thai restaurant. "It's like I'm riding this big lie about Gar's fate."

"This was his wish, Anton. Don't think that for one minute some French movie crew wouldn't go in search of Garwell Sorrentino and the A'kun if they knew they existed." She paused as their meals arrived. "You know, this may sound silly, but start forcing yourself to think of him as Gara'kun all the time. Not 'Gar' or worse, 'Garwell.' Gara'kun. Works for me."

"Do you think it means anything to him?" Kovac said. "All the honorifics: a new family, genus, species. Do you think he really gives a shit?"

"My God, Anton, sometimes you can be so dense," she replied. "He did all this for you."

The specimens and field books from Gara'kun's plots continued to roll in until they didn't any longer. No warning. They just stopped. Luis confirmed this via email. His friend was finished, having made good on his promise. "I wish you well, Gara'kun," Kovac muttered.

As predicted, half of the material represented species that had never before been described. The diversity in the *terra firma* forests of this portion of Peru was extraordinary. Some specialists were prompt in their determinations of the specimens, others, not so much. It was

Kovac's duty to canvass all the data and begin pulling it together in a floristic inventory of this part of the Peruvian Amazon, a region that had been soundly ignored by most botanists, in part because of the difficult logistics in penetrating its trackless forests, compared to working out of Iquitos. Garwell Sorrentino and Oscar Crescente had contributed most of the accrued knowledge.

Cincinnati was enduring a snowy winter that year, and while the first snowfall always cheered Kovac, by January he was ready for a break. He took time off and accompanied Nell to Brazil for two weeks. They worked out of a museum in the small city of Santa Teresa, a bucolic town in the mountainous State of Espirito Santo with which she had established a productive collaboration and found a cozy but reasonably priced apartment not far from the museum. While Nell interacted with her colleagues, Anton began working on his presentation about Sorrentino for Kevin's appearance before the U.N. general assembly in the spring. Nell had a wealth of photos of Gar in the field, accumulated over the years from friends and acquaintances of her ex-husband. "I was going to put together a photo book for the kids," she told him. "I ended up just giving them a copy of the archive."

There was a fair representation of photos from Gar's Ozark youth, from which he placed one in the "Use" folder on his computer. Gar was about 13 or 14, and he was emerging from the woods, a bow and arrows slung over his shoulder. He was smiling at the photographer or someone else off-camera.

The lion's share was of Gar in the jungle. From these he selected many, but there was one in particular that caught his fancy, and which he decided would be his introductory image, a medium closeup of his friend in his early 30's, standing in front of a tree, a kapok by the look of the flower in his hand. His clear blue eyes were not focused on this, but on something in the distance; neither was he smiling.

Near the end of their first week in Brazil, he accompanied two old colleagues from UNICAMP, the State University of Campinas, to an undisturbed fragment of forest along a stream. His friends were studying the amaryllid genus *Griffinia*, found only in Brazil, which like the Amazon lilies, had adapted to the shade of the forest understory with expansive leaves, but bore amethyst-colored flowers. What they speculated to be a new species was in flower when they found it, not too far up the bank of the stream. It was a welcome distraction for Anton.

He reviewed their herbarium's collections of *Clusia*, the genus that he had studied for his doctorate, providing determinations where appropriate. Botanists regularly provide this service to herbaria that they visit, a courtesy widely adopted in the community. One specimen piqued his curiosity, and he suggested to Nell that they visit the site, a narrow swathe of Atlantic close to the coast. It was estimated that the total extent of this biome's extent represented a mere eight to ten percent of the original forest.

The next morning, they set off along with one of Nell's friends, who knew the area. They started off on a trail that began at the terminus of a dirt road, but midway up the slope, it transformed into a clamber across large rocks, teeming with gesneriads, and a brilliant red amaryllis. It was upon these rocks that Kovac found his *Clusia*, in flower and in fruit, the jackpot for potentially describing a new species. The species had deep red flowers with a ring of white at the margins. Anton collected material from both a male and female plant and took many photos.

The two weeks wound down quickly, and he had to admit that he was less than enthusiastic about returning to winter. The museum in Santa Teresa processed the paperwork that would allow Kovac and Nell to take enough material back to Cincinnati to develop a description of the new species. Nell was also bringing with her some material of the coffee family.

To both their surprise, the city was experiencing one of those episodic periods of mild winter weather, and most of the snow had disappeared. The day's mail had delivered a stack of new identifications to the herbarium, and Kovac added them to his growing database of determined species from the Madre de Dios. He sent out polite reminders to scientists that still had specimens but had not yet provided an ID.

He continued to labor on his presentation. Talking about Gar was the simple part; supporting the fiction of his death was much more difficult. He constantly had to remind himself that these were the earnest wishes of his friend Gara'kun.

Sometimes he woke amidst the predawn darkness of a short winter day, in anticipation of some sign from the shaman of the

A'kun. He even went so far as to research providers of *ayahuasca* ceremonies on the west coast, figuring that perhaps he needed to jumpstart the process. He never acted on any of them, and with the passage of another month, he stopped fretting about it.

27

When Gara'kun and his son returned to the village, Te'bayna'kun called him immediately to the center lodge house where they could speak alone. "We had a visit while you and Pa'bayna were gone," the chief told him. "Two of the goldminers, the leader from before, and one new one, came into the village demanding to know where you were." He paused. "We pretended ignorance. Things got very tense." He shook his head. "We should have killed them that first night. This would not have happened if we had." He became quiet, but fixed his shaman with a hard stare.

"So, what did you do?" Gara'kun asked.

"Four of our best followed them, and halfway to the river, cut their throats."

Gara'kun's heart sank, though he knew there had not been much of a choice for the chief. Had they been allowed passage back; it would have been a small matter of time before the cartel would send a larger and better-armed crew in. Regardless, this would probably come to pass. This strike against them would allow a longer duration to develop the plan that he had begun devising on the way back from the research station. He would present it to the elders at the next council meeting.

◆ ◆ ◆ ◆ ◆

It was rare for the A'kun shaman to address the council of elders, of which he was a member, but he generally kept silent unless asked a specific question or had some shamanic insight about what was being discussed. The council meeting was open to any member of the tribe, including the women, of which a fair number attended. The novelty of hearing an address by Gara'kun had been enough to draw a crowd.

Te'bayna'kun gestured to the shaman and raised his ceremonial spear to indicate that the council was officially open for business. The elders usually had to adjudicate a handful of internecine conflicts between families or neighbors. There were fortunately none that had to be dealt with that meeting.

Gar stood in front of the assembly and began his speech. "My people, most of us can no longer remember the last time we left one place in the eternal forest and moved to another. That is not a task that we take lightly, for it involves much cost in our sweat and resources. But I believe that time has now come." A current of mutterings passed through the tribe. Gara'kun allowed it to die down. "Our current land is no longer a safe place for we A'kun. Twice, outsiders from beyond our forest refuge have confronted us. I believe that this will not stop. I believe that a future here means death for the A'kun." He paused and surveyed the faces of his tribes-people; he certainly had their attention. "We can stay here and fight, but ultimately it is a battle that we will lose to our great sorrow." He let that last statement sink in. "As you know, the most sacred place of our people is the mountain that rises heavenward and hosts our most potent plant medicine, the *m'kunaya*, which gifts us with miraculous health. Fewer of you know that the last time I went to gather the *m'kunaya*, there were ill signs for this giver of life." And here he gestured to his son, Pa'bayna'kun. "My son and I just returned from there, and he made an incredible discovery. Blocked from view by the mountain itself is a massive rift in the earth. And at the bottom of this chasm, there is a complete forest of our sacred plant. The rivers that flow from the mountain are not wide enough to allow even canoes to gain entry. We would be safe for many generations. And we would finally be in our true place on earth."

Everyone present started talking at once, causing such a cacophony that Te'bayna'kun had to command order be restored to the meeting. "It is time for the council of elders alone to debate our shaman's proposition." At this, the lodge emptied, yet all still abuzz with the prospect of uprooting their lives.

"Gara'kun," spoke up an elder, his son's father-in-law, "what is your plan to make this happen?"

"The chief will appoint a building crew from among our men. Pa'bayna'kun and I will lead them to the site, which they will begin clearing for our new village. We will save much of what we cut for construction. Pa'bayna'kun will return to our current settlement when the site is almost ready to build on. Te'bayna'kun will appoint another team to assist in what follows. Pa'bayna will lead the crew back to the mountain, accompanied by his sister, Na'bayna'kun, who is in charge of collecting cuttings and roots from the garden to propagate at the new site."

Several of the elders nodded in appreciation of these details.

"How many moons will this take?" a middle-aged man queried; Gara'kun recognized him as the father-in-law of his adopted son, K'naya'kun.

The shaman considered this carefully. "Six to eight," he replied.

The chief then requested that Gara'kun absent himself from the meeting before the elders made their decision. He returned to his hut and lay down in his hammock. He'd find out in the morning.

Gara'kun woke at first light and prepared himself some manioc porridge and fruit. When the sun crept above the forest canopy, burning away the early morning mist, he strolled over to the chief's house. Te'bayna'kun was playing with one of his grandchildren. He welcomed his brother-in-law inside and poured him a bowl of fresh *camu camu* juice, sweetened with honey. "You were very convincing," the chief told him. "Only one elder was opposed, but he is lazy and difficult." He paused. "There was one condition," he continued. "The council says, 'build it' and then they will advise whether we move or wait." The shaman wasn't fooled by the chief's language. Ultimately, the decision would be Te'bayna'kun's, and the caveat on proceeding was clearly his.

Gara'kun's plans transpired smoothly, for the most part. The site he had chosen to clear was situated on a small, relatively flat plateau that harbored a drier and less diverse forest composition. Despite the fact that most of the assembled labor had never done anything like this in their lifetimes, except for occasional enlarging of the current village as the A'kun's numbers increased, they worked efficiently and without serious injuries. His daughter set up a nursery at the edge of and slightly into the forest and placed all the propagules that she'd brought with her into a bed enriched with decomposed leaves that she dragged from low spots in the forest. After two months, the clearing neared the commencement of construction, and Pa'bayna'kun's headed home to fetch the second crew. Doubling the number of workers would speed the construction of shelters and completion of the new village, perhaps in even less than six months.

Gara'kun noted how much he was depending on his son for the day-to-day, sometimes lurching, movement forward on the new A'kun village. It filled him with pride, watching the young man's adaptation to a leadership role in the tribe.

Six and a half months it took before the first crew returned in rotation out of the new settlement. They prepared their families for the move, salvaging all re-usable components of their humble dwellings, while their wives or one of the older children supervised the smoking of meat for the trek.

This was, of course, what Gara'kun had hoped all along, that the men who had constructed their homes would see no reason not to occupy them. He spoke with Te'bayna'kun that day, having accompanied this crew back to the old village. "I will take the plant medicine tomorrow morning to see how far the invaders have progressed. Then I would like you to visit your new home, built, I should add, by your sons."

The chief gave his brother-in-law a tight embrace. "You have convinced me," he whispered in his ear.

In the early light of morning, the shaman took the *ayahuasca* in his favorite place to spread his mat, about a half mile from the old village. He would have to find a new site, most likely in the chasm near the new village. Gara'kun called for his diurnal spirt animal and soon heard the keening of the harpy as he connected. He was soon soaring above the treetops. The eagle's visual acuity caught the flurry of activity at the river village where he'd had the vision of A'kunayaz. The cartel group had twice as many people now. Their leader was talking to the village chief, asking for eight young men to go with them into the forest and through the old village. The A'kun had a matter of days to leave their old world behind.

He sent the eagle downward, which was risky and unnecessary since he had gathered all the necessary intelligence. Shots rang out, and this time they didn't miss. He was flung back into his body, in a meditative position on his mat, and immediately collapsed into unconsciousness.

When he returned to the old village, Pa'bayna'kun had just arrived with the second crew from the new village, including Gar's adopted son Ka'naya'kun. Gara'kun greeted his sons, but then headed directly to the now partially deconstructed house of the chief. Te'bayna'kun sensed the shaman's alarm. "We have four days at most, maybe only three." Gar informed him.

"I will call the council tonight. I will tell them my decision."

"Haven't they figured it out?" Gara'kun commented, gesturing toward the dismantled portion of the chief's abode.

"Tradition," Te'bayna'kun said with a shrug.

It took two days to exit from the old village. The chief and the shaman were the last to leave. Together, they set fire to the skeletal remains of what had been the A'kun's forest home for several generations. The tribe had stripped the orchard of its fruit and girdled the trunks of productive trees. They wanted to leave nothing of use for the interlopers. As they walked through the forest, they took pains to obscure signs of heavy human foot traffic. They crossed the river near the old village for the last time, knowing that the goldminers would soon despoil it with mercury.

When Gara'kun and Te'bayna'kun arrived at the new site in several days, the entire tribe was at work settling into their new homes. K'naya'kun joyfully welcomed his father and guided him to their family's new house. The structure had a big room in the middle and sleeping quarters for everyone on three sides. K'naya did the majority of the construction, sometimes getting help from Pa'bayna'kun and their sister Na'bayna'kun. "Come, *a'kunda*," K'naya beckoned. "Your shaman's place is over here." Set back away from their family's compound, was a sturdy hut, the walls replete with all manner of ingenious storage space as befit a senior shaman. "Pa'bayna moved all of your plant medicines," K'naya continued. "They're in the same order as before."

Gara'kun felt deeply moved. "I am thrice blessed by the hands of my children," he said with emotion.

A loud cheer suddenly erupted outside on the other side of the longhouse. The hunting party had returned with deer and fowl for tonight's communal meal, after which the chief and the A'kun's shaman would bless their new village.

The next day, Gara'kun led the chief to the crack in the earth on the other side of the mountain. Te'bayna'kun was flabbergasted. They circumnavigated the rim of the fissure, but through the forest where the way was less impeded, reconnoitering for any sort of approach to descend into the chasm. They were about halfway around the lip of the crater when the chief stopped and pointed. "There," was all he said. Gar followed his gesture and saw a small, rounded area that gently sloped downward. It was impossible to tell what lay at its feet; some large rocks obscured the view. "I will ask the women to begin making palm fiber ropes," he continued.

It took the A'kun weavers several weeks to construct two ropes, each approximately 200 feet in length. Gara'kun and Pa'bayna'kun would make the descent. They set off early, as the skies suggested rain later in the day. They reached the slope that the chief had first spied while the sun was still low in the sky. Each was encumbered by a lightweight basket affixed to their shoulders by straps of hide, these to collect fresh *m'kunaya*, and 200 feet of coiled palm fiber rope.

The rounded abutment was easy going; Gar wondered what they would find when they reached its terminus. To both his and his son's surprise, when they passed the large boulders that blocked their view, the slope continued on for another 1000 feet of elevation drop before they encountered a rock wall that required the ropes. They were now just above the tops of the elfin *m'kunaya* forest. The plants appeared incredibly healthy; many were in flower and fruit. The air was densely humid but chilly. "We never need to climb the mountain again for *m'kunaya*," Pa'bayna'kun declared.

They touched the bottom on a bed of rounded stones that rose slightly above a pond of cold water and filled their baskets with branches from the *m'kunaya*, spreading their harvest among many individuals so as not to tax any one tree in particular. When they finished, they took a short exploratory walk along the base of the canyon, at least five hundred feet below sea level. There were many interesting plants that competed for the shaman's attention, the majority concentrated on rocky outgroups that caught a few hours of sun. When they heard thunder in the distance, they began their ascent, and returned to the village just as the skies opened up.

Several months passed peaceably as the A'kun less and less thought of the village as novel; it just became home. With the *ayahuasca*, Gara'kun made one visit to their old settlement in the body of another harpy eagle host. The forest along the river fluoresced with alarming shades of mauve, and the music of the life stream was discordant and jarring. There was a shocking number of felled trees, and cuts sluiced into the riverbank in many places, where the trunks could be slid into the river to be then floated downstream. Dead fish littered the sandbars at the periphery of the waterway. The crew was busy extracting gold from the bed and banks of the river. Gara'kun remembered his vision of the future. Soon after, a plan formed in his mind.

He told his children that he would be away for a few weeks. They collectively had long ago learned to ask no questions whenever their father announced a prolonged absence.

Gar packed his old backpack with everything he expected needing for the task at hand. That included his old field clothes, and a small satchel in which he had accumulated a significant amount of gold nuggets fished from the doomed river over the years. He didn't take his bow and arrow but unearthed the 9 mm handgun one more time from its hiding place. Pa'kaya'kun came to his father's shaman's hut once as he prepared to leave. "Let me come with you, *a'kunda*," he said.

Gara'kun turned to his son. "Not this time, blood of my blood. I must do this alone."

The young man stood at the entrance for a moment, weighing whether to push the issue further. Finally, he sighed and departed, but not before saying "*Buena suerte, padre.*"[29]

---

[29] Good luck, father.

28

It took Gar five days to reach the Las Piedras River. On his last morning in the forest, Gar stripped himself of his sparse A'kun clothing and changed into his field clothes and boots. He had stored them clean in his few remaining sturdy plastic bags and had religiously administered them with dried flowers and crushed leaves of forest plants that had both antibiotic and insecticidal properties. And then he waited, just off the river where the *Ana Cariniña* would make a stop.

The boat didn't appear until the next day. While the passengers disembarked to wait for the crew to bring their goods to the beach, Gar found the captain and negotiated passage to Puerto Maldonado. As payment, he removed one modest-sized gold nugget from his satchel and placed it in the captain's hand. "*¿Suficientemente bueno?*" he said.

The captain's eyes widened, and he held up the piece of gold, occasionally glancing at Gar, as if trying to fathom where the scruffy old gringo had stumbled into it. He finally grunted with satisfaction and muttered, "*Sí.*"

Gar then requested enough spare change back to cover bus fare from the port to the small downtown center of the city and back again. The captain frowned, but withdrew an assortment of bills and coins from his pocket and handed them to the odd old man. Gar nodded. "*Gracias,*" he said.

The boat made three stops before pulling into Puerto Maldonado on the second night. The people boarding brought mostly crops to sell in the city. Gar melted into the forest on the flank of the Madre de Dios River, beyond where the road from the city to the harbor abruptly ended. He made a small camp, eschewing fire, and hung his hammock, drifting into a deep, dreamless sleep.

Gara'kun woke, hungry and thirsty, and found some palm fruits that staved off the worst pangs of both. He stuffed his sleeping gear into his backpack and headed down the road that led into the city, halting at the first bus stop, where he waited an hour for the next bus. Forty-five minutes later, he got off at Puerto Maldonado's central depot. He headed to the commercial district, alert and cautious. He did not want to run into Oscar Crescente, as much for Oscar's sake as his own.

His first stop was a small storefront advertising they bought and sold gold. A short, fat guy in his forties, with just the sort of skinny mustache one would expect someone in this business to cultivate, ran the place. There was no one else inside.

Gar was blunt. "*¿Me puede decir el valor de algunas pepitas de oro puro?*"[30] was all he said.

"*Claro, ven conmigo a la báscula,*"[31] the gold dealer replied.

Gar's gold came to eight ounces in weight, worth over $10,000 U.S. dollars. Gar would have no deficit of funds for his project he realized with grim satisfaction.

---

[30] Can you tell me the value of some pure gold nuggets?

[31] Sure, come with me to the scale.

"Te doy $8000 ahora mismo,"[32] the fat guy offered with a shrug.

Gar gave the dealer the tiniest bead of pure gold for his troubles, before pouring all the rest back into his bag, and bid him a good day. He took care to check if he was being followed on his way to his next stop; he did not entirely trust the gold dealer, but his fears were soon allayed.

When he entered the store called "La Selva," he walked around the store for several minutes, waiting for the few customers to leave. When only he and the sales attendant were alone, he strode forthrightly up to where the young man perched over the cash register. "*¿Puedo ayudarle?*" the clerk asked. — Can I help you?

Wordlessly, Gar handed him a list of items written on a blank page of a field book using the last of the indelible pens Luis had given him. The salesclerk studied the list and then more assiduously Gar himself. "*Necesitaré una semana,*" he said softly. — I'll need a week.

"*Bien,*" Gar replied. He handed several large gold nuggets to the salesman. "*Tendrás el resto cuando venga a buscar las cosas.*" — Good, you'll get the rest when I come to get the stuff.

Gara'kun had little recourse but to stay amid the stench of the city while he waited. He revisited the gold dealer, sold him a small nugget, so he'd have some ready cash, and bought a burner cell phone from another shop downtown. Gar found habitation in a flophouse where he could get a private room secured with a lock. He shared a shower and toilet with everyone else. The shaman in

---

[32] I'll give you $8000 right now."

disguise consumed mainly rice, beans, and local fruits, but eventually couldn't bear Puerto Maldonado any longer, or the prospect of encountering Oscar. He traveled back to the end of the line by bus and ventured deep into the woods. He found a small creek and a peaceful glade of sub-canopy trees, near a few fruiting *abiu* trees, within walking distance. Gar found two tree trunks from which to hang his hammock.

For the first time in a long time, Gar felt he needed help in getting to sleep, and before daylight was gone, he located two plants whose admixture as a tea would give him the relief he sought. He built a small fire, doused himself with A'kun insect repellent, and ensconced in a cotton blanket woven years ago by his wife, he watched the flames dance, illuminating his somber widower thoughts.

The next three days were lonely ones, which he passed by taking long walks through the forest. Only once did he encounter anyone, in this case two young men out hunting with shotguns. They exchanged pleasantries and went on their way. Though he had brought two draughts of *ayahuasca* with him, he felt compelled not to take it, at least not yet. On day six, he returned to town. He made his first phone call in over twenty-five years from the bus into downtown, to La Selva, confirming that everything he needed had arrived. And yes, the canoe would be found at the appointed spot and time.

The clerk, who was also the owner of La Selva, packed his goods into an empty backpack that Gar had purchased and asked him,

"*¿Estás seguro de que sabes lo que está haciendo?*" — Are you sure you know what you're doing?

Gar nodded and handed him the rest of the gold, slung his new backpack over his shoulder and made his way to the same room he'd rented before. He hung his hammock from two hooks in the wall, as much to avoid using the dirty-looking bed as for any other reason, and swung back and forth for hours, going over his plan again and again in his mind. Gar napped, setting his mental clock for midnight. He woke at eleven, and prepared to leave, both packs on his shoulders. He walked for an hour and arrived at a place on the river that was faithfully detailed to him by the owner of La Selva. Gar headed to the bank, where a teenager waited for him with the canoe. He tipped the boy a handful of soles, who then disappeared silently into the darkness.

Gara'kun loaded the small craft with his packs and pushed off from the shore. The spot had been chosen so that his return trip would be with the current. The center of the river was moving at a clip, and rather than fight his way upstream, he kept to a less strenuous parallel course.

It was about 2:00 AM when he reached his target. As the Puente Billinghurst loomed before him, he beached himself when the opportunity arose to briefly pause and consider his best approach. The bridge was lit up at night, but the maintenance crew was way behind replacing burned out lights. He scanned the river up and down; there were no signs of any boats. He paddled furiously now, heading for the first anchorage. He drew the canoe alongside, cloaked in shadow, and tied it to a metal post, then hoisted himself up to the base of the enormous support. From his pack, he withdrew the C4 explosive, affixing two charges on each of the reinforced concrete pillars. He attached detonators to each pair and wired these to an electronic device that would allow him to remotely set off the explosive by phoning a number and then inputting a code. With great stealth, he untied the canoe and paddled to the second support to do the same.

When he finished, he sped back downstream to the place on the riverbank where he'd picked up the canoe. The youth was waiting for him and took the canoe off his hands.

He took the *ayahuasca* as he walked back to his flophouse and settled himself into his hammock just as the plant medicine was coming on. He called out to his nocturnal spirit animal and made an effortless connection to a black jaguar that roamed in the forest where he had camped. Gara'kun sent the animal on a mad flight to the riverbank where he could see the bridge. There was only a single way to ensure no loss of life. Using his *ayahuasquero* power and the vision of the sigil, he bent time until the jet-black cat came to its place of vigil along the riverbank across from the bridge. There was no traffic on the bridge, nor any boats in the Madre de Dios. Gar broke the bond between his avatar and himself, which propelled him back into his physical body and the river of time. He dialed a phone number and waited for a tone. When he heard it, he keyed in a four-digit code. He quickly hung up and dialed a second number and input another four-digit code. Gara'kun grabbed his backpack and left the fleabag hotel, but first extracting and destroying the SIM card of the phone and depositing both into a trash bin he passed as he walked, heading further upstream where he could board the *Ana Cariniña* in the morning. He was far enough away that the explosions were muffled, like thunder in the distance.

The captain of the boat stumbled out of his hammock onto the deck in the early morning light and found the old gringo waiting for him on the dock. He put on a radio while making coffee. "*¡Mierda santa!*" he suddenly exclaimed. "*¡Alguien voló el puto puente!*"[33]

The captain reasoned that a hastened departure would be beneficial. Fortunately, they were at the furthest upstream moorage. He rousted his crew and bid waiting passengers to come aboard. Gar took all his remaining cash and placed it into the man's hand. The captain could see that he was being overpaid, but he said nothing.

It felt to Gar that he didn't breathe easier until they were hours upstream on the Las Piedras River. He felt stunned by the enormity of what he had accomplished and could only hope that the *ayahuasca* had guided him soundly and there had been no loss of life.

They arrived on the morning of the third day. He was the only passenger left on board and disappeared into the forest with nary a sidelong glance after a cursory nod of farewell to the captain. As soon as he was no longer in sight of the river, Gara'kun peeled off the trappings of the city, and stepped back into his much more comfortable breechcloths and bare feet.

---

[33] Holy shit! Someone blew up the fucking bridge!"

That night he burned his old backpack and its contents with the exception of the gun, which he needed for hunting on his trek back to the new village. He found it ironic that the only vestige of the life of Garwell Sorrentino was an instrument of death. The new pack he kept, and he used it to gather forest fruits and seeds as he made his way homeward.

Pa'bayna'kun was the first to meet him when he entered the settlement five days later. "Did you have success, *a'kunda*?"

Gara'kun looked at his son and replied, "As best as I can measure, *a'kundin*." Several of his grandchildren came running to greet him, bowling him over onto the floor of his quarters. He held them close for what seemed a long while and felt with an inner certainty that he had done the right thing. He turned to his son. "How about we climb the mountain tomorrow, you and me? I think that's just what I need."

His son smiled at him. "I will prepare the plant medicine."

29

"And so, in the truest sense of the word, Garwell Sorrentino sacrificed his life for the forests that he loved, not just loved, but understood at a level most people can't comprehend." Anton paused for effect. "And that is why we are here today, in a celebration of his brief life, and a plea for action in his name." The applause from among the General Assembly was polite, but not resounding. He glanced at the seat in the first row that he had vacated thirty minutes previously as he stepped up to the podium. Nell, Loren, and Rose were in attendance, and they were beaming at him in unison. He made his way back to his seat, passing Kevin Hobart, who was about to take the podium again.

"Great job, Anton," Kevin told him, squeezing his shoulder as he passed by.

Kevin Hobart then set upon what he did so well: demand the audience not to care about the scenes of destruction that he narrated: patterns between continents, the blinding statistics regarding extinction, tying these horrors to the scenes of fires across the Western United States, to famine in Africa, to the inevitable displacement of people in numbers that humanity had never before experienced, and which would have been unimaginable through most of our species' history. He explained the idea of a "tipping point" in Amazonian deforestation when the self-regulating interplay of canopy and moisture dynamics can no longer maintain equilibrium and the forests begin to transform into savannas. "And so, we lose the lungs of the world, and the last hope for a branch of human evolution that lives in perfect harmony in the untouched forests that remain, and who understands its value to our planet. We can no longer watch passively as the destruction proceeds unabated. It is finally time that the contributors of atmospheric carbon pay a price."

The flat tax of 3%, Hobart explained, would be levied on all profits reported by the fossil fuel industry. Administered by UNESCO, with representation from all participating nations, the funds would be used to start buying up vast tracts of Amazonian, African and Southeast Asian forests. Moreover, a conservation corps would be deployed in each region, populated by local people trained as both para-taxonomists and rangers. Law would arm and sanction them to confront poachers.

"I look at some of your faces," Hobart continued, "and I see disbelief, perhaps even cynicism in some of them; 'pie-in-the-sky,' you think. No, I beg of you, do not deny that we are already in the throes of an emergency. The time to act is now." He paused again theatrically. "For their sake," he concluded, as the screen filled with a photograph of a diverse rainbow assemblage of smiling children.

The auditorium erupted into thunderous applause, as the General Assembly audience rose to give Hobart a standing ovation. As he stepped down from the podium, Al Gore gave him a big embrace. "Kickass," Gore whispered in his ear. "Now comes the hard part. The really hard part."

They filed out onto the U.N. Plaza. Hobart and his wife invited them to dinner, to which Nell and her children acquiesced. Kevin had already made reservations uptown. They hailed two taxis and headed up the FDR parkway to an Indian restaurant of which he was fond.

They ordered drinks and studied the menu. Hobart reached over and rested a hand on Kovac's arm. "I thought that went pretty well," he remarked. Anton agreed, though even he had his doubts that Hobart's proposal would be adopted.

"What did Gore say to you afterwards?" Anton asked.

Kevin made a face. "'Now comes the hard part.'"

"Well, he's probably right," Kovac agreed.

"Difficulty be damned," Hobart declared emphatically. "I've got a media blitz prepared. Even FOX News."

Anton's eyes widened. "That'll be interesting."

There was a gleam in his boss's eyes. "Looking forward to blinding them with science."

Kovac laughed and placed his body into what he envisioned as the posture of a puffed-up pundit. "I'm not a scientist, but…" he intoned stentoriously. "Get ready to hear that."

"And I've got a book coming out. It's called "'The Best Last Chance.'"

Anton was impressed by how pumped-up Hobart was about his Sisyphean task. *May it be so*, he thought to himself.

After dinner, everyone bid each other farewell and went their separate ways. Anton and Nell were staying at the same hotel as Kevin and his wife, so they shared a cab to it. Halfway across Manhattan, Nell took Kovac's hand, and rested her head against his shoulder. Anton could have frozen that moment for posterity. He closed his eyes and allowed the traffic noise to place him in a reverie of dreams both lived and unlived. Kovac turned his head and breathed in Nell's perfume, squeezing her hand as he did.

They showered together back in the hotel, made love, and then showered again. They lay naked on the bed afterwards, speaking only with touches and shallow breaths. It felt like a timeless moment. He still was sometimes incredulous about him and Nell. Kovac was the happiest he'd ever been in his life, of that he was quite positive. There was an occasional twinge from the part of himself that he had considered vanquished by his *ayahuasca* adventure. It was more like a sibilant whisper, telling him he was undeserving of such feelings.

"Why did we wait so long for this?" Nell spoke up.

Kovac lifted his head, resting it on his hand and forearm. He didn't answer immediately. "I think I felt I didn't deserve you. Self-loathing blinded me." Anton grinned. "What was your excuse?"

Nell was momentarily speechless. "I honestly don't know. Maybe it was your closeness to Gar. Like I couldn't separate the two of you. So, I convinced myself that you weren't my type. I was vain in my younger days. I loved you for everything you were to my children, Anton; you know that." She laughed. "And you, my dear husband, made no moves."

The manuscript of his flora of the southwestern Peruvian Amazon continued to prosper as he, and secondarily Nell, labored on collating the determinations of specimens that had been sent to various specialists on different groups of plants. Several had willingly volunteered to write up the treatments of their specialties for the book. Anton welcomed such contributions and began inviting others to do so. Nell's on the coffee family was well underway.

Meanwhile, Kevin Hobart was becoming a media star. He accepted every invitation to discuss his proposal that was offered to him, down to Fox News, twice, no less. He became instantly famous on social media for rendering Tucker Carlson into a stuttering troll while he schooled him on how the atmosphere worked and the consequences of climate dysfunction. Several oil-producing countries had already signed on to the proposal, at least in concept. The petroleum industry was in an uproar and were doing everything in their power to present the envirotax, as it became popularly known, to be an expensive boondoggle that would have lasting, dire economic repercussions. The majority of the population supported it, not only in the U.S. but around the world, as poll after poll made clear. Its fate in the United States was less clear. Despite a sympathetic president, the opposing party dominated both houses of Congress, and it was an election year to boot. Obtaining buy-in from both legislative branches was doubtful.

One beautiful spring Sunday morning, Kovac and Nell arose, and while she began coffee, Anton fetched the New York Times from the front step. He tossed it on the dining room table and went into the kitchen to make breakfast: fried eggs and hash browns. Nell finished with the coffee and sat down at the table, unfolding the newspaper before her. She couldn't believe the state of elective politics in the nation. Kovac brought over two plates of eggs and potatoes and grabbed the sports section.

"Anton," Nell suddenly said. She sounded alarmed. The word "Peru" had captured her eye in a column towards the bottom of the page. "Oh my God," she murmured as she ruffled through the paper to continue the story inside; it had contributed only two paragraphs to the front page.

"What?" Anton queried through a mouthful of eggs.

Nell turned back to the front page and pointed to the headline: "Blast topples bridge in southeast Peru," it said. When his eyes met hers, their communication was silent but sure. They shared one thought and only one.

Anton recounted the maxim that Gar had told him that day at the foot of the Magic Mountain, when Gara'kun had given him a glimpse of what lay before the future earth.

"*So, what do we do?*" Anton had said.

"*We do what we've always done. We live. We love. And sometimes we fight.*"

EPILOGUE

The aftermath of the bridge's collapse soon overcame the human resources of local law enforcement, and the Peruvian Federal government mustered three jungle brigades from the Fifth Army Division into the area. By some miracle, not a single life had been lost in the blast and its repercussions. The Army first installed massive pontoons to restrict river traffic in both directions, and all boats had to show papers before being allowed passage either upstream or downstream. At certain times during the week, this created sizable logjams, but they never lasted too long.

Perhaps motivated by memories of trespasses in the past, the military was mostly on their best behavior. Moreover, they began to do some good in the reserves that surrounded the city. Patrols disrupted illegal activities in indigenous lands and confiscated equipment used for unauthorized road construction. There was even a gunfight with cartel goons along a riverbed that had been egregiously destroyed for gold and poisoned with mercury. One soldier was killed, along with several cartel men, before the gangsters were subdued. Ironically, or perhaps not so, Gar's actions had precipitated the greatest victory against deforestation in decades.

Rose's biochemist friend had finally gotten back to Kovac on his results with the *m'kunaya*. The first thing he said on the phone after greetings were exchanged was, "Can you get more?"

"Not easily," Anton told him. "Probably not."

Rose's friend told him they had a low yield of extract. "We really needed fresh material, and lots more of it." The results had been more than encouraging, but with an insufficiently large sample size. The laboratory mice received either several oral doses of *m'kunaya* or a placebo. Then, both were injected with a common mouse respiratory virus. "The animals that got the *m'kunaya* never got sick. Only the placebo. Every single one of them. We've never seen anything like this. But like I said, we can't publish the study without a larger sample size, and trials with other diseases. Are you absolutely sure you can't get more material?" he entreated, the disappointment obvious in his voice.

"Maybe someday," Anton replied unconvincingly.

One afternoon, he received a call from Oscar. It was several months after the Puente Billinghurst explosions. "Oscar, what a pleasant surprise!" Kovac exclaimed.

"Likewise, *amigo*. Hey, I just wanted to give you an update. I ran supplies up to the research station recently. While I was there, Isidoro and I headed to where the army had grabbed the cartel gang. I think I found the old A'kun settlement."

"How did you know?" Anton asked him.

"Charcoal. Lots of it. I think the tribe burned the place down before they left." There was a momentary pause in the conversation. "Any idea where they might have gone?"

"Not a clue," Kovac replied. "It's a big forest." He wondered if Oscar suspected he was lying. "Do they have any idea who blew up the bridge?" he asked, changing the subject.

"They haven't figured this one out yet," Oscar replied. "I don't think they ever will. The owner of La Selva, the outdoor supply store down the street, was questioned, and he talked about an old gringo who looked like a derelict." A long silence passed between them that spoke more than words.

The months went by swiftly. A year after the Billinghurst collapse, the proofs of the "Sorrentino" flora, as it had become known, were ready for review. Kovac distributed the PDF file to all the contributors, of which there were many. Anton and Nell were the titular editors of the volume, quite a tome at 482 pages, and which was dedicated to the memory of Garwell Sorrentino.

Kevin Hobart continued his tireless peripatetic cheerleading of the envirotax. He'd even managed to corral DiCaprio into making a movie about it. Kovac and Nell experienced the stirrings of optimism.

And then came the election.

Despite his loss in the popular vote, the electoral college, in lockstep with a program of continuous disenfranchisement of the vote in critical swing states, had awarded the presidency to the most unfit individual imaginable. Moreover, his party had enlarged their majorities in both houses of Congress.

The next day, Anton visited Kevin in his office late in the day. The lights were off, and Hobart was slumped in his chair, tie off, a glass of bourbon in his hand. "Hello Anton," he muttered. "We're fucked."

Kovac was startled; it was rare to hear Kevin Hobart curse. He sat down in a chair across from his boss. A half dozen or so copies of Kevin's new book lay on the desk. "Take one for you and Nell,"

Hobart said flatly. "I'll even sign it." He pulled a pen from a bamboo holder on his desk and inscribed a copy.

"Thanks," Anton said. He stood up and took a glass from the bar in Hobart's office, which was disguised as stylish furniture. He poured himself some bourbon.

"You know, Kevin," Anton began. "An old friend of ours once said something to me I've never forgotten. I'll spare you the details, but it's the last part of what he said that resonates to this day. He said: 'Sometimes we fight.'"

Hobart swiveled in his seat so that he could face Kovac with his haunted-looking eyes. "It was him, wasn't it? Gar. The bridge." Kovac's silence was answer enough.

Kevin had written a splendid preface to the "Forests of Southwestern Peruvian Amazonas," as the chief editor suggested the book be titled. He referred to the project's nickname — the Sorrentino flora — and touched upon Gar's having built the initial foundation of understanding of the region's plant diversity. Anton received many email superlatives from his colleagues. It felt good. Yes, it felt better than good, but something was a little off. It nibbled at him persistently until he abruptly decided what he wanted to do. Nell and he were at their favorite Cincinnati Thai restaurant when he dropped his decision on her.

"I want to take *ayahuasca* again." His wife frowned but didn't say anything. "I've been doing some research," he continued. "My friend at the university in Quito has a trusted shaman she's used as a guide a handful of times. You could come with me to Ecuador. I'd like you to be there, even if you don't take the drug."

Nell considered this over her pad Thai, and finally agreed. "I haven't been to Ecuador in a while," she muses.

Kovac messaged his friend and asked her to set the ceremony up for the week after next and then bought two round-trip tickets to Quito.

◆ ◆ ◆ ◆ ◆

The retreat was outside of Baños, a private forest reserve owned by an ecotourism company on the flanks of the volcano Tunguragua. Anton had paid the premium for a private session; he didn't want any distractions, not for what he had in mind. He lifted the cup of bitter tea to his lips and swallowed it all in a few swift gulps. Unbeknownst to his guide, he had shortly before arrival self-administered Gara'kun's recipe for quelling the violent physical purge that *ayahuasca* usually inspired.

As the plant medicine worked its wonders, Anton was at first filled with energy, following the music and luminescence of the forest, with Nell alongside. He turned to her, drinking in the golden light that surrounded her. It filled him with such joy that it brought tears to his eyes. She held him in an embrace for a long time. The shaman guide emerged from the shadows and reminded Kovac that he was on a mission. Kovac suddenly became enervated, and Nell had to help him back to where a bed had been prepared upon a woven cotton mat under a rain tarp. Anton lay down and listened inwardly to the network of life. He felt as if he was being drawn out of his body, and he surrendered to the sensation. The next thing he knew, he was beside his old friend, the Magic Mountain rising behind them. "You did it," Gara'kun's voice echoed in his mind. "I had hoped you would. Come with me, Anton; there's something I want to show you."

With the speed of thought, the tableau of the great crack in the earth lay before them. "The mountain blocked this place from our view," the shaman told him. He held out his hand and Anton took it in his own. They instantly transported down into the crevasse to the lowest rocky outcrop that placed them just above the shimmering green canopy of the *m'kunaya* forest. "Do you know what that is?" Gara'kun asked him.

Anton didn't need to answer. "And what of the population on the mountain?" he asked instead.

"Time will tell," the shaman replied. In a flash, they stood on the gentle slope above The Garden, which was resplendent as ever with flowers and hummingbirds. To Anton's spirit eye, the aura about the trees seemed dulled, their tones edged with discordance. There were more leaves exhibiting brown necrosis. They shifted to the platform-like promontory that overlooked the seemingly endless canopy of forest.

"Is Nell with your body?" Kovac heard inside his head.

"Of course," he answered.

"I have a message for her." Anton laughed when the shaman told him. "As for the rest; you don't need to ask." He paused for a moment. "Every *ayahuasquero* eventually learns when his life will end. I have fifteen years." Gara'kun kissed him, and with that, Anton was propelled back into his body. His first sight was the worried face of Nell, who clenched his hand. He managed a wan smile and saw her relax. "Gar had a message for you," he told her. "He said to keep fucking my brains out." And then he lapsed into unconsciousness.

He woke in early morning, wrapped beneath several wool blankets, entwined with the body of his wife. She stirred against him. "Tell me all about it over breakfast," she said.

♦ ♦ ♦ ♦ ♦

Kovac held an uncracked copy of "The Forests of Southwest Peruvian Amazonas" in his hands, just extracted from its shipping cardboard. He rushed into his office, where Nell sat at the other workstation and presented it to her with a flourish. He pulled up a chair beside her as they combed through the volume. His photographs of The Garden came out better than he expected, but his favorite was one he had taken from the last place that he and Gara'kun had visited in spirit form on *ayahuasca*.

Six months later, a large box addressed to Kovac arrived at the Garden from its research station deep in southeastern Peru. Anton was perplexed as it didn't resemble the typical cartons used for herbarium specimens. When he saw what the contents were, a chill traveled up his spine. It was bottle after bottle of *m'kunaya* extract.

At the bottom of the box was some writing that had been inscribed with charcoal on a flattened piece of light-colored tree bark.

"Go save some lives," the message said.

Plants Referenced in the Text

Abiu: *Pouteria caimito* (Sapotaceae).

Aguaje: *Mauritia flexuosa* (Arecaceae).

Alloplectus: a genus in the African violet family (Gesneriaceae).

Alstroemeria family: a monocot family (Alstroemeriaceaae) consisting of four genera.

Amaryllis: *Hippeastrum* species (Amaryllidaceae).

Amazon lilies: *Urceolina* species (Amaryllidaceae).

Andean bellflowers: species in the genera *Burmeistera* and *Centropogon* (Lobeliaceae).

Ayahuasca: a preparation of the inner bark of the vine *Banisteropsis caapi* (Malpighiaceae) or related species and most commonly the leaves of *Psychotria virens* (Rubiaceae), widely used in the Amazon for shamanic rituals.

Blue amaryllis, imperatriz: *Worsleya procera* (Amaryllidaceae).

Bomarea: a large tropical American genus of herbaceous, often twining, perennial plants with edible root tubers and showy flowers (Alstroemeriaceae).

Brazil nut: *Bertholletia excelsa* (Lecythidaceae).

Brea-caspi: *Symphonia globulifera* (Clusiaceae).

Bromeliad: any member of the Bromeliaceae, the pineapple family, a large group of epiphytic (air plants) and terrestrial plants found entirely in the Americas except for a single species in Africa.

Cacao: *Theobroma cacao* (Malvaceae).

Camu camu: *Myrciaria dubia* (Myrtaceae).

Capi, yage: *Banisteriopsis caapi* (Malphigiaceae).

Capirona: *Calycophyllum spruceanum (Rubiaceae).*

Capirona macrophylla: the only recognized species in its genus (Rubiaceae), found throughout the Amazon region and elsewhere in tropical America.

Cassava, manioc, yuca: *Manihot esculenta* (Euphorbiaceae)

Clusia: several hundred species of shrubs, trees and vines found only in tropical America (Clusiaceae).

Copal: *Copaifera reticulata* (Fabaceae).

Cumala, epená: *Virola* species (Myristicaceae).

Cupuaçu: *Theobroma grandiflorum* (Malvaceae).

Curaré: *Strychnos* (Loganiaceae).

Cypripedium reginae: showy lady slipper (Orchidaceae)

Gesneriad: any member of the Gesneriaceae, a large family of tropical plants.

Griffinia: ~16 species of eastern Brazilian forest understory bulbs (Amaryllidaceae).

Guarumo: *Cecropia* species (Urticaceae).

Heliconia: a large genus of banana-like plants with showy flowers (Heliconiaceae).

Hot lips plant: *Palicourea tomentosa* (Rubiaceae).

Huacapú: *Minquartia guianensis* (Santalaceae).

Ice cream bean: *Inga edulis* (Fabaceae).

Inayuga: *Attalea maripa* (Arecaceae).

Ipê: *Handroanthus impetiginosus* (Bignoniaceae).

Kapok: *Ceiba pentandra* (Malvaceae).

Kohleria: a genus in the African violet family (Gesneriaceae).

Manioc, cassava, *yuca*: *Manihot esculenta* (Euphorbiaceae).

Meriania: a large genus of Melastomataceae.

Ñejilla: *Bactris brongniartii* (Arecaceae).

Qantua: *Cantua buxifolia* (Polemoniaceae).

Sacha inchi: *Plukenetia volubilis* (Euphorbiaceae).

Sangre de grado: *Croton lechleri* (Euphorbiaceae).

Sasparilla: *Smilax* species (Smilacaceae).

Spanish cedar: *Cedrela* species (Meliaceae).

Surprise lilies: *Lycoris* species (Amaryllidaceae).

Tumbo: *Passiflora* species (Passifloraceae).

Tropical blueberries: various genera of Ericaceae (rhododendron family) subfamily Vaccinioideae, the majority growing as epiphytes in cloud forest.

Tropical lady slipper orchid: *Phragmipedium* species (Orchidaceae).

White oak: *Quercus alba* (Fagaceae).

Vellozias: several genera of the monocot family Velloziaceae.

Yacu sanaga: *Faramea* species (Rubiaceae).

Yuca, **cassava, manioc:** *Manihot esculenta* (Euphorbiaceae).

Acknowledgments

I thank Daniel Riggi, Linda L. Fisher, Sara Neuner, and Erica Meerow for their critical reading of various drafts of the manuscript, with excellent suggestions for revision. Cathy L. Brandstetter performed some near final proofreading.

Author's Note

The events depicted in this romance as occurring in "modern times" take place in the recent past, before the COVID-19 pandemic.

Dedication

For my family.

About the author

Alan Meerow worked as a tropical botanist for nearly 40 years, publishing over 200 books, book chapters, and both scientific and lay articles about plants. He divides his time between Arizona and western New York. This is his first novel.